P9-DCY-226

THE BLACKMAILER'S GUIDE TO LOVE

Also by Marian Thurm

Floating
Walking Distance
These Things Happen
Henry in Love
The Way We Live Now
The Clairvoyant
What's Come Over You?
Posh (pseudonym Lucy Jackson)
Slicker (pseudonym Lucy Jackson)
Today Is Not Your Day
The Good Life
Pleasure Palace: New and
Selected Stories

THE BLACKMAILER'S GUIDE TO LOVE

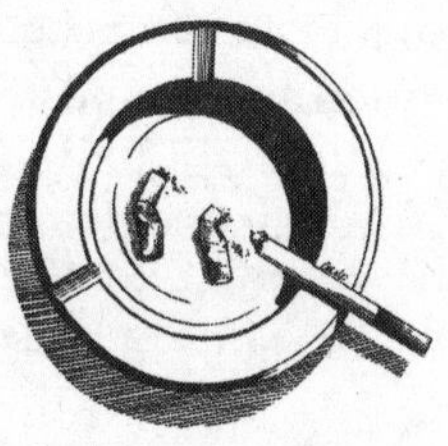

A NOVEL

MARIAN THURM

DELPHINIUM BOOKS

THE BLACKMAILER'S GUIDE
TO LOVE

Printed in the United States of America

For information, address DELPHINIUM BOOKS, INC.,
16350 Ventura Boulevard, Suite D
PO Box 803
Encino, CA 91436

Library of Congress Cataloging-in-Publication Data is available on request.
ISBN: 978-195300200-6

21 22 LSC 10 9 8 7 6 5 4 3 2 1
First Edition
The first chapter appeared in somewhat different form in *Narrative Magazine*.

Illustrations and Cover Design by Colin Dockrill, AIGA.

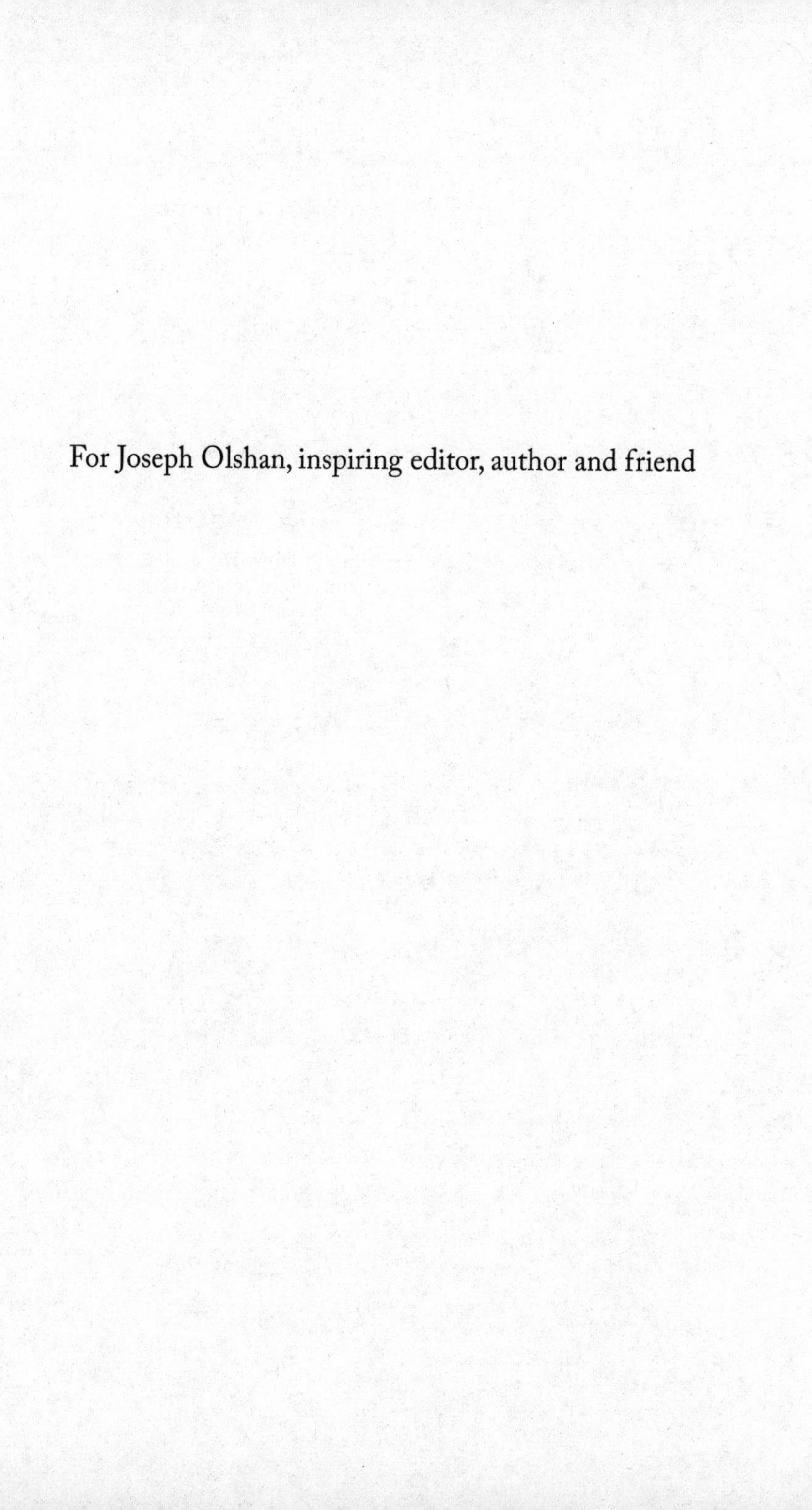

For Joseph Olshan, inspiring editor, author and friend

“I long for the raised voice, the howl of rage or love.”

—Leslie Fiedler

PART ONE

1
Mel

It is 1978 and Mel is twenty-five years old, and this is the most excruciating sore throat she's ever had.

The timing couldn't be worse.

She had, several weeks ago, nailed her first real job after a steamy, humiliating summer devoted to looking for work in Manhattan, a search that required her to submit to one typing test following another. After the briefest of these mortifying tests—sixty words a minute was the best she could manage, but she's an Ivy League alumna and evidently that mattered more—and then a short, skimpy interview with a magazine editor who was in the market for an assistant, Mel was hired at an annual salary of $7,800, which worked out to a princely $150 a week. Barely a living wage during these early post-Nixon years. At this new job on Madison Avenue at one of those glossy magazines, she will, it's been promised, be meeting (over the phone, anyway) some famously brilliant writers and will be able to smoke as many cigarettes as she likes, anywhere she likes—at her desk, at the Xerox machine housed in the alcove near the elevator, or in the ladies' room, which has an anteroom with a couch, a pair of comfy upholstered armchairs, and a few extra-large ashtrays that the housekeeping staff empties and Windexes every night.

In the office, Mel discovered on her first day of work, IBM Selectrics are coveted by editors and their assistants, but the typewriter assigned to her is merely an electric version of the manual Smith Corona she had in college. A minor disappointment, one she can easily live with.

Google and Wikipedia are decades away and unimaginable, as are cell phones and their many apps, Instagram, Twitter, and impulsive, ill-considered text messages that can swiftly bring down a career. Or a marriage. In these pre-Internet days at the magazine, a triumvirate of fact-checkers rely on the telephone and big fat volumes of facts and figures that they consult repeatedly throughout the workday. All three fact-checkers are, like Mel, in their twenties, and are deadly serious about their work; they are rarely seen smiling. Except for one guy named Simon, who likes to talk about his Birman cat, a breed he rather formally refers to as "the Sacred Cat of Burma." Mel and her husband, Charlie Fleischer, to whom she's been married for close to four and a half years now, also have a beloved cat—his name is Birkin and he is part Himalayan and part Maine coon; when she brought in a snapshot of Birkin on her second day at work, Simon was unimpressed with this majestic, long-haired cat of hers, and Mel's feelings were hurt by the apathetic shrug of his shoulders.

On this Wednesday in the middle of September, when that fiercely painful sore throat first hits, Mel has been an assistant for all of sixteen days, and she panics at the thought of being fired if she allows herself any time off to recuperate from what will turn out to be a relatively severe case of mononucleosis. But she needn't worry: her boss, Austin Bloch, a slender, handsome middle-aged man, is more than generous when it comes to the issue of a brand-new employee asking for a leave of absence of sorts. He instructs Mel to give herself as much time as necessary; he'll get a temp to take her place until she's well enough to return to work. Which she manages to do through sheer force of will just a couple of weeks later, still feeling not quite herself, and weighing in at ninety-four pounds, a number her father, an orthodontist here in the city, worriedly deems "the critical weight." (No doubt her adored mother—gone from this earth for two years now, and an always-confident Legal Aid attorney but a famously big worrier when it came to Mel—would have been anxious about her, too. Mel can, without any effort at all, hear her mother's openly loving voice saying, *But are you absolutely sure you're feeling well enough to go back to work so soon, mamaleh?*)

Austin, that generous-hearted boss, has eyes that are sea green, and a head of beautifully thick black hair graying at the temples. He wears Top-Siders and a safari jacket to work every day, along with a thin silk scarf tied around his neck. There's a lovely-looking wife whose sort-of-sexy, professionally photographed black-and-white portrait hangs on the wall of his office; and, too, the family includes his impressive three-year-old daughter, Skylar, who has, mysteriously, somehow taught herself to read. Austin also has a pair of sulky ex-wives who call the office from time to time complaining—Mel has heard from a colleague or two—about alimony and child support. He generally answers the phone himself, and once a month or so, Mel will come to observe, Austin will speak in the urgent, intimate voice that lets her know it's one of those ex-wives at the other end, wanting something from him, something he clearly isn't happy about handing over. But when the voice at the other end belongs to one of those brilliantly talented writers, Austin's own voice turns boisterous and is pitched at a higher volume. "Wayne, my boy! I was *just* thinking of you!" Mel hears him say, and by the end of the conversation he's persuaded Wayne to send him the new story that has already been reworked again and again, a story Austin promises to whip into shape for him. According to Austin, Wayne Morrissey is a boozer and an occasional wife-beater, but his stories—at least when Austin gets through with them—have begun to attract attention out there in the literary world once they appear in the magazine. Austin has an unusually heavy hand when it comes to whipping those stories into shape; he sits for an hour in his windowless office across the hall from Mel's desk, an extra-fine-point pen poised between the fingertips of his left hand, *deleting deleting deleting*, while in his other hand there's that ever-present True Blue. From her desk near the end of the linoleum, typewriter-lined hallway, Mel watches, mesmerized by the swiftness with which Austin's arm sails from left to right and back again across the pages of Wayne's manuscript, the pages themselves illuminated by the column of light that shines from the single draftsman's lamp clipped to the side of Austin's metal desk; his office is mostly dark, and Mel looks on as the smoke from his countless cigarettes rises straight up and into the lamplight. When he finishes editing, he calls out to her, "Melissa, dear heart, will you take this to the Xerox machine for me?" and each time, as he transfers the typed pages of Wayne's story from his own narrow hands to hers, she instinctively winces at the mercilessness of his editing. She's not yet officially a writer herself—the publication of her first story in a similarly glossy, and even more distinguished, magazine is several months away—but after only a few weeks on the job she finds herself aching for Wayne and what has been banished from those stories of his that Austin pares down so brutally. Though Austin is overbearing in his editing, in truth Wayne's work will gain from Austin's efforts. And Wayne, like the best of Austin's discovered talents, will, in the end, surpass him and find his way back to his own unforgettable voice.

Wayne is talkative and friendly over the phone, eager to chat with her while Austin is out to lunch, eager to listen when Mel tells him, prematurely, and in her softest, shyest voice, that she, too, is a writer. He occasionally sounds drunk when the two of them talk, but that doesn't mean she needs to discount his encouragement, does it? So what if she can readily imagine Wayne's drunken smile as she talks earnestly about her writing, about those stories focusing on her accordion teacher from her childhood or her long-widowed grandmother or her father's best friend who ended up in the slammer for drug-dealing but eventually went on to graduate from medical school. So what if her writing is severely limited to what she knows and *only* what she knows?

It occurs to her that Wayne must be lonely—why else would he be spending all that time schmoozing with her about this and that, about the omelet with whisky-infused bacon he made himself for breakfast or the toe he smashed against the bathroom door when he got up in the middle of the night to take a whiz. And where's his wife, she muses. It's difficult to envision Wayne chasing his wife around their Seattle home with a beer bottle aimed at the back of her head, as Austin has told her he's done; eventually Mel will hear that he has stopped drinking entirely. Sometimes when Wayne and Mel are talking, their conversation is interrupted by another call, sometimes from yet another brilliantly talented writer, one who sounds so whiny and childlike that Mel comes perilously close to laughter each time the guy takes pains to identify himself. *I know I know*, she wants to tell him, *of course I recognize your voice, Lincoln Pastorelli,* and *yes, of course I saw you in the spring on* The Tonight Show—pot-bellied, in a light-blue turtleneck and blazer, wearing dark sunglasses and seated next to Joan Rivers as the audience and an attentive Johnny Carson learned about that childhood friend from Mississippi, "*the girl who wrote* Blackbird in the Dead of Night." *"The girl" was thirty-four years old when* Blackbird *was published—be respectful!* Mel wants to shout into the phone, but how can she? Instead, she tells Lincoln, politely, as she invariably does, that Austin is out to lunch but will return his call as soon as he gets back.

"Out to lunch," she learns from an older colleague, is a euphemism when referring to Austin: the arrangement of those particular words will be something Mel will put in air quotes years later whenever the subject happens to come up. But today her wiser, hipper colleague Daphne has taken it upon herself to sit Mel down at the very back of the office at lunchtime and spell it out for her in the simplest terms, which trigger in Mel a frisson of alarm, immediately followed by overwhelming disbelief. She is still a suburban-bred innocent, so unworldly that she can count on two fingers of one small hand the number of friends she has whose parents are divorced. In college she smoked some pot on weekends, and she and Charlie began sleeping together when she was a freshman and he was a senior, but that's the modest extent of the ways in which she strayed from her parents' very clear instructions about life. She has no idea how to navigate a universe where husbands and wives betray each other or snort coke with straws off glass coffee tables while their toddlers are asleep in their beds down the hall.

The universe she's inhabited, beginning in childhood, has nearly always been rooted, it seems, in obedience, about doing what she's asked, or implicitly asked, and getting it right. It's what has led her to a career of straight A's, a long history of being handed one seal of approval after another from her mother and father, and most recently, her professors. She can't even imagine what it might be like to be told she's done a shitty, unsatisfactory job in any arena of her life.

"Hell, yeah, Austin likes to fuck around," Daphne repeats—zestfully, this time. "He tried to convince me to sleep with him as soon as I started working here, in fact, but I had no interest whatsoever," she goes on. "And I'm still not interested, and he was perfectly fine with that." She's glamorous in her emerald-green capri pants and sleeveless blouse on this surprisingly warm October day. She, too, is a graduate of a top-tier school in New England, but she's thirty-six years old and unmarried, and Mel thinks of her as womanly and sophisticated in ways she senses, regretfully, she herself might never be.

"You know that briefcase he always takes with him when he goes out to lunch?" Daphne asks her now. "The one he took with him today? Do you know what's inside it?"

"Manuscripts?" Mel guesses. "Advance copies of the new issue?"

"You crack me up!" Daphne says, but she is shaking her head impatiently. "You're really kind of unbelievably clueless, aren't you?"

"Am I?" Mel is feeling a little woozy; she can't get the words *Austin likes to fuck around* out of her head.

Though Daphne is one of the few people in the office who almost never smokes, she extracts one of Mel's Tareytons from the pack and flicks Mel's fluorescent-pink plastic lighter smartly. "Listen to me, inside his briefcase are the following items: one neatly folded clean white towel, one travel-size bar of soap, and one stick of Ban deodorant. And believe me when I tell you he's not heading out to the gym at the Y."

Mel thinks of Austin's briefcase, its battered, mahogany-colored leather, its shiny golden clasp, and the casual way he tosses it onto the chair in his small, dark office every morning. She listens as Daphne explains that Austin evidently has, at any given time, a stable of a half-dozen women to choose from, women who are more than happy to meet him "for lunch" at the East Village pied-à-terre belonging to a married friend of his—someone named Richard, who is ardently devoted to his own adulterous affairs, and is, by profession, a sharply insightful book reviewer for the paper of record. Mel is blushing now at her own thickheadedness, her babe-in-the-woods dopiness: how many times has she dialed Richard's number for Austin, week after week, never understanding the connection between them? As Daphne tells it, all Austin needs from his friend is the key to that East Village apartment, conveniently left for him downstairs with the doorman on days when Richard himself has no plans to bang any of his girlfriends. Who knows how many times Austin has been disappointed to learn that sorry, no, he absolutely may not use the apartment this afternoon.

But how does she know all this, Mel asks Daphne, who rolls her eyes, and says, "Are you serious? Are you familiar with the phrase 'common knowledge'? Everyone in the office knows."

So who are all these women so eager to sleep with him?

"Wannabe writers?" Daphne says. "*Lonely* wannabe writers?"

"Okay, okay, I get it," Mel says, but the truth is, she doesn't. Superficial though her thinking may be, isn't Austin something of a geezer, forty-five or forty-six, his hair already flecked with gray?

"Why do you look so skeptical, Mel? By most people's standards he's an attractive guy," Daphne reminds her. "Not my particular cup of tea, but that's irrelevant."

Mel's phone is ringing, and she leaves Daphne and walks a couple of steps away to answer it.

"Hi there," Austin's wife says; as usual, Hillarie's soft voice sounds just the slightest bit tremulous.

"Hi there, sorry, he's still, uh, out to lunch," Mel says all in a rush, and this will be a memorable day for her, the first time—the first of so very many—that she will knowingly lie to, or at least withhold information from, Hillarie. She feels a pinch of something uneasy deep in her gut, a hint that she may have to make a run for the ladies' room, but then it's gone and she's relieved to see she's going to be okay.

She turns around to watch Daphne expertly blowing a line of smoke rings in her direction.

When Hillarie calls again, an hour later, Mel hears herself asking about her young daughter, Skylar, and immediately engaging Hillarie in conversation about Skylar's pregnant babysitter. She's surprised at how smoothly she's able to advance their exchange from one subject to the next, as if she and Hillarie were friends and had much in common. But Hillarie is fourteen or fifteen years older and, unlike Mel, has been married for more than a decade to a remarkably successful adulterer.

And here's her husband now, cruising along the waxed linoleum hallway leading to his office, a cool half smile at his lips, briefcase clutched possessively against his middle, as Hillarie returns to the subject of Skylar's babysitter, who is planning to give birth not in a hospital but in a birthing center run by midwives. "Obviously she must have a passionate dislike of doctors," Hillarie is saying, "but who knows why? Who knows *anything*?"

It's twenty minutes after three; Mel wonders if Austin showered in Richard's apartment and, if so, what he's done with his wet towel—maybe rolled it up and shoved it into a plastic bag he found under Richard's kitchen sink?

But how will Austin explain to his wife why he's pulling a wet towel from his briefcase tonight?

And why does Mel care? Surely it's none of her business.

Yet somehow it seems that surely it is—that, in truth, part of her job is to protect him. She looks at Austin's pretty eyes set in his smiling, handsome face, and there it is again, that deeply unpleasant feeling in her stomach; it's almost as if it hurts to look at him.

"It's Hillarie," she offers now, holding out the receiver from the phone on her desk, but Austin, with nothing more than a scarcely perceptible nod, disappears into his office.

"Hey, hon!" he says cheerfully as he picks up his phone, and Mel can hear the warmth in his voice, the unmistakable sound of what she would have to say is simply the essence of love.

She doesn't understand, just doesn't get it; and worst of all, feels so very stupid.

Now Austin closes the door behind him, something he virtually never does.

Over dinner in their studio apartment, Mel and her husband discuss Austin and Richard's arrangement, and Charlie is shaking his head, saying he has come to believe that anyone might be capable of anything. "Listen, babe, even good people are, under the right circumstances, capable of screwing up big-time," he tells her.

Charlie spent five years studying in a clinical psych program at Columbia, where he got his PhD and, after a year of practice under the supervision of a licensed clinician, is now flying solo. He was an inspired, diligent student while he was in grad school, and is, Mel is sure, an excellent therapist, not to mention a loving, attentive husband. She appreciates him all the more whenever she contemplates Austin's rampant infidelity. Which she tries not to do very often because it's all just too, too disillusioning.

"Okay, look, this is going to be our one and only conversation on this sickening subject," she promises Charlie, and hands over the Pyrex cup of balsamic vinegar and olive oil, the homemade dressing he prepares for their salad almost every night. Lucky for her, he's routinely made dinner since the start of their marriage; he still makes fun of her for the uninspired meals she fixed for herself in college—Campbell's cream of mushroom soup heated up in her toaster oven, accompanied by a tuna sandwich on a hamburger roll.

Charlie is laughing at her now, and she can already guess what he's going to say. "You? You'll never put a lid on this," he tells her. "You obsess about these things—I know you, babe."

"Yeah yeah yeah, and who better than a shrink to accuse someone of being obsessive?" She punches his arm playfully, and he grabs her fist, raises it to his mouth, and kisses it.

Though fielding multiple phone calls from Hillarie almost every day is apparently part of her job, there *is* one thing Mel refuses to do. One morning, Austin comes toward her with a long tube of festive wrapping paper, a pair of scissors, and a metal dispenser of Scotch tape, then returns to his office to gather up a pile of shiny white gift boxes of various sizes.

"Would you mind helping out with these?" he asks Mel. "It's Hillarie's fortieth today."

She is in the middle of reading through the slush pile of manuscripts that now and then may hold something of genuine interest; looking up at Austin standing before her with his impressively balanced tower of gift boxes, she thinks about what she might say to him and the diplomacy with which she needs to say it. She would like to say, *Are you kidding me? Do I look like someone in the gift-wrap department at Saks? And by the way, how about ditching this ridiculous pile of boxes and giving Hillarie the gift of your faithfulness instead?* But she sighs, and reminds Austin, just a bit nervously and apologetically, that she has a bachelor's degree from Brown University and an MFA from Columbia, and that wrapping birthday gifts just isn't in her job description. And, too, she would have to categorize herself as all thumbs when it comes to scissors, paper, and tape, she adds.

This all-thumbs excuse is a lie, but so what? No way is she wrapping those damn gift boxes of his.

"No problem," Austin says with a shrug, and hands everything over to Daphne, who briskly gets to work and, to her dubious credit, Mel thinks, does a beautiful job.

She is proud to have said no, she realizes, proud to have turned down the brainless, time-consuming task Austin is too lazy to deal with himself. She is not, after all, his secretary; what she is, is an *editorial assistant,* a discriminating reader of manuscripts who's adept at separating the wheat from the chaff. She doesn't do windows, and she doesn't do gift wrapping.

"Hey, isn't that wrapping paper pretty!" Bonnie, the copy editor, is saying; she's come by with some page proofs she needs to ask Austin about. She has a head of frizzy dark hair and has been seen with bruises up and down her arms, which Daphne has made clear are from Bonnie's S&M escapades with her boyfriend, a bearded, burly guy who works in the Art Department.

What would Mel do without Daphne, from whom she is learning more and more about the world every fucking, amazing day.

Mel has stopped smoking Tareytons and switched to True Blues, probably in emulation of Austin, though she's not fully persuaded of this, not even sure she prefers the taste of Trues over her old favorites. So what made her switch to Austin's brand? No idea. Certainly she knows, as any sane person would, that she should consider quitting smoking altogether, but this doesn't seem like a possibility, not when nearly everyone in the office has an open pack sitting invitingly on their desk. One of the editors, in fact, has stopped by Mel's to bum a cigarette on her way into Austin's office now. Sally Steinhart, tall and thin and on occasion oozing a surfeit of self-confidence, is in her mid-thirties and has already made a name for herself as a stellar journalist; but here she is helping herself to one of Mel's True Blues.

"I really should quit," Sally says. "So should you," she adds, winking. She fires up her cigarette, and walks away, without bothering to say thank you. Sally is prodigiously smart and darkly funny, but just last week she shrieked at Mel for failing to answer her phone when her own assistant had left for the day.

Every so often over the next few weeks and months, Mel will recall the sound of Sally's supremely pissed-off voice shouting—loud enough for everyone in Editorial to hear—*Goddamn it, Mel, I told you to answer my damn phone!*

While Sally is in with Austin, their heads bowed over an open book of photographs, his phone rings, and he calls out to Mel to pick it up.

"May I please, if he's not too busy?" the writer on the other end says shyly. A member of the American Academy of Arts and Letters, Nina Levinthal has won the Pulitzer for one of her novels, and she possesses the sweetly girlish voice of an angelic kindergartner. Barely able to conceal her reverence for Nina's books, all of which Mel has read, she has to stop herself from confessing, again and again, "Oh God, I'm such an admirer of yours!" each time Nina calls.

Nina's modesty and divinely sweet voice have made her Mel's favorite caller, but while Austin is admiring as well, one time, after he'd met Nina for a drink, he came back and reported to Mel, *Not the comeliest of women, alas.*

Asshole, Mel had mumbled to herself, worrying, an instant later, that Austin might have heard, though, thankfully, he gave no sign that he had.

"I'll call back at a better time," Nina is saying now, and then another call comes through; it's one of those exasperated ex-wives, and it pleases Mel to yell out, "It's Kathleen again!"

"Shit," Austin says, but he takes the call nevertheless, and Mel returns to the slush pile, which today includes some manuscripts messengered over by a number of literary agents whom Austin has let her know he can't afford to waste his time on. "Type up a letter saying 'thanks but no thanks' and go ahead and sign it, what do *we* care?" he directed her during her first week. But she sympathizes with these agents who have so hopefully, so foolishly, spent money paying people to hand-deliver work that Austin will consider for less than a moment.

A guy in his forties sporting a pure-white suit and matching white tie is swanning down the hallway now; he doesn't have a walking stick but he does have a white Homburg, which he tips in a courtly way at Mel, and then says, "Okay if I poke my head in?"

Mel has to smile—who wouldn't love to get a glimpse of this journalist, this Brad Foxworthy, who's so formally dressed all in white on such a cool autumn afternoon? Brad is the only man who's ever tipped his hat at her, and she will always smile when she sees him even though he'll never remember her name.

Austin is loudly shooting the breeze with Sally and Brad; at her desk, Mel enjoys their intermittent hoots of laughter and continues sifting through the slush pile, searching for today's nonexistent gems.

Later, after the sun has set, Austin approaches her desk with a manuscript in hand, and in an instant, her heart begins pulsing at some crazy rhythm that frightens her. Stupidly, she lights a cigarette to calm herself as Austin drops the manuscript—its eleven pages held together by a gleaming violet paper clip—on top of her typewriter, "Lauren Silver," the pseudonym she'd added to the title page looking laughable to her now.

"You asked me if I thought this was publishable?" Austin says. "Well, you know what, dear heart? Shit always rises to the top, that's what."

Mel has never heard this expression before, but her face is scorched with humiliation; she knows enough to silently acknowledge that what he has said is deeply insulting, the mother of all insults, as a matter of fact.

He shakes his head, turns away, then turns back to her, perhaps reconsidering. "This story isn't yours, is it?" he says gently.

"No, of course not! I would never ask you to read anything of mine! Ever!" She's already on the road to the ladies' room; she's not going to break into a thousand pieces, but she *is* going to wipe away her embarrassing tears in private.

It turns out that something else she has a genuine gift for is steering Austin's wife away from all manner of dangerous subjects, including why he is still at lunch at three or four in the afternoon; whom, exactly, he is out with; and what he might be discussing over this endless series of protracted lunches. Sometimes while she and Hillarie talk, Mel cradles the phone receiver between her chin and shoulder, and proceeds to slit open envelopes of manuscripts, or take large paper clips from the box on her desk, unfurl them, and shape them into abstract designs. While chitchatting with Hillarie, she has also taught herself to write, in both cursive and print, with her right hand, starting with the alphabet itself and then progressing to whole sentences with which she ornaments sheet after sheet of typing paper. She is ambidextrous now, at least with a pen!

As if she were some lovesick thirteen-year-old, she writes her initials and Charlie's and draws a heart around them. She draws a line of these hearts, each successive one larger than the previous, and then she outlines them all in red Magic Marker. She and Charlie love each other as only a couple of people in their twenties can. They take showers together and tenderly pat each other dry afterward, and in the pitiless fluorescent light of their bathroom, they admire each other's skinny bodies with superlatives that strike Mel as absolutely accurate. She and Charlie will never cruelly disappoint one another, Mel knows, but if there are disappointments, it will only be because she might have forgotten, on her way home from work, to buy a banana for his breakfast, as she'd promised him, or because he left her favorite bra in the basement laundry room of their building when he went down to collect their stuff from the dryer. These are forgivable lapses, and any marriage can survive them.

Unlike what Austin has done, and will continue to do, as long as lust continues to inform his life.

His marriage is none of your business, Charlie keeps reminding her. *Don't even* think *about spilling those crappy beans to Hillarie*, he warns her.

But maybe Hillarie already knows.

She's telling Mel over the phone now about the monkey she saw on TV last night. "He was sitting in a kitchen sink full of soapy water, scrubbing a frying pan with a sponge. And doing a fabulous job," Hillarie says.

Though Hillarie is laughing, Mel can sense her nervousness, can hear the way her voice is edged with worry. As always.

None of your damn business, Mel berates herself.

Tonight, just before she goes home, Austin has her type up a letter to the parents of a young writer whose work interests him. He rarely asks Mel to type anything at all, but this letter, he says, needs to be on the magazine's official, full-size stationery, which he normally doesn't use when he sends out encouraging, handwritten notes to authors, as he does most every day.

Apparently this young writer is one more VIP in Austin's Rolodex.

Dear Mr. and Mrs. Beller,

I'm writing on behalf of your wonderful daughter, Victoria, whose work I admire more than I can say. She is a remarkably gifted writer, and I beseech you both to give serious consideration to supporting her financially so that she may devote herself to her work as a writer, work that I strongly suspect will lift her to a prominent place in our literary universe here in the US, and even internationally as well. Her literary gifts are such that it would be altogether criminal for her to continue wasting valuable time in her job as a receptionist when instead that time would be infinitely better spent on her writing.

I beg you to find it in your generous hearts to help Victoria achieve what she so richly deserves.

With deepest gratitude—
Austin Bloch
Literary Editor

* * *

The next day, when Mel tells Daphne about the letter, Daphne once again rolls her eyes. "Honestly, Mel? Please don't say you're surprised to hear that he's been banging this Victoria Beller chick for months already."

"Of course he has," Mel says, and wonders aloud what Victoria's parents would think if they knew.

"Better that they don't," Daphne says. "She's married to some NYU law student, by the way."

"Of course she is," Mel says. "Of course."

At home, Charlie's arms looped tightly around her middle as they lie in the double bed that seems to swallow up half their apartment, Mel acknowledges that in this world with a population of more than four billion souls, she can't imagine ever finding herself so deeply in love with anyone but this guy dozing alongside her, his unshaven cheek noticeably scratchy against the thin veneer of her see-through T-shirt. There is no one else to whom she is this well-suited, no one else who shares their quirky sensibility, their mildly snarky view of the world, their ability to make each other collapse with the kind of laughter that has her eyes actually overflowing with tears.

After four and a half years of marriage, she knows every bit of his long, reedy body; she's deeply familiar with the smooth skin behind his ear, the bony knobs of his spine, the vitiligo that mars, though only mildly, the surface of several of his fingers and toes. And there's the sweet, curious mouth of his that has explored nearly every inch of her.

And, too, his moral compass is sterling. If a stranger ambling along ahead of him anywhere in the city were to accidentally drop a quarter, a dime, or even just a nickel on the pavement, Charlie would stoop to the ground, sweep up that coin, and go running after that stranger, yelling, "Hey? Sir? Excuse me? You dropped this, sir!"

But sometimes she worries about him.

Every now and again he wishes, enviously, Mel knows, that he could be more like his brother, Jeff, who ultimately was tough enough to disregard their parents' aspirations for them and now owns and runs a New Orleans–themed restaurant near the Village Vanguard. Like Mel, Charlie was raised with those well-meaning Jewish parents and their exasperating, conventional expectations that he and Jeff would become either lawyers, or physicians like their mother and father—both of them psychiatrists. A PhD in psychology was acceptable but, perhaps, not quite enough, not fully satisfactory in his parents' eyes, he's told Mel. She knows, too, that it drives his father crazy when Charlie refers to the people he sees in his own practice as "patients." She was there in her in-laws' dining room in Westchester once as Charlie began, "One of my patients, the one who was raised a Christian Scientist and never saw the inside of a medical office until she was old enough to leave home and get a job working for a pediatrician—" And that was when his father interrupted him, saying, "Jesus Christ, Charlie, they're 'clients,' not patients. *Physicians* treat patients; you *psychologists* treat 'clients.' How many times do we have to have this conversation?" And Charlie looked so deflated, if only for a moment, that Mel wanted to say to her father-in-law, *What is it with you? You're a psychiatrist and you take pleasure in humiliating your son*? *Are you crazy?* Instead, she helped her mother-in-law clear the table and then carried out a key lime pie and a fistful of dessert forks from the kitchen. *I hate it when he does this to you*, she whispered in Charlie's ear, and they both knew that when it came to this particularly touchy subject, this age-old conflict between psychiatrists and PhD psychologists, Charlie was always going to insist on using the word *patients,* no matter *what* his father—or the psychiatrists—thought.

She knew that his beloved grandfather Morris, an immigrant cigar-maker who taught Charlie how to ride his two-wheeler on Wild Currant Drive in the placid suburbs of his childhood, was born in the early 1880s in a miserable shtetl in Lvov, in southeastern Poland, and had grown up with five sisters, with dirt floors beneath his feet, in a tiny wooden house heated by a coal-burning stove. No way, Charlie was made to understand by his father, would he or Jeff be allowed to disappoint their paternal grandfather by becoming less than they were capable of, less than their parents envisioned for them.

Maybe, he once told Mel, sounding a little mournful as they were lying in their darkened bedroom one night, maybe grad school in psychology had been a mistake; maybe he'd chosen it for himself simply because he couldn't come up with something that might have made him happier . . .

You have your whole life ahead of you, sweetie—you're free to do anything you want, she consoled him that night. *Anything at all.*

Listening to the news on the radio as she gets dressed the next morning, she hears that Sally Steinhart and her boyfriend, a celebrity at *The Washington Post*, had, as the WMCA announcer puts it, "tied the knot just minutes ago at City Hall." So Mel is astounded, a few hours later at work, when she runs into Sally in the ladies' room. The bride is dressed in a navy-blue linen pantsuit and black patent-leather high heels, and is smoking a cigarette as she checks her makeup in the long, smudged mirror above the row of sinks.

"Wait, *really*? What are you doing here? Didn't you get married this morning?" Mel says, and then remembers to say "Congratulations."

Sally smiles. "Thanks. Do you mind if I bum a cigarette from you for later?"

"Aren't you supposed to be out celebrating or something?"

Sally smiles again, then lifts one shoulder in a half-hearted shrug. "It's a workday—Greg has deadlines, and so do I. He's already on his way back to DC."

If you say so. Feeling uneasy, though she doesn't quite know why, Mel fishes around in her bag for her cigarettes, and gives Sally two more than she asked for. "Congratulations!" she says again, wishing she had more to offer—something suitably celebratory, a glass of champagne to be shared in the ladies' room, empty except for her and Sally at eleven o'clock on this weekday morning that appears as ordinary as any other, the metal garbage pail stationed next to them stuffed with crumpled paper towels, the old-fashioned black-and-white ceramic tiled floor splashed with water here and there. She finds herself wishing, benevolently, that Sally were on that short flight back to DC with her husband, the two of them miles above the city, celebrating their marriage in first class, with extra legroom and unlimited champagne.

It will be impossible for Mel to forget this day in the ladies' room, this day when surely Sally should have been somewhere else, her hand linked with her husband's as they boarded their very first Boeing 727 as husband and wife.

After she and Sally go their separate ways and Mel is back at her desk out in the hallway, she notices a tiny blond child in an Oscar the Grouch sweatshirt worn over pink corduroy pants emerging from Austin's office, followed by Hillarie, whom she's never seen before, but whose face she knows from the portrait hanging above Austin's desk.

"Melissa?"

"Hi there," Mel says, and is startled when Hillarie draws closer, only to shake her hand. So businesslike, she thinks, as if the two of them hadn't spent, over these several months, all that time on the phone, Mel, the underpaid assistant, never failing to reassure Hillarie that of course her husband would be back from lunch—*soon, shortly, very soon, any minute now . . .*

She's struck by how insubstantial Hillarie looks in her black pants and silk T-shirt, her thin arms pale and exposed, her hair the palest blond, just like her daughter's; their eyes an identical rinsed, pale blue.

"Say hello to Daddy's friend Melissa," Hillarie says, but Skylar declines, swiveling her head from side to side, and then regarding Mel coldly.

There's no denying she's a beautiful child.

"Can you show me how you read, Skylar? I'd love to see," Mel says, but there's that ice-cold stare again, focused directly at her; she's reminded of *Children of the Damned* and wants to laugh.

"Hey, Hill, what's going on now?" Austin calls out to Hillarie from the doorway of his office. "Something going on out here, ladies?" he says. "Anything I need to know about?"

"I guess we're leaving," Hillarie says. "Too late for breakfast, too early for lunch. I told you, we only stopped by because Skylar wanted to see her daddy, that's all." She instructs Skylar to give Daddy a hug and some kisses, but none of this is forthcoming. "Skylar!" Hillarie says. "You need to listen to Mommy."

"I wanna go home." Now Skylar is looking at her mother beseechingly. "And I want Doritos."

"Not to worry," Austin says. "Someday when I least expect it, those kisses will come showering down upon me."

Mel thinks of him promenading down that linoleum hallway after one of his three-hour lunches, carrying himself with such smiling assurance, as if he had nothing to hide—*nada!* He's proud of himself, she now understands; he relishes every fucking minute of this double life of his.

"Really? I wouldn't count on it if I were you," Hillarie is telling him. She is forty years old, but to Mel she looks fragile; even her voice sounds thin and exhausted. It hits Mel in this moment that Hillarie has been married too long to a man who loves her but who can't be trusted, and this must be why, at forty, she looks so bone-weary and used-up. When Hillarie rubs the heel of her hand very deliberately back and forth along the soft sleeve of Mel's shirt just below her shoulder, and then says goodbye, Mel almost grabs her hand and says *don't go*, almost says, in a whispery voice, *waitwaitwait, there's something we need to . . .*

But instead, regretfully, as she will so many times over the next few years, she lets the moment pass.

2
Julia

Julia Myerson, current PhD student/dog-walker/occasional cat-sitter, and forty-hour-a-week caregiver for the elderly, is in the market for a new shrink. Tough times: it's only with difficulty that she has been able to pay her rent after her three-year marriage and adjunct teaching job ended, one right after the other, this spring. The adjunct gig she started in the fall of '77 and lost after the spring semester of '78, was in the English Department at Queensborough Community College; despite her outstanding references, Julia hasn't been able to find another teaching position like the one that slipped through her tightly crossed fingers just a few months ago. Not her fault, all those cutbacks in the English Department, but no matter what, it continues to sting.

Though months have passed since Julia's divorce became final, she is still struggling to understand what lay beneath the very heart of things but keeps coming up empty. Even from the beginning of their marriage, she and Daniel made love by appointment only, in either her bed or his; afterward, Daniel, naked under that thin, aqua-and-gray tattersall bathrobe with the ripped pocket and missing belt, would retreat soundlessly to his own bedroom at the back of their book-strewn Union Square apartment. No one seemed to have a fix on what it was all about, not Julia herself, or a single one of her closest friends, and not even her generally insightful therapist at the time, Dr. Safran.

According to Daniel, it was all about savoring his privacy, his *alone time,* but wouldn't you think there was more to it than that? He'd insisted, from day one, on separate bedrooms;

on the night he asked Julia to marry him, he spelled it out for her with remarkable precision, so there'd be no mistaking the very stringent rules of the game, no mistaking the way things had to be.

But you always think, don't you, that you can change people, that if you just give it your best shot, you can talk them out of their wacky ideas.

Guess what: Sometimes you simply can't, no matter how hard you try to appeal to a person's reason, common sense, common decency. No matter how hard you try to persuade him to come with you to marriage counseling or to see a therapist on his own.

And what about love? Isn't love supposed to trump everything?

You'd think so, wouldn't you?

Well, in this case, you'd be dead wrong.

In the summer, not long after the failure of her marriage and the loss of her teaching job, Julia lost Dr. Safran as well. She was, it turned out, the very last patient he ever saw. An hour or so after her appointment ended, on a memorably hot day at the end of July, Dr. Safran left his office in the West Village, got into his spanking new BMW 528i, drove to the George Washington Bridge, and jumped.

The next night was so rainy and windy, Julia's umbrella had been of no use to her at all as she returned home from her new job as a caregiver on the Upper East Side; flipped inside out by the wind, the umbrella had to be abandoned in the tall garbage pail stationed outside the apartment building where she now lived. The apartment, on Twelfth Street, was only a few blocks from the two-bedroom she'd shared with Daniel, but this one was just a studio, and not a generous-size one, either.

Arriving home, Julia had ducked barefoot into the kitchen for a dish towel, using it as a mat for herself as the water dripped steadily from her clothes and hair. Even the bra under her thin camisole had been soaked in the downpour. She headed directly for the shower, washed her hair, and went into the galley kitchen to make herself some dinner. Never much of a cook, she found that she missed Daniel's excellent meals every night when she sat down to whatever lackluster dinner she'd fixed for herself.

Just before she was about to start on her grilled cheese, with a side of badly crushed, bottom-of-the-bag potato chips, one of her friends called, having seen the story about Dr. Safran's suicide on the local six o'clock news. Stunned and horrified, nearly breathless, Julia had to walk away from the dinner table. She immediately felt sick with guilt; she couldn't stop thinking it might have been something she'd confessed to Dr. Safran in their last session that compelled him to leap from the GW Bridge.

But what could she have done differently? She'd been complaining about her failed marriage, of course, and Dr. Safran had been noticeably distant, come to think of it, somewhat preoccupied, rubbing his palms together again and again, then lighting a cigarette, blowing smoke from the side of his mouth toward the large black-and-white photograph of a severe-looking Sigmund Freud in a tweed suit, thick cigar fixed between two fingers. Underneath the portrait were the words, *All my life I have had to tell people truths that were difficult to swallow.*

Just days after Dr. Safran's suicide, Julia happened to read in *Newsweek* that, mysteriously, physicians were more than twice as likely as everyone else to take their own lives, and that four hundred doctors in the United States killed themselves every year.

Was this supposed to make her feel any better, any less guilty?

It did, but only a little. Eventually, she understood, she would have to start seeing a new shrink to help her cope with, among other things, this gut-wrenching loss of her old one.

According to the small, paid obituary that appeared in *The New York Times* two days later, Dr. Safran left behind a wife, a son and daughter-in-law who were also doctors, and a German shepherd named Zeus. Reading the obituary, Julia almost expected to see something about herself: *The Final Appointment*, *The Last Patient*, the one who had, perhaps, unwittingly sent him over the edge.

But of course there was nothing about her in the obituary—she was, after all, just another patient Dr. Safran had dealt with in his practice, someone who had suffered through a fairly shitty childhood, but who had managed to tough it out.

Other than her parents and her younger brother, there was no one on her end who knew about that fucked-up childhood except Dr. Safran and Julia's oldest friend, Emily. She finally told Emily when they were sophomores in college, on a Columbus Day weekend when Emily was visiting her at Penn, and they'd had a couple of beers too many in Julia's dorm room in Hill Hall.

Remember my broken arm? Julia said. *Remember I told you I fell down the stairs to the imaginary basement in our house?*

Emily remembered. And remembered, too, the long-sleeved shirts Julia and her brother wore even on the hottest days.

Now I can tell you, Emily said. *I was always kind of afraid of your father but I never knew why. There was something, but I couldn't put my finger on it.*

Well, now you know, Julia said.

Emily asked if she could give Julia a hug. They were both standing in the doorway of Julia's closet, looking for a pair of flip-flops for Emily so she could use one of the quartet of mildewed showers in the bathroom across the hall.

"As you know, I'm not much of a hugger," Julia said. "But never mind about that." They were both a little drunk, a little unsteady on their feet. They hugged and then kissed, and Emily played with Julia's hair, which had finally been dyed the extreme black she'd longed for when she was twelve or thirteen.

She and Emily found themselves collapsed on Julia's twin bed.

They both had boyfriends; Julia's lived a five-minute walk away in a dorm in the Quad.

Despite the two boyfriends, Emily unbuttoned Julia's shirt with her good strong teeth.

Listen, these things happen; these things *happened*. Though they never happened again. Not in Julia's life anyway.

In the morning, they were embarrassed, both of them equally so, Julia thought, to discover that all of their clothing had somehow found its way to the dusty wood floor beneath them. It was her father's fault, she decided, and Emily didn't argue with her. *Your father's a piece of shit*, Emily assured her.

When Julia told this to Dr. Safran the night of his suicide—how Emily had partially undressed her with her teeth—he seemed to be smiling, something he seldom did. So at least she had been able to make him smile on the very last night of his life.

The evening she learned of his death, she couldn't get back to her dinner; couldn't even look at her buttery grilled cheese sandwich surrounded by those crumbled potato chips. She considered calling Daniel and asking if she could come over and smoke some of his weed, a hit or two just to get herself into a better frame of mind. But the thought of calling her ex and hearing that familiar scratchy voice was too much. Too much on a rainy night only twenty-four hours after a fifty-seven-year-old guy made a decision to leave his family behind and throw himself into the darkness of the Hudson River. Julia wondered what Dr. Safran's last thoughts had been, and if he might have been thinking of her, thinking of her and that night well over a decade ago when she and Emily experienced a bit more of life than they had bargained for.

Had he been thinking of her? Probably not, Julia decided. Because to believe that, you'd have to be a raging narcissist, and she knew that wasn't who she was. She was just someone who'd had a hard time. And was having a hard time still. Out of work, out of love; and, it seemed, with no prospects for either in the foreseeable future.

Soon she will confide much of this to her new shrink, Charlie Fleischer, who comes highly recommended by a couple of grad-school friends of hers. His specialties, he will tell her, are generalized anxiety, depression, and family conflict.

Perfect.

"Going back into therapy after Dr. Safran's suicide is really a no-brainer, don't you think?" Julia asks Dr. Fleischer, this new therapist of hers. He's a lanky guy with wire-rimmed glasses; his nearly shoulder-length, wildly curly hair is dirty-blond, and as she stares at him from the Ultrasuede couch large enough for three where she's seated all by herself, she hears him say, "Please, I'm a very informal guy, just call me 'Charlie.'"

"Cool," Julia says, and is charmed by the warmheartedness of his smile. His framed diplomas are hanging just the slightest bit off-center on the wall behind the armchair in this small, modestly furnished office on the Upper West Side; she can see one diploma is from Columbia, the other from Brown, and she is comforted by the knowledge that, at the very least, he's a well-educated guy with a manner distinctly kinder than Dr. Safran's.

"Please talk to me," he says. He takes off his glasses and breathes on them, then polishes them with the bottom of his sweater. "About anything at all," he says. "It's crucial that you feel comfortable revealing anything, no matter how distressing or painful. I want you to think of my office as your safe space, a place where you can be absolutely free to unburden yourself." There's such sweetness in his face, she thinks, and so she's not surprised to hear him say, "I'm here for you, Julia. I don't want you to experience the least bit of embarrassment or shame in talking with me about anything you feel the need to explore; nothing is off limits. Always remember that I'm your confidant," he says, leaning forward in his seat encouragingly. "You should always be able to trust that I have your best interests at heart. Remember, too, that my job is mostly to listen, very, very carefully and, in doing so, help you navigate the challenges your life may present."

Okay then, she's good to go. She tells him that when she and Daniel were first married, the welcome mat that stood neatly outside their front door was a red-and-white rectangle ornamented with the words "OH SHIT—NOT YOU AGAIN!" It was Daniel who thought it was hilarious when they found it in some junky store on the Lower East Side just after they'd signed the lease on their apartment, that very small two-bedroom near Union Square. He instructed Julia to take the larger bedroom for herself, but she hadn't been sure if this was meant to be regarded as a gift and whether she was expected to say thank you. They had each furnished their own room, Julia with a rose-colored comforter and a swiftly sinking heart, but still nurturing the hope that she could talk Daniel out of this inexplicable lunacy of his. He was one of four siblings and had always shared a room with one of his brothers. Was this the reason he needed his own? But Daniel merely shrugged when she asked. He liked to smoke weed by himself in his bedroom every night after dinner while Julia did the dishes, and he didn't like her coming in and interrupting him when he was getting high. Was that what this was all about? His response was always to remind Julia he loved her enough to marry her, and that of course she returned that love, didn't she?

She did, she assured him.

So, hey, what's the problem? he always said. *Indulge me, Jules, okay?*

Or: *I really, really like my privacy, my alone time, Jules, what's not to understand?*

They had met while Daniel was still in law school, before he'd decided to drop out and become, instead, a freelance journalist.

Julia wondered if his friends knew about their sleeping arrangements, and if they thought Daniel was nuts.

Even Fred and Wilma Flintstone shared a bed, she reminded Daniel.

But Julia was convinced she was still in love with him—with his sandpapery voice, with the way his perfectly straight hair fell forward and had to be swept back by a reflexive flick of his left hand, the one wearing the smooth, unadorned white-gold ring she'd given him at the close of their brief wedding ceremony at City Hall. In certain ways he was very good to her. He made labor-intensive dinners for them that required marinating, basting, chopping with a dangerous-looking cleaver, sautéing in a fry pan, stir-frying in a wok. He helped her with the laundry, gathering it in steamy armloads from the dryer in the basement of the apartment building and conscientiously folding her T-shirts and nightgowns, displaying them in orderly piles on their living-room couch. When they made love, he did everything he could to bring her to a kind of euphoria that struck her as one of the very best things in life.

She'd thought, mistakenly, that she could live with Daniel's stipulations but discovered, after a couple of years of marriage, that she could not. There was that ache of the most acute sort of loneliness, when, after making love, Daniel sent her back to her own room, as if she were a hooker being dismissed after the job was done.

Gonna go to sleep now, he would announce, and slide the pillow out from under her head, yawning in a way that seemed a little theatrical, a little forced.

I'm tired, too, Danny, she would tell him. *Too tired to go back to my room. Why can't I just stay here with you?* She knew how pathetic it sounded, but couldn't figure out what other words to use. She and Daniel were both lying curled up on the futon that opened into a double bed, and she raised his arms and positioned them around her, but a few minutes later, he would remove them and, very quietly, tell her it was time for her to go.

Please, she would say, and he would silence her with a kiss and a small, gentle shove.

Let's not make a big deal out of this, it's nothing, Jules. See you in the morning, okay?

Nothing? It was a lot more than nothing, and it was most definitely messed-up, but for some reason Daniel just didn't get it.

Back in her own bed, Julia would find it impossible to doze off, and sometimes, as she had too frequently throughout her childhood, she cried herself to sleep.

There were so many of these failed attempts to get permission to stay overnight in her husband's bed. If they were in *her* bed, she would beg him to stay, hating the sound of that begging, and trying, instead, to add something playful to her voice, as if she were really just teasing him.

If you stay, I'll give you a special treat.

Oh yeah, like what?

Something you really like, Danny.

One bj per night is all I need, Jules, he told her, and left a kiss under her neck. He was already sitting up at the side of her bed, arranging his bathrobe over his shoulders.

It wasn't that, *Danny. It was something else,* she said, but this was a lie.

Get a good night's sleep, and I'll see you in the A.M., Jules.

And then he was out of there.

She hated waking up to find herself alone, the sheets on his side of the bed cool to the touch.

It's destroying me, kind of, she finally had to tell him. *I'm losing myself to loneliness, moment by moment, minute by minute, every single night in my bed.*

Baby doll, he said, and wrapped her warmly in his bare arms, but what was the point, really? Because, in the end, he wouldn't, or couldn't, give her what she needed in order to breathe, to live, from one day to the next. You couldn't underestimate the weight of that loneliness and how, late at night—after the dinner plates and silverware had been rinsed and loaded into the dishwasher, and Daniel was in his inner sanctum getting wasted—it was that loneliness that made her slip out of the apartment and into the stairwell with one of the lighters Daniel used to fire up his blunts, and that *she* used to burn herself here and there. A small magenta-color burn on the underside of her wrist, a slightly larger one behind her knee, a tiny one on the tender skin between her thumb and index finger.

It calmed her to do this, there in the quiet stairwell where no one could see her or hear the satisfying click of the chartreuse plastic lighter in the instant before she brought it to her skin. There was something satisfying, too, in being able to do this, in being able to give herself what she wanted, what she longed for, really.

There were many things she would never have, many things she would want. This was only one of them, one of the things she could have every night if she wanted it.

Oh God, I'm sorry, she hears her new therapist saying, and he's looking at her with such compassion that she almost has to restrain herself from rising from the fake-suede couch, heading straight for him in his fake-suede armchair, and offering this Dr. Fleischer/Charlie an exuberant, thankful hug.

3
Mel

That tall, intense-looking guy leaving Austin's office now will never know the debt Mel will come to feel she owes him, will never know how many times she will, in the years that follow, think of what he has done for her, and how wild it is that he will never even know her name or his connection to her. As he saunters slowly past her desk in his rumpled suit, taking no notice of her as he's about to head down the hallway and back to the elevator and out into the world, Mel leans over in her desk chair, and puts one hand out to touch his elbow.

"Excuse me," she says impulsively, and she will soon come to regard this moment in which she pronounced those simple, commonplace words as the one that will have ignited her new life in the most significant of ways.

"Hey," the guy says. "Hi." His name is Chris Altman and he works in the typing pool at *The New Yorker*, typing other people's stories even though he, too, is a writer. A very good one, in fact; so good that Austin has been courting him for a while now. He's just about Mel's age, but she is too shy to look directly into his face and stares instead at the wrinkly denim shirt he is wearing under a suit jacket that's badly in need of ironing.

"Can I ask a question, please?" she says. "Would that be okay?"

"Sure."

Looking up at him now, into what she sees is his pleasingly good-natured face, she explains that she's, *uh, actually a fiction writer herself*, and then asks for the name of his editor, *if that's okay with him, if he wouldn't mind*, watching as he hesitates for just a moment, and then listening carefully as he says the name aloud, a woman's WASPy, suitably impressive name. Mel writes it on the palm of her right hand in the green ink of her favorite Pentel rollerball pen that she brings with her from home every morning.

When she thanks Chris not once, but twice, adding *so very much* the second time around, he nods and smiles vaguely, saying *sure thing*, and then he continues down the hallway and out of sight.

She promptly writes the name—Elizabeth Greenwell—on a small piece of note paper imprinted with the words *From the Desk of Mel Fleischer* and slips it into the pocket of her itchy woolen pantsuit. That night, after dinner, she asks her husband if he can please take a walk around the block for a little while so she can concentrate on the last paragraph of the new story she has been working on.

"Are you kidding me?" Charlie says. "Come on, Mel, gimme me a break, will you? It's, like, forty degrees out there. Why can't I just sit here at the table quietly reading my *Journal of Abnormal Psych* while you're working? Come on, don't be nutty, I won't disturb you, I promise."

From their bed, where she's sitting with her legs stretched out in front of her, her back against the corduroy study pillow she used every day in college, Mel points out, apologetically, as she has many times before, that she can't fully concentrate knowing he's in the room with her, that she simply needs to be alone to finish up her story. "Maybe someday, if we're incredibly lucky, we'll have a one-bedroom apartment instead of a studio," she half-teases him. "And when we do, I'll just go into that bedroom and close the door and I won't have to rudely kick you the hell out into the cold."

"Okay okay okay," Charlie says, going to the front closet to get his jacket. "I'll be back in half an hour."

"Are you pissed off at me?" Mel says, and kisses the tip of his ear when he comes over to say goodbye. "Come on, honey, please don't be pissed off at me. Give me that half hour to finish up my story and I'll be forever grateful."

"*Forever* grateful? Really? I believe that's what they call 'hyperbole,'" Charlie says. "Big-time hyperbole." But he's smiling, and Mel is, indeed, grateful.

Birkin, the cat, has arranged himself next to her on the bed; at her other side are her leather-bound thesaurus and dictionary, gifts from her grandmother when Mel graduated from high school. Over the years these books will be opened and shut so many times that their bindings will break and Mel will have to repair them with thick layers of masking tape. But, for now, the bindings remain sturdy and the leather, which is the color of burnt sugar, is unblemished. Though she doesn't really know anyone to whom she might confide this—except perhaps Wayne Morrissey or the Pulitzer Prize winner, Nina Levinthal—Mel can't envision her life without that pair of leather-bound books.

The thought of them lost or destroyed brings something like tears to her eyes, but she can't explain why, exactly.

During her lunch hour, Mel stays at her desk addressing a dozen large brown envelopes, each containing a copy of her new story, which is only nine pages long. It is a quiet, understated story; the words *chemotherapy* and *small tumors* appear at the bottom of the second page but never again. The dozen copies were made several minutes ago at the Xerox machine where she copies Wayne's stories for Austin, and all the other stories Austin edits. Mel doesn't feel guilty about using the machine for her own work—her salary is so absurdly low, the least the magazine can do is allow her unlimited access to their supply of paper and ink, right?

With a can of Tab at the side of her desk, along with the

half of a tuna sandwich she brought from home, she types, on her electric Smith Corona, the same note to eleven of the dozen magazines she will submit her story to:

Dear Sir,

Thank you for taking a look at the enclosed short story, "Untroubled Lives."

Working at a magazine, as I do, I know how easy it is to dismiss the manuscripts that turn up in your slush pile. But it is my hope that you will give my story the careful reading it deserves and read it all the way through to the end.

With high hopes,
Mel Fleischer

The twelfth copy of the story will go to the editor at *The New Yorker* whose name she wrote on the palm of her hand in green ink. "With high hopes" was a lie: Mel recognizes that, in all likelihood, all twelve of those editors will turn down her story.

There's a post office not far from work, and she tucks all the envelopes under one arm and heads out onto Madison Avenue. Waiting in a long line to have her envelopes weighed and stamped, she smiles at a child riding on his father's shoulders, one tiny finger confidently up his nose. The little boy smiles back at her, removing his finger from his nostril and wiping the tip of it on the shoulder of his father's jacket. His father, staring straight ahead, has no idea what has just transpired and Mel considers passing along the information, but surely this, too, is none of her business.

A homely dog in an ugly orange sweater is glaring at her now; Mel turns away. It will be a long wait, she suspects, before she hears back from any of these magazines and their editors. Probably a month or two or more; who knows? Then she'll be back in line at the post office, with dogs glaring at her and toddlers with fingers up their noses.

She forks over a five-dollar bill to the cashier, collects her change, and returns to the office, where Austin is, of course, nowhere to be found, because it's only two o'clock and this is one of those lucky days when his pal Richard, the book critic at *The Times*, has given him the green light to head downtown to that pied-à-terre of his.

Mel will never, she believes, get used to this. And will continue to remind herself that, as her-husband-the-shrink has counseled her, this guy's marriage is none of her damn business.

4
Julia

Julia had grown up on a street called Fortunate Lane on the south shore of Long Island in a family of four, plus a variety of cats. When Midnight or Snickers or any of their successors died of natural causes or skipped out the back door and never returned, he or she was replaced after a quick visit to the North Shore Animal League a half-hour's drive from Julia's home. Her parents strongly preferred cats over dogs: cats were a cinch to take care of and required, beyond a small plate of liver-colored food and a steel bowl of fresh water, little more than a cozy lap to snooze in and a litter box to be scooped out once or twice a day. That was nothing compared to the annoyance of walking a dog late at night in even the worst weather, and all that frenzied barking every time the doorbell rang or the mailman innocently made his way along the path to the front door. *Too much aggravation*, Julia's parents told her when she was growing up and she'd begged for a cheeky little Maltese like the one her best friend Emily had.

"So that's the story, no dogs in the family when I was a kid," Julia is saying to the Mishkins, the nonagenarian couple she is paid five dollars an hour to keep watch over until 4:30 in the afternoon, Monday through Friday, in their Upper East Side high-rise apartment. She is thirty-three years old, and this is about as far from her dream job as you could get.

"Hmmm, many thousands of years ago, when *I* was a kid, we had a cat named Minnie," Walter Mishkin says, and asks Julia if he can please have a banana sliced up into his bowl of breakfast cereal. He's a geezer with a hearing aid in each ear, and a good head of hair for a ninety-three-year-old. Unlike his wife, Molly, whose memory is still relatively sharp, for Walter, absorbing and retaining new information has become something of a challenge. But Molly, who recently turned ninety, has her own problems—near-blindness and a half-dozen different pairs of glasses that don't seem to make a whit of difference. She and Walter are among the most bullheaded people Julia has ever known, and sometimes, after a full day of looking after those two, Julia can feel as if she just can't take any more of them. On the other hand, her grandparents having died years ago, there's something to be said for being paid to spend time with a couple of old people who eagerly open their door to her every morning, their faces illumined with genuine happiness, and who mark her cheek with fervent smooches that are only the slightest bit slobbery.

Her own parents have always had an entirely different vibe about them and might, on a good day, learn a thing or two from the Mishkins. Today, however, is not one of those days. When Julia arrived at the apartment this morning, flames were dancing above a pair of burners on the gas stove, not a pot or tea kettle in sight. Shutting off the burners and trying, gently, to let Walter and Molly know how disastrously things might have turned out, Julia failed to get her point across. She decides to give it another shot now as she peels a banana and carves it up for Walter.

"Don't look at *me*," he says. "The kitchen and I have never been friends, if you know what I mean. I have nothing to do with what goes on in there, except maybe when I want to get a glass of water for myself. Or maybe a tangerine. Other than that, I keep my distance. If you know what I mean."

"You guys will burn the whole building down if you're not careful!" Julia warns them.

"Listen, darling, what can I say, life is full of danger and there's no disputing that," Molly reports, sounding annoyed.

"We've got homeowner's insurance," Walter says. "Even if the whole place goes up in flames, there's nothing to worry about. So don't worry!"

Don't worry? How can Julia not worry about these two—one legally blind, the other perpetually engaged in a struggle to hear. Molly, despite her blindness, all too pumped to continue cooking and cleaning, Walter blithely seizing his wife's hand and heading out across Third Avenue, never mind the cars and taxis and trucks and buses speeding uptown and in no mood to slow down for two frail old people heedless of the dangers that await them as they make their excruciatingly slow way to the drugstore on the other side of the avenue.

If there were family members to contact, Julia would have quietly made a call about the gas stove Molly refuses to keep her hands off. But the Mishkins are childless and there are no relatives to be in touch with except an elderly sister in Fort Lauderdale who apparently has issues of her own. Standing above the upright piano that no one plays anymore are several steel-framed photographs of their daughter Debra, who, Julia was told, had cruelly died in childbirth along with her stillborn baby, over three decades ago. There had once been a son-in-law, but other than the photos of a teenage Debra and a single picture of her as a little girl (nursery-school age, dressed in shorts, with a sweater tied around her waist, balancing on a fence somewhere while a young, dark-haired Walter held her hand), there's no evidence the Mishkins ever had a family of any sort at all. Julia feels a twinge of sorrow every time she studies the pictures of Debra, their sweetly smiling daughter, who'd worked as a high school chemistry teacher and who lost her life, at close to the age Julia is now, in the labor-and-delivery suite of Doctors Hospital, across from Gracie Mansion. Though Julia has asked about the Mishkins' former son-in-law, all that has been offered in response is silence, pursed lips, and a mournful shrugging of shoulders. She knows enough to just leave it alone . . .

Also resting on top of the piano no one ever touches is a heart-shaped box made of royal blue porcelain tricked out with silver-and-gold butterflies. The box contains Debra's ashes, and can be balanced in the palm of your hand. The first and only time Julia happened to pick it up, Walter roared "STOP!" as if she were in imminent danger, about to be mowed down by an eighteen-wheeler going ninety on the L.I.E. She couldn't imagine what had made him shout at her like that, couldn't imagine what she might have done wrong. And then, a few moments later, couldn't imagine what it had been like for Molly and Walter to lose their only child, and their grandchild, on what should have been a brilliantly happy day, the day that marked the birth of their granddaughter. *Those poor, poor Mishkins,* Julia thought then and is thinking now.

She's thinking, too, that probably *any* sort of family is preferable to no family at all.

Though, in all honesty, sometimes she isn't completely convinced of that.

"You guys need to be extra careful about everything when I'm not here," she reminds them as Molly begins pouring orange juice from a half-gallon carton down the V-neck of her shirt instead of into the glass poised so perilously at the edge of the kitchen counter.

"Oy!" Molly says, and Julia shoves the glass across the laminate countertop and toward the sink, then grabs a dish towel to mop up the juice that's already soaked through Molly's gray blouse, turning it black. Molly is laughing at herself, but Julia doesn't find it amusing, and neither does Walter, who is watching from his seat at the dining-room table and shaking his head in disapproval. Something that looks like water is running from his nose; Julia isn't certain if she should wipe it or not. On occasion Walter has thanked her for it, but other times he's said, *What do you think, I'm a child? Do us both a favor and don't insult me like that, Miss.*

"The Jewish Guild for the Blind. I can't stomach the words," Molly says. "Just because I'm old, and what they call legally blind, doesn't mean I can't see the handwriting on the wall. I can see *plenty*, let me tell you."

Walter's nose is still dripping. Taking a chance, Julia reaches in front of him with a napkin and cautiously swipes it under his nose. Walter says nothing, and continues eating his Special K. It's as if Julia is invisible.

She puts an arm around Molly and leads her from the kitchen into the bedroom, where she opens up the walk-in closet and picks out a clean blouse for her. Molly doesn't want any help, not even with the buttons, but there's an unruly thread suspended from the front of her big white cotton bra: Julia snips it off with the pair of nail scissors she's plucked from the medicine cabinet. All of a sudden, scissors still in hand, she's thinking anxiously of her unwritten doctoral dissertation, which she's decided is going to focus on violence in the work of Flannery O'Connor and a couple of other female southern writers; most likely Carson McCullers and Eudora Welty. But she hasn't been in touch with her thesis adviser in several months, and really ought to give him a call.

Molly has just now decided she wants to take a shower this morning, even though she took one last night. Can Julia help her out of her clothes and into the shower?

Of course Julia can. She unhooks Molly's bra, slips the straps gently over her fleshy, freckled shoulders.

Forgive me, but I still miss my daughter, she is saying, and presses her soft face hard against Julia's collarbone. *I miss my baby.*

I know you do, Julia whispers. *Of course you do.*

5
Mel

Several weeks have passed since Mel's visit to the post office and her story has already been rejected by a couple of second-tier literary magazines; at home she rarely thinks about it, but when she's at work, reading the slush pile, she wonders if "Untroubled Lives" is as hopelessly amateurish as the worst of what she sees on her desk every day. And so when Charlie, home early from work, calls her to report that there's a letter addressed to her from *The New Yorker,* her pulse and blood pressure remain stable; she doesn't even think about lighting up one of her cigarettes.

"Okay if I open it?" Charlie says.

She can tell there's food in his mouth, and when asked, he admits to selfishly eating the very last brownie in the batch she made at the beginning of the week. "No offense," he says as he opens the envelope, "but why would *The New Yorker* possibly be writing to you?"

"Maybe," Mel says, flicking her lighter with one hand and extracting a True Blue from her pack with the other hand, "maybe they lost the story I sent them and they want me to send another copy?"

"Let's see what they have to say," Charlie begins, and reads the letter aloud to her:

Dear Ms. Fleischer—

Not only have we read your story all the way through to the end, but we have decided to take it for the magazine.

Although we normally do not like to publish stories about cancer, we felt the need to make an exception in your case.
Our payment rate is fairly generous, about a dollar a word, and once I do a preliminary edit of your manuscript and we have set the story in type, you will be receiving a check from us.

I want you to know how happy we are to have your story. It seems thoroughly original and makes us hope for more fiction from you. I very much look forward to working with you.

Yours,
Elizabeth Greenwell

"*What?*" Mel says. She forgets to inhale her True and exhales instead, then puts out the cigarette. Her face is on fire; raising her hands to her cheeks, she can feel the heat.

"What the hell?" Charlie says. "I mean, really, holy shit!"

"I think I have to call you back," Mel says.

"Congratulations, sweetheart," she thinks she hears Charlie say. "Mazel tov and all that jazz."

She hangs up the phone using both hands; one isn't sufficient for the job. When she tries to get up from her chair, she's a little woozy, as if she were still in high school and had unwisely helped herself to one beer more than she should have. Pulling herself up slowly from her seat, she walks across the hall and into Austin's office, forgetting to knock on his open door first, as she usually does.

"Melissa, everything okay?" he says. "You look, I don't know . . . shaken . . . Something wrong?" He appears genuinely concerned; she appreciates that.

As she tells him about the letter, she feels herself rising through her disbelief and floating toward something that feels like elation. Austin offers one of those barely perceptible nods of his, and then he says something she wishes she could instantly forget but will, instead, remember for the rest of her life.

"All very well and good, dear heart," he says gravely, "but how long do you think it's going to take before you sell them another story of yours? Three years? Four years? Ten? This could, after all, be *it* for you." He narrows his sea-green eyes. "You might simply be one of those writers who have only one story to tell and then they're finished. Could that be you, do you think?"

What she thinks is that he wants to crush her with his contempt, but maybe she's got it wrong; maybe he's just testing her to see what it will take to bring her to her knees, if she really *is* that weak. She had expected him to be proud of her, in a fatherly way, but then it hits her that possibly he's envious—because she's twenty-five years old and this is the very first story she's sent out into the world and things aren't supposed to happen with such ease. Such grace.

So she won't even bother to answer him.

She can go home soon; it's almost the end of the workday, and when she gets home she will hold that tiny 4 x 5 envelope from *The New Yorker* in her hands and silently read the note from Elizabeth Greenwell and then read it out loud and she and Charlie will celebrate with pizza ornamented with sliced artichoke hearts, her favorite meal. And she will go back to work tomorrow and pretend, for the sake of her job, that nothing has changed.

When, in fact, everything has.

Only now, she thinks, is her life, her real life, *finally* beginning.

It occurs to Mel the next day that she needs to write to the nine remaining literary magazines where she submitted her story and inform their editors, with her apologies, that she is withdrawing "Untroubled Lives" from consideration. It's not necessary to tell them that *The New Yorker* is where her story will be published, and yet there's a small, childish part of her that's dying to tell them—to tell the doorman in the lobby of her building; the maintenance guy who is mopping the muddy footprints in front of the elevator; and every stranger she sees as she troops uphill toward the Lexington Avenue subway this morning. She wants to announce that she's been officially anointed, by the magazine she admires more than any other, to the status of *a real writer*.

When a couple of those editors she's written to eventually write back, she will be astonished by their responses, both of which arrive in her mailbox on the same day.

Dear Ms. Fleischer:

We've given your story a second look, and the hard truth is, we wouldn't have published it anyway. It is simply, by our standards at least, not a very satisfying story.

Yours,
The Editorial Staff
Santa Fe Review

Dear Mel:

"Untroubled Lives" did not impress us. And frankly, we've been scratching our heads here trying to figure out why the hell the NYer wants to publish it. We wish you good luck nonetheless.

Yours truly,
The Great Lakes Review

Her husband, the shrink, will comfort her, using all the right words (*envy, envy, and more envy,* he will explain) and taking her out to dinner to a neighborhood diner where she will order the cheeseburger with mozzarella and mushrooms she's so fond of. But the sting of rejection will disturb her sleep that night; it is her first experience with this particular sort of vindictiveness, and she's shocked by how much it hurts. She reads and rereads Elizabeth Greenwell's note to her over and over again until, at last, she no longer needs to look at it, and carefully puts it to rest inside her velvet-lined jewelry box, next to a prized necklace of colorful glass beads, the one she will wear four and a half years from now, when an esteemed photographer will take her author photo for the back cover of her very first book.

6
Julia

Sex in the movies, or on TV, is often something so remarkably, so absurdly, spontaneous, Julia has observed; the first thing exchanged is a look, and before you can count to ten, a guy, breathing heavily, has tilted his date or colleague or best friend's wife or wife's best friend backward against his desk or the back of a restroom door, raised the woman's skirt (conveniently, she is almost always wearing a skirt), and there you have it, noticeably hot sex in a public place—with one partner generally remembering to lock the door—over and done with in what seems the blink of an eye. In the next shot, the woman is always adjusting her skirt and smoothing her hair with her manicured hands, and the guy is tucking his shirt back into the waist of his pants and straightening his tie, if he happens to be wearing one. He leaves the room first, looking both ways before crossing the hallway, smirking, maybe even whistling blithely; his partner will casually follow two minutes later, perfectly groomed, neither her face nor her clothing revealing anything at all about where she's been and what she's been up to.

Julia has never had sex in a public bathroom or on top of or against a desk, and she's pretty certain she doesn't know anyone who has. During her marriage to Daniel, she's explaining now to Charlie, her therapist, just getting herself into her husband's bed was often a challenge. *By appointment only* was his mantra, and he wasn't kidding around.

She remembers telling Daniel she'd be ready in ten minutes, one April night in the first year of their marriage, one night when she was ardently looking forward to lying in his arms, her bed or his, it didn't matter where.

Daniel was standing behind her at the kitchen sink, and he put his lips to the side of her neck. *Well, okay, there's just this Monaco Grand Prix I have to finish watching. Honestly, there's nothing like watching Formula One cars race around the streets of Monte Carlo. You understand, right?*

Yeah, right. Well, she understood it was a guy thing, along with those small, 3,000-cubic centimeter, high-revving engines, but that didn't make it any easier to deal with.

Daniel thanked her; his breath was steamy at just the right spot under her earlobe, and she could feel herself growing excited.

They settled on 6:30, the moment ABC's "Wide World of Sports" would be off the air. *Your place or mine?* Julia wanted to know. She was hoping to be invited into his bedroom, where they hadn't been together in a couple of weeks, but *her* bed had a more comfortable mattress and Daniel seemed to prefer it. His was that old futon he had from his law-school days; it folded easily into a couch, though Daniel usually kept it open unless company were coming and, Julia assumed, he wanted to pretend to his buds that sometimes a den was merely a den and not a second bedroom where you would stay overnight all by yourself.

After the Grand Prix ended, Daniel insisted he had to smoke some weed, and then he fell asleep for hours and then they had to have dinner, and so it was close to midnight when he finally came to her and led her down the hallway toward his bedroom. She had to teach her classroom full of freshmen the next morning, but Daniel was working from home and could stay in bed for as long as he wished. He was a little stoned and a little sleepy that night, but he gave her what she wanted, his hair and breath scented with weed.

Afterward, as usual, he kicked her out, almost tenderly,

and sent her back to her own bed. Where, she tells Charlie now—as she has told him once before—she'd been losing herself to loneliness, moment by moment, minute by minute, every single night.

"What you've been through is awful, so painful and humiliating," Charlie says. "But you know what, ending your marriage as you did, it seems to me you're saying you recognize you did the right thing, recognize that being denied the intimacy that's absolutely fundamental to any healthy relationship, is . . . well, that denial of intimacy is simply unacceptable . . ."

Now he's sounding like a therapist, and she's tuning him out, a little disappointed; the truth is, she likes him better when he sounds more like a friend with impressive emotional intelligence, one who just happens to have a PhD in psychology and can gently steer her in the right direction.

"In future sessions, I think, we should be focusing on skills to help you meet and overcome all the issues, all the challenges, you have to contend with." Charlie takes out his spiral appointment book, flips it open, and asks, "So . . . same time next week?"

Julia's wondering now what he looks like without his shirt on, standing in front of his bathroom sink barefoot, wearing only his pajama bottoms, brushing his teeth late at night, his crazy, wild hair tucked behind his ears, the water running in the sink muffling the sound of his wife's petulant voice as she calls out to him to hurry it up and come to bed. Julia wonders, wistfully, if he is happily married to that wife he's mentioned a couple of times, wonders if he knows intimately the texture, the feel, of a good marriage. *Tell me what it feels like*, she wants to say.

At dusk, on her way home from Charlie's office, Julia swans past a row of stately townhouses, and through the illuminated ground-floor window of one of them catches sight of a woman in a puffy black blouse turning over a page of sheet music against a metal stand; at her side, in the yellow light, a little girl glides her bow back and forth serenely across the strings of the violin tucked beneath her chin. And the envy Julia feels at the delicate beauty, the sheer loveliness of this scene from the girl's childhood, has her blinking back tears.

What she remembers at this moment is her piano teacher, Mr. Rabinovici, occasionally dozing on a folding chair beside her while she labored on that hard, varnished bench at the keyboard of the upright secondhand Baldwin in her parents' living room, playing the same simplified version of "Somewhere Over the Rainbow" again and again, her seven-year-old self failing to engage Mr. Rabinovici's attention long enough to keep him fully conscious during a weekly half-hour lesson. Mr. Rabinovici had to have decided, so many years ago, that she was a no-talent, yet one with parents who were determined she take lessons, as if, miraculously, the talent she would never possess would, one fine day, spring from her fingertips. Or maybe her soul.

But he was a gracious, courtly man, and when he awoke, he would look around in confusion for just an instant, then take Julia's hands in his and say, "Let's try that again, shall we?" She delighted in the feel of her hands nested in his powdery-dry palms, loved the thought that, in some other universe, some other life, a man like Mr. Rabinovici might have been her father. He was *someone's* father—why couldn't he have been hers?

She stands too long now staring into the tall window of that Upper West Side townhouse, gazing at a nameless family she does not belong to, pretending she can hear what the little girl might be playing: "Greensleeves", a Bach minuet, Schubert's "Ave Maria." Or, perhaps, Beethoven's "Ode to Joy."

7
Mel

"Whoa, that's cool!" Wayne Morrissey says—so loudly that Mel has to pull the phone away from her ear—when she reports she's sold her story to *The New Yorker*. After Austin's odd and rather creepy response, she's decided, for the moment, not to tell anyone else at the magazine. But when Wayne calls the office, she senses he might actually be sympathetic, and so she confides in him about Austin's less than generous reaction.

Hearing Wayne exhale what she knows to be a stream of smoke, she lights up a cigarette of her own, and worries that she should have kept her hurt feelings to herself.

"This is strictly between us, but hey, how fucked up is that!" Wayne says. "If you were here with me in Seattle, I'd give you a congratulatory hug, how's that, Melissa?"

"Thank you, that's so sweet," she says, and feels a rush of both relief and gratitude. She's thankful, too, that Austin is still down at the other end of the hallway talking with the editor-in-chief, a little duckfooted guy who always has an unlit cigar installed in the corner of his mouth. Inexplicably, even though he has degrees in literature from both Yale and Cambridge, it's clear that, for the most part, he scarcely cares about the short stories Austin buys for the magazine.

"So you're *how* old?" Wayne asks her. "You're not a child, are you?" he teases.

"Twenty-five . . . well, closer to twenty-five and a half, to be completely accurate," Mel says.

"Damn, you *are* a child!" Wayne says. "Congratulations,

baby! And you know what, I'm a little jealous myself, that's what!" he says exuberantly, and now she suspects he's probably blitzed. But still she's grateful for his honesty and his kindness.

"I'm no one to be jealous of, trust me. I live in a studio apartment and make a hundred and fifty dollars a week," she confesses.

Wayne laughs, as if she's said something truly amusing. "Cry me a river, Melissa," he says, but then he offers her a gift. "Hey, you know what, I'm coming to town in a couple of weeks and our friend Austin's gonna take me out to a nice expensive lunch. Why don't you come with us?"

Not gonna happen, Mel wants to say. *Well, maybe on an ice-cold day in hell.*

"You don't understand," she tells Wayne. "I'm the one who calls the restaurant to make those reservations for you and Austin, and to him, believe me, for the most part that's pretty much *all* I am."

"Old news," Wayne says. "Things are changing."

On a glacial day in hell, maybe.

8
Julia

Exhausted from a day spent scrubbing down the Mishkins' none-too-clean kitchen and bathroom, changing the linens in the bedroom, doing two loads of their laundry, and accompanying Walter and his wife back and forth to his podiatrist appointment, Julia wants nothing more than to take the subway home and sit in front of her TV tonight watching *Taxi*, a show she knows can always be counted on to make her laugh so hard, her nose begins to run.

"Bye now," Molly is saying, one palm cupping each of Julia's ears. "Don't forget to come back to us tomorrow." Walter is standing behind his wife at the door, waiting in line to deliver his goodbye embrace. The golf shirt he is wearing is stained with the ravioli in tomato sauce the three of them had for lunch today, and there's a spot of saliva pooled in both corners of his mouth.

"I have to tell you, Miss, that we can't live without you," he says. "What will happen to us if you don't come back tomorrow?"

"Of course she's coming back tomorrow," Molly says.

"What?"

"Where else is she going to be? OF COURSE SHE'S COMING BACK TOMORROW!" Molly shouts for Walter's benefit.

"How do *you* know? Maybe she's got something better to do, somewhere better to be. Maybe she's going into the wilderness of the Arabian Desert or for a walk along the Champs-Elysées. How do *you* know what her plans are?"

"You're crazy." Molly rolls her failing eyes.

"What?"

"YOU'RE CRAZY!"

"Come on, guys, no fighting. We'll see each other tomorrow," Julia promises.

"Tomorrow we're going to Dr. Whatsit, the orthopedist, the knee man," Walter says cheerfully.

"Why do you sound so happy?" Molly says. "What's wrong with you?"

"I can't hear you."

"WHAT'S WRONG WITH YOU?"

"I have a hearing aid in each ear and neither one of them really works, that's what's wrong with me."

"That's not what I'm talking about," Molly says.

"Bye, you two!" Julia sings out, and closes the door behind her. Walking toward the elevator, she can hear, as she often does, one of the neighbors, a middle-aged woman, shrieking behind the closed door of her apartment, "Go to hell, you miserable prick! If I catch you looking down my shirt again, I'll have you arrested!" According to the Mishkins, she lives alone and never has any visitors.

Julia slips the earpiece for her transistor radio in place, and listens, with relief and pleasure, as she waits for the elevator, to the Beatles singing "Across the Universe," drowning out the Mishkins' schizo neighbor.

If only she could go straight home now and unwind.

But she can't; first there are a couple of litter boxes to be carefully scooped out, and a dog to be walked, right here in the neighborhood.

Money to be made to help pay her fairly reasonable New York City rent.

After walking a good-natured Pomeranian named Toby, who enjoys peeing on piles of plastic garbage bags set out on the sidewalk, Julia brings him back home to his apartment on the thirty-seventh floor in a building directly across from the Mishkins. Toby's owner, Heather, who works for a health-care company and is attending a conference out west in Portland until the end of the week, has made it clear that Julia is free to help herself, anytime she likes, to whatever is in the refrigerator. Looking over the scant offerings now, she indulges in some club soda and a sliver of a caramel tart, which she cuts with a butter knife, and then arranges daintily on a napkin. She eats standing at the kitchen counter, then washes the knife with detergent, dries it diligently with a paper towel, and puts it back in the silverware drawer, precisely where she found it; with Toby at her heels, she makes her way down the hallway to Heather's bedroom.

She's so tired.

Too tired to walk to the subway on Eighty-Sixth Street that will get her back home to Union Square. She confides this to Toby, and lifts him up onto the bed with her—a king-size bed covered by a pure-white comforter made of some kind of satiny material. Hard to figure out why anyone would want a pure-white comforter that your dog could so easily soil in any number of nasty ways.

It's a bit after six on a late-fall evening, and she's snoozing with Toby snuggled against her folded knees.

When she awakens a couple of hours later, she realizes that, inexplicably, she has sweated through the turtleneck she's been wearing since early this morning. She heads to Heather's linen closet for a pair of thick towels that smell faintly of strawberries, and then into the bathroom, where she strips off her jeans and turtleneck and underwear, and enters the shower, which is ornamented with a wall of glass blocks tinted mint green. She has to admire it, and the shower head as well, a large shining circle of stainless steel that looks nothing like the crappy little nozzle in her own shower at home. Sampling a squirt of conditioner, she can tell it's some super-luxury brand, and then she shaves her legs with a pink plastic razor she finds hidden behind the soap dish. She gets a kick out of the soap itself, which is citrus-scented and resembles a big pale Lego block.

Toby is waiting for her when she gets out, his fleecy tail wagging; he's not going to pass judgment, he's just going to follow her around loyally and keep his sweet little mouth shut.

The pleasingly fragrant towel feels velvety wrapped across her body; she uses the second towel for her hair and then winds it tightly around her head like a turban. There are pristine-looking, backless lavender slippers in Heather's bedroom closet, and she slides her feet into them after a moment's hesitation. She sees a light-blue silk kimono decorated with pink roses hanging right up front on an upholstered hanger; it's so easy to slip it off the hanger and over her shoulders.

She's feeling nice and cozy in Heather's silky kimono. Nice and laid-back for the first time all day.

Though lazing around in this particular apartment on the thirty-seventh floor is a first for her, it's not as if she is unfamiliar with making herself at home in other people's fancy digs.

But how, she wonders, has she become the sort of person who showers in her clients' homes when they're away for the weekend or on an extended business trip? How has she become someone who helps herself to her clients' fluffed towels and the softest bathrobes and kimonos and then relaxes with her heels up on their coffee table, sipping their wine, but mostly their Coke or Pepsi, which she occasionally knocks back straight from the bottle and then returns to the refrigerator, always taking pains to wipe off the neck of the bottle with a napkin first.

She is not, after all, a slob.

She's a woman who's *this* close to earning her doctorate, if only she could find the time to start that dissertation on violence in the work of those prominent female southern writers.

But she's been so busy cleaning and cooking for the Mishkins, accompanying them to the podiatrist; the audiologist; the optician; the dentist; the orthopedist; the ophthalmologist; the glaucoma specialist; the retinologist; the barber; the hairdresser. Then there are all those runs to the drugstore, the supermarket, the dry cleaners. She manages the Mishkins' life for them and does a bang-up job.

If only she could hire someone to manage her own.

Toby stares at her with those obsidian eyes. He seems to be regarding her sympathetically, but who knows what's really on his mind?

"What is it, kiddo?" she asks him. He makes a yapping noise and nips at the toe of one of those illicit violet slippers on her feet. He knows they belong to Heather, knows that Julia has no right to be wearing them; he's offended by the sight of them on her feet and wants her to know it. He expects better of her; shouldn't she expect better of herself?

Fine, she tells him. *Take your damn slippers back*.

What would her parents think of her lounging around in Heather's kimono, the scent of that expensive conditioner still clinging to her hair? Or even the Mishkins—what would they think of her, helping herself now to a scarlet bikini bottom straight out of the top drawer of Heather's dresser? She's going to bring it back tomorrow, *swear to God*, washed by hand and perfectly clean, when she returns to walk Toby. Look, it's not as if she's a thief; she's just a borrower, someone who needs clean underwear and can't stand the thought of getting herself back into what she was wearing all day today, sweaty stuff you can't reproach yourself for not wanting to put back on.

Frankly, why should she care what her parents think about *anything*? She barely talks to them these days, and why should she?

Her mother has two degrees from Sarah Lawrence, works as an assistant curator at the Vanderbilt Museum on the North

Shore and is not a moron by any means. So would it have killed her mother to step in now and again when Julia's father was in one of those crazy pitch-dark moods of his and had the urge to fling her or her brother against the wall of their bedroom?

You kids are driving me fucking insane.

Julia hears those words and knows what's coming and her heartbeats per minute accelerate to a number so outrageous, it zooms right off the charts and flies straight into the upper reaches of the stratosphere.

You couldn't blame alcohol or drugs; there was none of that, just a boiling anger that grew hotter and hotter until that pathetic excuse for a father *had no choice*, her mother said, *couldn't stop himself*, her mother insisted, from slamming his eight-year-old daughter against the wall.

And then threw a few punches while he was at it.

He passed the CPA exam—a *very difficult test*, her mother always said proudly—on the very first shot.

I think you and your brother need to forgive him, she said. *I think he feels bad enough as it is.*

Forgive?

Really?

Does her mother think Julia and her brother are idiots?

Our brains are not sieves, Mom. My frontal cortex, the memory keeper, is working just fine.

Why would you ever forgive the six-foot-two guy who, from time to time, showed up in your bedroom at night just to torment you?

Always in the dark; the lights were never turned on, not even for an instant. Like some nocturnal primate, her father knew just where to go in complete darkness.

School nights, holidays; it was all the same to him. New Year's Eve was the night he broke Julia's arm, as a matter of fact. She and her brother, Andrew, who was five years younger, had been allowed to stay up until midnight to usher in the new year; they were wearing festive paper hats and drinking ginger ale from plastic champagne glasses, just like all the other children on the block. They went to bed giddy from fatigue, from savoring the privilege of having stayed up hours beyond their usual bedtime. It felt so good to fall right to sleep so effortlessly.

And then, who knows what time it was—one a.m.? one-thirty? two a.m.?—their father came charging in, in a rage about something he never bothered to explain—and hauled them out of their beds, first Julia and then Andrew.

You kids are driving me FUCKING INSANE.

This was a Saturday afternoon long ago, in the late fifties, Julia is telling Charlie, when she and her parents were, despite her father's ill-concealed displeasure, well on their way to the Washington Irving mall—no doubt the only shopping center in the world where lines from *The Legend of Sleepy Hollow* were engraved in the building's façade. Her father, Steve Myerson, a certified public accountant in Manhattan, had been forced into the role of chauffeur today because Julia's mother, Roz, had failed her road test for the third time and would not ever, not in the twentieth century or any other, get her hands on a driver's license. For Julia and her mother, a couple of suburbanites, nothing was within walking distance; everything was out of reach. Her father was willing to drive the two of them and Andrew, her brother, anyplace at all, but everything lay in the asking, in the piling up of debts he seemed to hint could never be repaid.

When they arrived at Macy's that afternoon, Julia's father seated himself in an upholstered chair on the sidelines of the Young Miss department with a copy of *The New York Times* folded back lengthwise and then in half horizontally, still wearing his caramel-color suede coat and a tweed hat with a small red feather tucked in its brim, and looking as if he might abandon his family at any moment. (Andrew, who was seven, and hated shopping of any kind, was with a friend for the afternoon, playing with his fleet of Matchbox cars, which included a tiny dump truck and a cement mixer, and which twelve-year-old Julia and her mother were tired of tripping over in the bedroom Julia and Andrew still shared.)

"Twenty minutes, Stevie," her mother promised, "that should do it for Julia and me," and she went through the racks with notable speed, glancing frequently, and maybe a little uneasily, in his direction, as if to make sure her husband was still there. When they were finished, her mother kissed the top of his goofy hat with the feather, saying, "You're a prince, Stevie," and the words made little sense to Julia, because one thing she understood with full clarity, even as far back as the very end of her childhood, was that her father could hardly deserve the title that had been bestowed upon him.

There was bumper-to-bumper traffic on the return trip, and when they finally reached home, close to an hour later than they should have, her father was in a quiet rage. Even though he claimed to have a headache, he chain-smoked until dinner, seated grimly on his leather Barcalounger, the ashes falling from his Camels and speckling the knees of his olive-green corduroy pants, the scent of his mood filtering throughout the apartment-size, one-story house until even Julia's hair smelled smoky.

You kids are driving me crazy.

How many times can you hear this in your head before it starts to drive *you* crazy?

Julia's hands rest obediently in her lap; she uses her right to caress the protruding, knobby bone of her left wrist. "My father broke my arm," she hears herself saying to Charlie. "It was my wrist, actually. I was eight when he pitched me against the wall on New Year's Eve." And now she is remembering the look of fury on her father's face, lit only by the overhead light in the hallway, and the grim determination in the set of his jaw. "My father, Steve Myerson, CPA. My mother must have told us a hundred times that he passed all four sections of the accounting exam on the very first try."

"How awful." Charlie appears genuinely stricken. "I mean, what he did to you, not about the CPA exam." He gets up from his seat and Julia thinks he's coming over to comfort her, but, in fact, he's on his way to the minifridge stocked with cans of Coke and Diet Pepsi and glass bottles of Gatorade. He asks Julia what she would like, and hands her a can of Coke, but first he pops the top for her in a gesture Julia finds touchingly thoughtful. Back in his seat, Charlie rubs his shoulder, meditatively, and asks, "Would you like to tell me more about it?"

What Julia would like is to relax in silence with her soda.

And to receive an apology from the guilty parties, even one delivered more than twenty-five years late. But *that*, she knows, will never be granted. Certainly not by her father and, in all likelihood, not by her mother, either.

She appreciates Charlie's kind demeanor, noticeably sweeter than Dr. Safran's, and the Coke, icy and full of fizz, is just the way she wants it. She observes, as she sips at it, that Charlie is studying her in a way that strikes her as intimate, as if now she were something other than his patient—instead simply a woman seated across from him—and that clearly he likes what he sees.

"I feel as if you know me," she tells him, "I mean, that you really know who I am."

"I do," he says, and it's the best, and most gratifying, thing anyone has said to her in what feels like a very long while.

9
Mel

In the office next to Austin's, there's an editor who doesn't seem to do much of anything except read portions of book-length manuscripts and talk quietly into his phone; his name is Martin Glass, and it's hard to figure out exactly what his job is, though he's listed on the masthead as an associate editor. He's a prematurely white-haired guy who dresses every day in the same dark-blue suit and brown penny loafers. And nearly every *other* day, it seems, he and Austin somehow end up standing out in the hallway arguing about who-knows-what. Which is where they are this morning, six inches from Mel's desk.

"You're really something, you know that?" Martin is saying now.

"I don't know what you mean," Austin tells him.

"What I mean is that you're SUCH an idiot. You're stupid, really," Martin explains.

"In what way? I have no idea what you're referring to, and that's because you're the first person in my life who's ever called me stupid." Austin turns to Mel, and says, "Have *you* ever heard anybody call me that, dear heart?"

Looking down at her typewriter, Mel pretends not to hear him. It's both bewildering and uncomfortable listening to these two grown men belittling one another, as if they have nothing better to do on a workday.

"I don't even know why I even bother to talk to you," Martin says.

"No one's holding a gun to your head, buddy," Austin says,

but he smiles, weakly, as he says it, and shrugs his shoulders as he walks past Mel's desk and back into his office.

"Thanks a lot!" Martin says, and gives Austin the finger, though it's only Mel who can see it.

Phillip, the editor-in-chief, is duckfooting his way down the linoleum; he comes to a stop in the middle of the two offices and says, "You children need to grow up." He's not smiling; in fact, he looks like a disapproving father who's just about had enough. It occurs to Mel that these three dudes are nothing more than a family whose members just can't get along with each other, and have long ago given up trying.

10
Charlie

He's parked in the driver's seat of his Volkswagen Rabbit reading about anxiety in adolescents in his *Journal of Generalized Anxiety Disorder.* And he's not happy about it. It's not the article that disturbs him, it's the fact that Mel has—apologetically—kicked him out of the apartment once again so she can work on a new story. He understands, though not fully, why she can't concentrate on this or that paragraph of hers while he's sitting in the same room with her, and he's sympathetic to her ambitions. But it's almost nine o'clock on a Sunday night, and he's been here, two blocks from their apartment, for nearly an hour; frankly, he's had enough of indulging her. He wants to go home and lounge cozily with Mel on the couch in their studio apartment and watch *All in the Family* together, as they usually do on Sunday evenings.

Then it comes to him that this distressing feeling of exclusion is more familiar than he realized. And it's not so much exclusion from Mel's fiercely stubborn attempts to master whatever story she's struggling with, but rather that feeling of living a life unmarked by a genuine passion for a particular sort of work—work he might love in the unwavering, utterly tenacious way Mel loves to write her stories. It reminds Charlie of his brother Jeff's insatiable enthusiasm for cooking, an obsession inspiring unforgettable meals that wowed everyone in the family and made it easier for his parents—despite their objections to Jeff devoting his life to anything other than medicine or the law—to accept that decision to abandon his already-lucrative career as a litigator and open a restaurant down in the Village.

Jeff, he knows, loves being a chef/restaurateur the way Mel loves being a short story writer, and even though Charlie feels a sense of purpose and commitment to his own work helping his patients, that's where it ends. And so, now and then, he finds himself feeling painfully unfulfilled.

But of course, like almost everyone else, he has his passions; every word of Kurt Vonnegut's novels, every bit of Dylan's music and the nasal twang of his voice, and Lennon and McCartney and the Kinks and the Rolling Stones and Procol Harum and the black leather interior with its white piping of his very first car, a three-year-old, British racing green MGB that he bought in 1968 for twelve hundred and twenty-five dollars. One time and one time only, he drove that beloved MGB a hundred miles an hour on the newly opened Seaford-Oyster Bay Expressway on Long Island, the convertible top lowered in the summer sun, his right hand gripping the walnut gearshift, the glorious sound of the MGB's motor a thrill to him as he accelerated; a sound that he will always say brought him to life like nothing else. He loved the feel of the mahogany steering wheel beneath his fingers, and the wrinkle-finish metal of the dashboard, the ashtray filled with shining quarters to pay the twenty-five-cent toll to get him across the Triborough Bridge and into Manhattan, where he could hear Led Zeppelin play in Central Park and Jefferson Airplane at the Fillmore East and the Stones at the Garden in the fall of 1969.

But at least his practice is going fairly well, thanks to referrals from his mentor at Columbia, and referrals from his patients themselves—those who are pleased with Charlie's gift for intuitively sensing just how long he needs to listen to the details of their laments, their worries, their terrors, before gently interrupting them and asking just the right questions. Today one of his patients was a teenager who'd been asked to take a medical leave of absence from her boarding school in Massachusetts, where she continued to struggle with anorexia.

He sat in his office and listened to this fifteen-year-old named Jessica talk about how she stared longingly at a package of Hostess Twinkies in her parents' kitchen this morning, until finally putting her nose up against the cellophane and inhaling the sugary scent of what lay beneath it. This was all she allowed herself, all she could manage to offer herself, and it almost broke Charlie's heart listening to her. That clinical distance between him and his patient had evaporated, for only a moment, and it worried him.

He's pretty certain this isn't the sort of lifelong career he wants for himself. Really he's still trying to figure out what that career might be. And he's still in his twenties, surely young enough to keep searching for a satisfying place for himself in the world, isn't he? If only he cared less about what those parents thought of him; in fact, he's asked himself, why should he care at all?

It's uncomfortably cold in the car now and the flashlight he's using to read his journal seems to be losing its power. He could turn the heat on but doesn't want to keep the motor running.

He rubs the tips of his chilly fingers together.

No one ever warned him this was what it would be like to be married to a writer.

11
Mel

It's no surprise when Austin deems Wayne Morrissey's suggestion that they include Mel in their lunch plans at Tre Scalini on Madison and Sixty-Third *wildly inappropriate*. And yet she is surprised at how wistful she feels as the two of them leave the office together, Austin's long slim arm slung over Wayne's bulky shoulder as he says, "Let's head out, my boy," Wayne turning his head toward Mel and mouthing the single word *sorry*. He's dressed in jeans and slightly scuffed, pointy-toed black boots, never mind the four-star restaurant where he and Austin will be dining. He hugged her, enthusiastically, when she introduced herself out in the hallway across from Austin's office; he looked like a cowboy of sorts, and Mel could imagine him with a holster strapped under his arm, carrying a loaded semiautomatic. Then she thought of Wayne pointing this imaginary pistol at Austin and saying, *Listen up, dude: delete any more of those simple but meticulously crafted sentences of mine, and I'll blow your fucking head off!*

In the mostly empty office she eats her homemade cream-cheese-and-green-olive sandwich at her desk, plucking Cheetos from a fifteen-cent bag she bought downstairs at the newsstand in the lobby, and then browsing through the collection of bound galleys of soon-to-be-published books—sent by sadly uninformed publishers hoping the magazine will review them in its defunct book column—left for the taking on the long, plastic-laminate table positioned outside the fact-checkers' office. Before helping herself to a pair of short-story collections, one by John Updike and the other Alice Munro, Mel quietly licks the neon-orange Cheetos dust from her fingertips. A couple of years from now, when she is introduced, in a members-only library in downtown Boston, to Updike, whose every sentence she worships, he will take her hand in his and flatter her charmingly.

You must be rather brilliant, Melissa, to have had those stories of yours published in The New Yorker *when—look at you!—you're so very young.*

Look who's talking! she will want to say to him. And seriously—brilliant? Come on, don't be ridiculous! She's just a storyteller, she will explain, dying to tell these stories of hers as best she can.

Hours later, when Austin and Wayne return from their lunch at that four-star restaurant, both of them reeking of alcohol, Wayne hands her a brown paper shopping bag containing their smelly leftovers in cardboard containers.

"Linguini alla puttanesca and chicken parmigiana!" he says grandly, and his Italian accent isn't bad at all.

"For me?"

"For you, *Signorina* Mel."

Sometime in the next decade, when she reads in *The New York Times* that Wayne has been inducted into the American Academy of Arts and Letters, one of the things she will remember most distinctly are these sweetly offered leftovers smelling of tomatoes, anchovies, and garlic.

12
Julia

Steering a couple of nonagenarians from one side of a Manhattan street to the other isn't as easy as you'd think. Especially if one of them has a bad knee and the other insists on trying to walk and talk simultaneously. When you hit ninety-three, you have to choose: You can either walk, or you can talk, you just don't have the concentration for both, at least not at the same time. Julia discovered this on her first day on the job with the Mishkins, when all three of them were nearly clipped by a station wagon the color of dried blood. The fault lay entirely with Walter, who couldn't be dissuaded from stopping halfway across Lexington Avenue just to point out a little guy on the corner sporting buckled shoes and a bright green velvet leprechaun costume; over the costume he was wearing a poster advertising O'Shea's Bar & Grill. Both the Mishkins seem to have forgotten the leprechaun and their close call with the station wagon; whenever Julia raises the subject, as she does now, Molly and Walter stare at her and claim they don't know what she's talking about.

"But what was a leprechaun doing advertising a bar?" Molly wants to know as Julia guides her and her husband across the street now. It's 8:30 in the morning and they're on their way to the podiatrist again. "Why do leprechauns even need to earn a living?" Molly teases. "What could they be saving up their money for?"

An enraged toddler, kicking the heels of his black-and-yellow Batman sneakers angrily against the plastic footrest of his stroller, is wheeled past them. "I don't WANT orange joo!" he squeals.

"What's he carrying on about?" Walter says, but Julia doesn't answer. She notices a bevy of teenage girls in the same private-school uniform—gray jumper, white blouse—ambling along Third Avenue on the other side of the street with their coats open and flapping in the wintry breeze, and the sight of them brings to mind her lost teaching gig. It's disquieting to see uniformed schoolgirls when you're out of a job, out of the classroom, and instead, out on the street with two extremely elderly people who don't like taking orders from you, even though it's for their own good.

"Life is remarkably interesting," she hears Molly saying. "It's boring and stupid, but also interesting, and that's because of all the crazy ways things turn out. Remember that two-headed turtle you saw on television, Walter? Each head had to be fed separately, and it was such hard work, the owner had to give it back to the pet store?"

"All right, let's forget about the two-headed turtle and concentrate on getting to the podiatrist," Julia suggests. Just as the traffic light changes, and she begins to escort Walter and Molly across the street, she sees Charlie Fleischer, her therapist; for some reason, she's almost too shy to even look at him though she just saw him in his office last Thursday and has another appointment scheduled again for this week.

He's moving past her along this Upper East Side street humming with pedestrians and buses and trucks and cabs, busy talking to a short, brown-haired chick in her twenties in plaid woolen bell-bottoms who, curiously— Julia thinks—is drinking from a glass bottle of Tab before nine in the morning. What kind of a weirdo drinks soda for breakfast, she wonders.

Julia calls out to Charlie, but too shyly, too quietly for him to hear. If she had a free hand, she would extend it to wave at him, but both her hands are occupied at the moment, her left grasping the thin, bony crook of Walter's arm, her right holding on to Molly.

He walks right past her, talking earnestly to the chick drinking her soda, saying to her, "Not Edgar Allan Poe, Edgar Allan *Pearl*," and though Julia's not sure why, she feels more than a pang of disappointment not to have been recognized as Charlie vanishes, somewhere along the west side of Third Avenue.

"I'm tired and I'm hungry," Walter complains in the podiatrist's cramped waiting room, and he sends Julia across the street to Dunkin' Donuts for one Boston Kreme and one chocolate glazed. "Remember: no powdered sugar!" he yells after her. "If it's powdered sugar, I won't eat it, Miss!"

Hurrying across the street as the "Don't Walk" sign flashes red, Julia mouths the words *thanks a lot* to the driver of the cab making a wide, reckless right turn that could have been the end of her.

The driver rolls his window down just in time to call her a stupid bitch.

Though she's not a great fan of donuts, she takes Walter's Boston Kreme out of the bag anyway and picks at it indifferently. She's sitting at a low counter in the window of Dunkin' Donuts while, across the street, the ninety-three-year-old with two hearing aids waits for his snack. She's feeling guilty and selfish, but she remains in her seat nevertheless, just not in the mood to deal with the Mishkins this morning.

She looks out the window and sees a man in an ankle-length coat making the sign of the cross as a fire truck speeds up the street. What's he thinking about? His sins? The guy comes into Dunkin' Donuts now and proclaims to the two employees behind the counter, "Let God arise. Let His enemies be scattered." His voice is dull, oddly uninflected; in the background, on someone's transistor radio, Bonnie Tyler's distinctively scratchy voice can be heard singing "It's a Heartache."

"Let those who fear Him flee before His holy face," the guy advises. He has an unkempt gray beard that reaches to his collarbone, though his face is surprisingly youthful.

"Would you like a donut, sir?" a woman behind the counter proposes. "And maybe something to drink?" One of her arms is embellished with dozens of the thinnest silver bracelets, and she smiles tentatively. "I've got a Bavarian Kreme for you, and a couple of powdered sugar, and some coffee, all right, sir?"

"Decaf," the guy says, and soon collects his free donuts and coffee, but instead of *thank you*, he says, "Let the wicked perish in the presence of the Lord."

He turns away from the counter with his goodies in both hands, and stares at Julia. "As wax melts before the fire, so let the wicked perish in the presence of God."

"Understood," Julia says, already on her way to the counter to buy another donut for Walter, whose Boston Kreme she's ruined.

Eleven years after graduation, Julia and her best friend from college are still close enough that they're in touch every week. Rachel's split-level house is deep in the suburbs of New Jersey, where she lives with her four-year-old, Brady. She and her husband, Peter, are separated, but won't be for long, Rachel has predicted, though Peter recently confessed he knew they had made a grievous mistake even before they'd gone halfway down the aisle on their wedding day. It hurts Julia to view her old friend as hopelessly optimistic, but really, *what* is Rachel thinking?

How different could their lives be from one another? Though Julia has no burning desire at this moment for a four-year-old of her own and a 4,500-square-foot house in the suburbs (and you can forget the husband who's gone AWOL and only stops by to see that four-year-old from time to time), it feels to her as if her dearest friend Rachel has *something*. While she, Julia—husbandless and childless and employed by all the wrong people—feels as if her life is pretty thin, pretty impoverished.

"Wanna say hi to Aunt Julia?" Rachel is asking Brady. "Here, angel, talk into the phone."

"Brady!" Julia says. "I miss you, so come into the city and visit me, all right?"

"I'm having chocolate-chip pancakes for dinner," Brady reports. "With caramel syrup. You want some?"

Reclaiming the phone, Rachel whispers, "Dinner is going to be mac and cheese, but that's between you and I."

"*Me*," Julia says, and is unable to stop herself from sighing.

Why does everyone mistakenly think "I" instead of "me" and pat themselves on the back for it? And why does this continue to drive Julia crazy, she who has yet to write even a word of her dissertation.

"Me *what*?" says Rachel.

"Between you and *me*, Ray, you who have a degree from an Ivy League school should know better," Julia teases.

Rachel doesn't respond at first, then lowering her voice, she says, "Actually, I've been thinking a lot lately about when we were at Penn and all that really, truly memorable sex I had with Marc. Of course, I was only a sophomore, and laughably inexperienced, but I have to say he was one of the best. Ever."

"Oh God," Julia murmurs. She is someone who's not altogether comfortable talking about sex, even with her dearest friend, and she doesn't want to linger, even for a moment, on images of Rachel and their middle-aged Critical Reading and Writing professor dampening the sheets in one bed after another at the Do Drop Inn in Philly. "Can we please not talk about this again? Please?"

"Brady, NO!" Rachel says. "His sweaty little hand is down the front of my shirt!" Now Julia can hear Brady shrieking, "Bosoms bosoms bosoms!"

"Those were the halcyon days," Rachel reminds her. "Me in my size-3 jeans, sneaking around in motels Mondays and Thursdays in the late afternoon, after Marc's last class was over. Gotta tell you, it was pretty romantic, all that sneaking around. He never really seemed afraid the wife would find out, he just kept coming back for more."

She and Rachel would sit around late at night in their dorm room sophomore year, Julia remembers, smoking a little weed, and there would be tears in Rachel's eyes as she talked about what it was like to be in love with the wrong person. *I mean, what am I doing?* she would say. *It's not like we're ever going to* be *anything together, not like this is ever going to* go *anywhere. He's told me this, like, fifty times already.*

Don't sleep with married guys if you can help it; what kind of genius do you have to be to figure that *one out?* Julia always wanted to tell her, but even if she had, would Rachel have listened?

"Bosoms bosoms bosoms!" Brady continues exuberantly, and Julia can hear how he's made a song of it. "Bosoms here, bosoms there, bosoms ev-ry wher-ere!"

"Fabulous lyrics, Brady!" Julia yells into the phone, as if he could hear her. How did people summon up the infinite patience required for parenthood, she wonders. She questions whether she'd be a whiz at raising a child, but this seems to be her default position, always being hard on herself, scarcely if ever giving herself a break. In fact, she and Dr. Safran had spent way too much time on that particular subject, and she can still hear him urging her to give herself "a fucking break now and again." His exact words; that was how frustrated he'd been.

Not like Charlie Fleischer, who never loses patience with her, and will, she thinks, figure out precisely how to guide her along the right course.

13
Mel

Mel may be nobody and nothing at the office, but here at *The New Yorker*, waiting for the very first time in front of the glassed-in reception box high above Forty-Third Street for Elizabeth Greenwell, her editor—and oh how Mel savors being able to silently say those words *my editor!*—she feels like the tiniest bit of a somebody. Or at least not an unequivocal nobody.

Elizabeth Greenwell, Mel discovers in an instant, is everything Mel herself is not: starting with tall, hazel-eyed, and red-haired, and ending with beautifully soft-voiced, quietly self-assured, perfectly dressed, and oh yes, supremely WASPy. Someone, Mel knows, whom her mother, the Legal Aid lawyer, would have referred to as *classy*. (If only she were still here, how excited she would be for Mel; it brings brief but embarrassingly sentimental tears to her eyes just to think of what her mother is missing out on hearing about today.)

"Such a pleasure to meet you in person," Elizabeth is saying now in front of the receptionist's window, her hand extended, charm bracelets tinkling, to shake Mel's own.

"Oh gosh, me too," is all Mel can think to say, feeling an unsettling combination of lesser-than and supremely lucky to be standing here next to Elizabeth, with whom she's already, in some strangely intoxicating way, fallen in love. The words *love at first sight, sort of,* are what come to her; but really it's more a profound awe and reverence for everything Elizabeth Greenwell embodies, especially that quiet self-assurance.

She is leading Mel into her own office, one almost as spacious as the duckfooted editor-in-chief's, and beautifully decorated with an immaculate-looking linen couch, a large oriental rug, and a couple of stylish lamps, all of which, Elizabeth confides, she's brought from home.

The little-more-than-adequate furniture back at the office will look all the more unimpressive when Mel returns to work this afternoon—this is what she is thinking when Elizabeth slips on her coat and politely announces that she and Mel will be having their lunch at the Algonquin, which is only a block away. Mel nods calmly, as if to say, *Yeah, yeah, of course the Algonquin—where else would you be taking me?* But honestly, could her life get any more thrilling than this?

Highly unlikely, she thinks.

She needs a cigarette right now, though she hardly feels confident enough to light up in front of Elizabeth; her fingers would probably be trembling too fiercely even to strike a match or flick her lighter.

Riding down in the elevator, she thinks of the pink-and-white cover of her copy of *The Portable Dorothy Parker*, a small paperback that fits in the palm of her hand, though it's over five hundred pages and cost a dollar and eighty-five cents, and which she bought as a freshman at her college bookstore, only a few years after Dorothy Parker's death. She tells this to Elizabeth when they reach the lobby, tells her that Dorothy Parker is someone whose stories she has read and reread four or five times since college.

Elizabeth is a decade older and wiser—a woman in her mid-thirties who most likely knows all there is to know about Austin and his compadre Richard at *The Times*. She looks at Mel and offers her a kindly smile. If only, Mel thinks, she had the nerve, the boldness, to confide in Elizabeth about Austin and Richard. But then again, Elizabeth, so poised and self-possessed, would, perhaps, look down on Mel or dismiss what she might regard as lurid gossip. It's just much too risky to even raise the subject, Mel realizes.

Elizabeth is offering the same sort of gracious smile now as Mel hears herself confessing that all of her stories are handwritten in an official Brown University spiral notebook she bought as an undergrad; only after the story is in its final draft will she type it up on the sleek, two-tone gray electric Olivetti her parents bought for her when she graduated. And, oh yes, the pen she uses—her lucky pen—is a twenty-nine-cent extra-fine-point white plastic Bic pen with a blue plastic cap. But what else will they talk about as they walk over to Forty-Fourth Street, Mel worries. It's only a single block, but she knows she's not an expert at face-to-face small talk, particularly with someone like Elizabeth, whom she can't help but think of as her superior in every way.

On this arctic January afternoon, she will soon turn up the space heater beneath her desk until it glows orangey-red and toast her icy hands in front of it. And in less than a week, her name will appear in the table of contents of *The New Yorker*. (At work, she's seen her name on the masthead, one of the half-dozen names preceded by the words *Editorial Assistants*: not really anything that stirs much more than a whit of pride in her.) She can't yet imagine what this will feel like, or what anyone she knows—friends, family, people at work—will think of her story. Or if they will even care enough to read it. Her family is filled with dentists and lawyers, a couple of social workers and high school teachers. Her friends are in PhD programs, med school, law school; a couple of them are copywriters at advertising agencies. She shouldn't, she knows, expect any of them to fully grasp the meaning that all of this—her name in the table of contents, her story occupying a few pages of the magazine in its distinctive font—holds for her, but even so, she wants it from them. She wishes, too, that she could talk about these expectations of hers with Elizabeth, about whom she knows so little, really.

In the Algonquin's dining room, she stares at "The Vicious

Circle," the vividly colorful mural of the Round Table, where Dorothy Parker, the only woman in the group, is wearing a broad-brimmed hat and a decidedly pissed-off look on her face. Mel and Elizabeth are seated next to each other on the same side of a table for two; Mel is a little confused by this, but flattered that her editor wants to sit so close to her.

Elizabeth, it turns out, doesn't need to study the menu; why would she? She's been here so often, she explains to Mel, the waiters know her and the things she's likely to order—today it's steak tartare, she tells the server standing over them now, and to Mel this is so exotic, it is, mortifyingly, something she's never even heard of. She orders a Cobb salad for herself, though she hates the velvety texture of avocado and can't stand the bright yolk of hard-boiled eggs. She doesn't want to bother the waiter and ask him to make even the smallest changes to her order; she doesn't want Elizabeth to think of her as hard to please.

When their food arrives, Mel can't quite believe what she's seeing on Elizabeth's plate: something that looks like a raw hamburger on toast . . . but *now* what? The waiter is breaking a raw egg over it, though it's only the yolk that lands neatly on top of the burger. Elizabeth is smiling and thanking him, and Mel is still in a state of shock at what she's seeing—a raw hamburger? Embellished with a raw egg? But where's the steak?

"Would you like a *cor nee shon*?" Elizabeth asks her, gesturing toward the little pickles garnishing what Mel continues to think of as her raw hamburger.

"*Merci bien*," Mel says, and both of them smile when she jokes, "A.P. French and then some."

"By the way, that table over there? That's Mr. Shh—" Elizabeth begins in a whisper.

"I'm sorry?"

"That's his table over there. Do you see Mr. Shh—" Her voice is barely audible.

"Excuse me?"

"That table is his and his alone," Elizabeth says.

Mel knows that the small, solitary man hunched over his plate at his table in the middle of the room is Elizabeth's boss, and now understands that his name is never to be uttered aloud except in the most muted of whispers.

And if that's the way he wants it, so be it.

She overhears two men at a nearby table, both of them in suits and ties, talking animatedly about a woman one of them refers to as "a fucking psycho bitch." Apparently Elizabeth has heard them as well; she glances at Mel and shakes her head. Mel looks beyond them to the table where Elizabeth's boss is sitting, wiping his mouth now with a linen napkin. She wonders if he, too, has overheard the guys discussing the *fucking psycho bitch. Not for us*, she can imagine him saying, which is what he wrote in the margins of the galleys of her story, commenting on a paragraph where she used the word *asshole* in a simple line of dialogue.

And if that's the way he wants it, so be it.

How hilarious—and gratifying—it will be to Mel, when in the next century, three decades from now, variations of that word *fucking* will appear fourteen times in a single, wonderfully artful piece in the magazine.

It seems odd that she and Elizabeth haven't talked at all about "Untroubled Lives," she's thinking now. Or even much at all about "Autumn," the new story Mel recently sent her for the third time and which Elizabeth has asked her to keep working on, explaining that one of her characters, even after two revisions, remains a bit of a cipher. And it's still not quite believable, Elizabeth is saying now, that the two women in her story could be so wildly in love with this guy, each of them knowing the other exists and yet not really caring. "There's got to be something truly compelling, something galvanizing about this man, but I'm just not getting it from you. Not yet, anyway." Then, fixing her gaze thoughtfully on Mel, Elizabeth says, "I think there's something blocking you here. You keep returning to this guy, but for some reason you still haven't been able to transform him into a fully realized character."

"Got it," Mel says. "I'm very grateful."

"Don't be silly." Smiling, Elizabeth begins talking about a new Wayne Morrissey story that she'd admired in a literary magazine. "I hear, as I'm sure *you* have, that he has a serious problem with alcohol, but who knows, maybe his writing is all the better for it . . . On the other hand," she says, and offers Mel another cornichon, "I'm reminded of John Steinbeck, who wrote in his diary about 'a fine depressed hangover in which nothing seemed any good and I myself the most no good of all.'" She says this so beautifully, so elegantly—almost as if she were reciting poetry—that Mel doesn't know what to say; all she can do is chew on this tiniest of cornichons from Elizabeth's plate.

Mostly, they talk about their families and husbands—Elizabeth's husband, she reports, is a vice-president in the asset management division of Goldman Sachs. Nodding her head, Mel says, *Oh, so interesting,* when really she is far more engrossed in the story of Elizabeth's father. Who, she learns, served in the US Army Air Corps in India during World War II and was shot in the stomach while innocently waiting in the mess line for his dinner when a gun someone was cleaning nearby went off accidentally. "The bullet killed the man waiting in line directly behind my father," Elizabeth says softly, "then went through my father, and then through the man standing in line in front of him, wounding them both rather seriously. I don't know why, but when I was a little girl, and we were all in our bathing suits at the beach, I loved running my finger along the outline of the scar across my father's stomach. But why would I have done that?" she says, looking over at Mel, as if for an answer.

Mel can see that five-year-old Elizabeth, her tiny finger

stroking, so lovingly, the scar from her father's World War II injury.

Later, when she and Elizabeth go off to the ladies' room together, Mel is a little apprehensive, unsure if she can feel comfortable enough to pee in the same room as her editor. The ladies' room is just about empty and perfectly silent except for someone rinsing her hands at one of the sinks before touching up her eye shadow. Mel doesn't know which stall to choose: she doesn't want to be too close to Elizabeth, but doesn't want to insult her by going to the one at the other end of the room. She decides on one that is two stalls away from Elizabeth and then waits until she hears the sound of her editor peeing before she feels comfortable enough to do what she herself is there to do.

Peeing together in the ladies' room in the Algonquin—a bonding experience between writer and editor never to be forgotten.

At least by one of them.

14
Julia

In the months that have passed since she walked away from her marriage, Julia has allowed herself one blind date, a get-together engineered by that best friend of hers. As soon as it comes to an end, Julia calls Rachel to complain. "I'm telling you, there was something weird about their relationship," she says, taking pleasure in the withholding of critical information, which involves Rachel's neighbor, Henry, and the long-hair Chihuahua he brought along on their dinner date.

"Whose relationship?" Rachel says. "And what kind of weird?"

"Weird," Julia says, "as in, a single father dragging his little kid along on a blind date. Though in this case, the kid was a Chihuahua named Winston." To his credit, Winston had been on his best behavior all night and sat meekly in Henry's lap, Julia says as she sponges off her tiny kitchen's tiny Formica countertop. "The poor little guy has cataracts. According to the veterinary ophthalmologist Henry brought him to, the cataracts aren't ripe yet, but he'll have to have the surgery eventually."

"This is what you talk about on a date? Canine cataracts? In any case, was the food good?"

The restaurant Henry chose for dinner was the kind Julia wasn't really able to patronize on her own; it was high-end Japanese, where a Pepsi in a miniature glass bottle went for an outrageous dollar and a half. Julia had two of them and felt guilty when she ordered the second round. Watching Henry chow down so enthusiastically, chopsticks in hand, she found herself missing Daniel more piercingly than she had in a while. She could picture him, short and sort of scrawny, slumped in his seat at their dining-room table as he ate his broccoli and brown rice and talked about an article he was writing for *Rolling Stone* on father-and-son directors in Hollywood.

With Henry, who worked at a corporate law firm where he handled antitrust cases, there was nothing much to talk about except his dogs, past and present, and before too long Julia had enough and just wanted to get going. "No more blind dates!" she tells Rachel now. "Not that I don't greatly appreciate your wanting to help."

"But what if I find you someone who'll show up alone, no Chihuahua tagging along?"

"Sorry, no, so not interested, Ray. I'm fated to die alone, no husband, no kids, no partner, no job, no nothin', " Julia says. She tries not to listen too carefully now as Rachel delivers a lecture, the substance of which is well-meaning but uninspired—on the importance of keeping an open mind about meeting new people even if, at first, they don't seem to be precisely what you're longing for . . .

And what, precisely, *is* she longing for? If only she knew.

"*Fated to die alone*—what part of that don't you get?" Julia says. Even *she* can hear how prickly she sounds. "What about *you*? When was the last time *you* were out on a date, big shot?"

"What?" Rachel says, and then there's the click of a cigarette lighter. "I'm sorry, why would I be dating when it's obvious Peter has every intention of moving back in here as soon as he gets his act together." It sounds as if Rachel is blowing smoke directly into the phone.

"Can I have a drag of your cigarette, please?" Julia teases. She and Rachel are forty-seven miles apart, but she swears she can smell cigarette smoke, then realizes it's burning weed she smells, and that it's coming from the apartment a few doors down the hall. If only she could remind Rachel of Peter's confession, that he'd known, walking down the aisle, that this marriage of theirs was no less than a huge mistake. But there are *some* things, no matter how much you may want to voice them, that are better left unsaid.

Someday, she predicts, Rachel will recognize that contrary to what she has long believed, Peter is, most assuredly, not the love of her life. But until that day arrives, it will continue to be rough going.

"I'm sorry, Ray," she says. She thinks of the Mishkins, and how, after more than six decades of marriage, they still get on each other's nerves. Every day, multiple times a day. Marriage can be such a fucked-up thing, no matter how ardent, and generous, the love at the center of it—you can't convince Julia otherwise. Look at her parents: married nearly forty years, her mother still in denial over her father's unforgivable behavior, and all too willing to have sacrificed both daughter and son to keep that marriage afloat. Better to have let it sink under the weight of her father's fierce, poisonous, uncontrollable anger.

Why stick around that dickhead and grow old together? Why bother?

Hey, Mom: Why not 'fess up and tell your kids the truth—that the guy you so unwisely fell for in his World War II Navy uniform is unworthy of every bit of that mystifying, unwavering love of yours.

"Hey, Julia? Brady wants to say goodnight to you, okay?"

"What? It's eleven o'clock, doesn't he have nursery school tomorrow?"

"Fine, I'm a bad mother," Rachel says. "What's Brady gonna do, fire me?"

"Put him on the phone and then put him to bed," Julia instructs her, as if she knows anything at all about parenting. "You know I'm kidding, of course," she adds. "I'm obviously the last person you should be listening to about raising your kid. When it comes to pets, on the other hand, I'm your guy."

"What about when it comes to old people?"

"Yup, I'm a genius when it comes to getting them across the street an instant before the 'Don't Walk' sign stops blinking."

Rachel laughs, and Julia feels better, less worried about this beloved person she's long considered her best friend. The scent of her neighbor's smoke is seeping under the door powerfully now, and she decides not to fight it. Getting a little secondhand high after a crappy blind date seems more than a little enticing.

15
Mel

Her story comes out in *The New Yorker* on a Tuesday—or at least there it is on the newsstand downstairs in the lobby at work this morning, along with *The Atlantic Monthly*, *Mademoiselle,* and *Seventeen*. It's crazy, Mel knows, but she would swear she can hear the sound of her heart pulsing excitedly under her coat, under her sweater, under her bra, under her skin, as she stands before the tidy, stacked piles of magazines she's seen here every morning before she steps into the elevator on her way upstairs to the editorial office on the fifth floor. Shyly, she contemplates how many copies of *The New Yorker* to buy, but not wanting to seem extravagant or show-offy, she can't bring herself to scoop up more than three. Worried she may possess an inflated sense of her own importance, she puts back one of the copies and forks over two dollars for the other two she has in hand, each magazine with a drawing of a large colorful abacus set against a dazzling yellow cover. She will give one copy to her father later this week and he will have the cover laminated and then display it on the wall in his den, next to an oversize print of a huge black-and-white photograph of Andy Warhol planting a kiss on John Lennon's cheek, Warhol looking sweet, but Lennon just staring straight ahead, a kind of mysterious half-smile on his face, as if maybe he likes that kiss but maybe he doesn't.

In the next century, when a single issue of the magazine will cost a penny short of nine dollars, Mel will remember this day when she paid only a dollar.

She feels very protective of these two copies of the magazine—these treasures—she's just bought, and when she gets home tonight after work, will have Charlie embalm them in layers of Saran Wrap, along with the three copies he bought at a newsstand on Eighty-Sixth and Lex, just before he hopped on the crosstown bus en route to his office.

Such extravagance, they will tell each other gleefully—five copies of a single magazine! Tonight there will be spare ribs and fried dumplings at their favorite Chinese restaurant, something they would ordinarily never do on a Tuesday, in the middle of the week like that. But today, this Tuesday in early January, marks the beginning of Mel's life as a published writer, and so she and Charlie will be as extravagant as they've ever been.

Those two copies of the magazine will stay wrapped in plastic all the way into the twenty-first century, when, on a whim, Mel will search her apartment for them. Finding them deeply embedded in the back of a closet, she will cradle them in the crook of her arms as tenderly as if they were something akin to her precious children. She will, as well, keep a Xerox copy of her very first check from the magazine, a check that, as *she* sees it, is made out for an extraordinary sum: one thousand four hundred and sixty-five dollars. The check is ornamented with a gold-and-white image of that monocled nineteenth-century dandy, Eustace Tilley, holding a letter—or maybe it's a manuscript—in one hand and a goose-feather quill pen in the other; two inches from his palm stands a golden owl set against a tiny bit of cityscape. Frankly, Mel would have given away the story to the magazine for free, just for the privilege of being published there—and she might even have done so in the twenty-first century, she will reflect years from now, when the check would have been worth over six thousand dollars; six thousand one hundred and fifty dollars and thirty-four cents, to be exact. While having lunch with

Elizabeth Greenwell, she almost seized her editor's hand and told her this, that Elizabeth could have her story for *nothing*, *nada*—but somehow she managed to resist making a fool of herself. Never would she want Elizabeth to think of her as such a laughably unworldly idiot!

When she gets upstairs now and goes to her desk, she sees that Austin, as usual, hasn't yet arrived, though it's already after nine. But there's a single, pinkish-red, long-stemmed rose arranged gracefully across the top of her pumpkin-colored IBM Selectric, that coveted typewriter she recently inherited following the departure of another editorial assistant, who left in pursuit of her doctorate in art history at Stanford.

"Hey there," Daphne says, leaving her desk and approaching Mel with a smile. "So, guess what: read it, liked it, passing it around the office even as we speak."

Mel is on the brink of offering her a hug but suspects her fellow editorial assistant would not be one to welcome it; despite their comfortable office friendship, Daphne isn't the squishy, touchy-feely sort, and so Mel simply says, "Thank you, and thank you, too, for the rose." Though she knows very little about how to care for flowers, she does know that this one needs to be in water so it won't shrivel and die.

"The rose? Not from me, actually," Daphne says. "It's from the guys over there," she reports, pointing to the fact-checkers' office down the road.

"You're kidding," Mel says, because the trio of fact-checkers still scarcely acknowledge her presence, even in the elevator or in line at the Xerox machine. Simon, the only one who talks to her from time to time—always about his Sacred Cat of Burma—hasn't said much to her lately either, come to think of it.

"But seriously, Mel, congratulations. I mean, I'm proud of you," Daphne says, and quickly looks away, though not before Mel—truly shocked—can see that Daphne's eyes are glassy with what appear to be momentary tears. This time Mel is overwhelmed by that urge to embrace her, but she knows to keep her hands at her sides and move on.

She needs to swing by the fact-checkers' lair; one of them is on the phone, and the other two, poring over books that resemble super-size encyclopedias, look up to smile at her and offer their congratulations.

"Good goin', Melissa!" says the fact-checker named Roger. "You like the rose I put on your desk?" Eventually he will leave the magazine to become a highly regarded fashion writer at *Vogue*, but at the moment, he's just an ill-paid fact-checker whose handful of kind words mean a great deal to Mel. She thanks all three of the guys for the rose, and it's Roger who says, "You bet!"

Like Simon, he will die an early death exactly a decade from now—from something that will come to be called acquired immunodeficiency syndrome, but his obituary in *The New York Times* will try and pass off the cause of death as an unnamed "blood disorder." And that long-stemmed rose placed so carefully across Mel's typewriter this morning will always be the image that will spring to mind when she finds herself thinking of this day, of him.

Here's Austin, turning the corner past the fact-checkers just as Mel is leaving; the two of them almost collide in the hallway.

"Sorry," Mel says, as if she were at fault when really neither of them is.

"What's going on? Fact-checkers got anything interesting to tell us so early in the morning?"

She's hoping he will notice the rose on top of her Selectric and then ask her about it, but he doesn't, and instead turns away from her and into his office and she's surprised at the weight of her disappointment. But she needs a vase or a glass, anything to keep the rose alive for the next couple of days, and now she has an excuse to go into his office and ask if Austin has anything she can use.

"No," he tells her, "I don't." He's taken off his coat and is opening a couple of large, manuscript-size envelopes that have been delivered by messenger, and she hears herself telling him that the fact-checkers gave her the rose sitting there on her typewriter and that she really doesn't want it to die.

"Is one of them in love with you?"

"Excuse me?"

"Are all three of them in love with you? Though frankly," Austin says, lowering his voice, "I think at least two of them prefer men."

"What?"

"I'm asking you, dear heart, what kind of man gives a woman a rose if he's not, shall we say, besotted with her?"

"No no no," she says, and laughs. She tells him it's just that her first story is officially out in the world today. He nods; the look on his face is unreadable.

"Very nice," he breathes. "And please ring up Richard and find out if he'll be home this afternoon."

Will do, sir. And by the way, screw you.

But first she will return to her desk and carefully open up one of her copies of *The New Yorker* and turn, even more carefully, to the table of contents, where her name is printed directly under "The Talk of the Town." And she will draw her fingertip across her name, across the page, again and again, as if she were blind and reading Braille, not fully believing what her finger is telling her.

His buddy Richard isn't answering his phone, a message she yells across the hall to Austin, who grunts something in reply.

In the ladies' room she runs into Sally Steinhart, whom she hasn't seen much of since the day Sally got married at City Hall and that celebrity husband of hers flew back to DC immediately afterward.

"Hiding your light under a bushel, I hear?" Sally says, and then, as always, asks if she can bum a cigarette.

"What?" Mel gives her a couple of True Blues and throws in a book of matches in the deal.

"Your *New Yorker* story? Word around the office is that it's quite good, and so I'm looking forward to reading it, Mel." Lighting up her cigarette, Sally tosses the match, without blowing it out first, into a sink decorated with one black hair loosely circling the drain. "Austin must be pretty proud."

"Of me?"

"Why are you looking at me like that?" Sally says. "Did I just say something incredibly stupid? Because that's just not me."

Mel hears herself confiding that Austin doesn't seem to be the slightest bit interested in anything about her or her story, and then Sally is saying, "What's wrong with him? I mean, seriously?"

Though neither of them knows the answer, Mel leaves the ladies' room feeling consoled.

At her desk, she's drawn back to *The New Yorker*, skimming an endless twenty-one-page profile of the director of the new museum of modern art at the Pompidou Centre in Paris; a hilariously vicious Pauline Kael review of a Neil Simon movie; an equally scathing review of an off-Broadway David Mamet comedy and its "ponderous irony."

She can't imagine, on this Tuesday afternoon—incontestably one of the most exhilarating days of her life—what it might be like to be Neil Simon or David Mamet and find oneself, now and then, insulted by a host of well-respected critics. But sometime in the next decade, one Saturday morning, a reviewer at *The New York Times* will reduce Mel to an exceedingly bitter flow of tears even as one kindhearted but clueless friend or family member after another will call to congratulate her and the lovely photo of her unwitting, smiling self in the paper of record. Her heart will be broken by a Princeton-educated critic who, like Pauline Kael, has a fondness for telling brutal truths. Or half-truths.

But today—though Austin clearly feels otherwise—is a day to celebrate. With two kinds of fried dumplings at Szechuan Garden followed by a reckless, joyous romp with Charlie.

16
Julia

The list of things the Mishkins need from the supermarket includes a half pound of kosher turkey from the deli counter, two quarts of nonfat milk—not a half gallon—but *two quarts*, and please don't forget the toilet paper, the soft, expensive kind, Molly reminds Julia, who doesn't need reminding.

As the elevator door slides shut now, Julia smiles at her fellow passengers, two little second-graders and Shirleen, the babysitter who's accompanying them. "Hey, Katie, let's play ticket-holders on line at MoMA!" one of the girls suggests to her playmate, her enthusiasm unmistakable.

"I don't know what game that is," Katie says. "It sounds stupid."

"When I was a small girl like you, Allyson and Katie," Shirleen says, "my father would shove a bar of soap in my mouth if he heard me use the word 'stupid.'"

"That's *really* stupid!" Katie says. She and Allyson giggle, and Julia smiles at them reflexively, at the sound of their innocent laughter.

Shirleen gives all three of them a dirty look. "It's not a joke, ladies," she says. "That bar of soap was so big and fat, I choked on it, and threw up. You think that's funny?"

Her father would never have pulled something like that, Julia thinks. She and Andrew were free, as far as their father was concerned, to use the word *stupid* anytime they pleased, along with "idiot" and "shut up" and "Shut up, you stupid idiot." They would never have spoken that way to an adult, of course, only to each other. Their father, unlike their mother, didn't pay much attention to them when they talked. He liked to read *The New York Times* and watch the news on CBS and listen to Leontyne Price and Joan Sutherland and Maria Callas on his stereo, one that came with tall speakers that occupied distinct places of honor in the den of their small house. Julia and her brother grew up with *La Traviata* and *Tosca* and *Manon Lescaut* playing in the background while they tried to do their homework. It was useless to complain that it was hard to concentrate—hard to solve quadratic equations and to memorize the differences between ionic, covalent, and metallic bonds—with all that powerful music blaring from the den. By the time they reached high school and finally had their own tiny rooms, their father simply told them to stop complaining and to shut their bedroom doors. Their mother, though, was sympathetic to them and said things like, "Stevie! Why can't you cooperate and just lower the music for them!" But he preferred not to, saying it was the most beautiful music the world had ever heard, music that was meant to be listened to at the highest volume. Finally, one year on his birthday, he was given the gift of a pair of headphones by their mother, big, clunky-looking ones that made him look like an air traffic controller, Julia thought. He didn't like wearing them, but evidently had decided to cooperate after all.

"I think your father should be put in jail, Shirleen," Allyson says to her babysitter as the elevator comes to a stop in the lobby.

"Oh yeah? Well, he's long dead," Shirleen says. "Gone gone gone."

"If he wasn't dead, I would put him in jail and make him stay there without TV because that's what he deserves," Allyson says.

"Yeah, that would be a terrible punishment!" Katie says, sounding exultant, her eyes shining. The two little girls agree that jail time for Shirleen's father would have been just the right price to pay for that bar of soap squeezed so cruelly into her mouth.

Julia doesn't have it in her to disagree.

"Let's go, ladies," Shirleen says, and all three of them, Julia included, follow her obediently through the lobby and out the door.

Shopping at the supermarket at the start of a weekday afternoon—who *does* that? Julia asks herself. Why isn't she behind her desk in her old Queensborough Community College classroom where she belongs? And why does she feel so lost here among the elderly, the jobless, the caregivers like herself who've been sent out by their employers to get this and that, a list often so long and detailed, that, like an old person, she has to write everything down on a note pad and remember to bring it with her.

It is, she realizes, time to hang a large oak tag sign from her neck:

I AM NOT AN UNEMPLOYED NITWIT
I AM, IN FACT, <u>THIS CLOSE</u> TO GETTING
MY DOCTORATE

All right, *this close* is something of an exaggeration, she'll own up to that, but she doesn't want to be mistaken for some pitiful loser who has nothing better to do on a Thursday afternoon than hang out at the deli counter at the A&P, begging for a free sliver of $6/pound prosciutto or a teaspoon of ridiculously expensive $15/pound foie gras.

As she waits her place in this line of only three at the deli counter for slices of kosher turkey breast and havarti for the Mishkins, the woman standing behind her is sounding off to an elderly man who looks like a benign, slightly confused soul. "How many times do I have to tell you, Dad—I'm NOT a neurosurgeon, I'm only a psychiatrist! Jesus, Dad!"

With another piece of oak tag and a Magic Marker, Julia can make a sign for *her*, too.

NOT A NEUROSURGEON—MERELY A
PSYCHIATRIST
AND DON'T ASK ME AGAIN!

She turns around for a better look at the woman who's so exasperated by her father, and sees that she is both very attractive and very angry. "I'm one thousand percent SICK of this, Dad!" the psychiatrist says a little too loudly, and Julia hopes that, like Walter Mishkin, "Dad" has significant hearing problems.

Rolling his eyes theatrically, the man working behind the deli counter says, "Fine, who's next?"

"No problem, you go ahead of me," the shrink says to someone who apparently has just taken a place behind her as Julia moves up to the counter now.

"Appreciate it," a familiar voice says, and this is when Julia swivels around to see who it is.

"Hey, Doctor . . . Charlie," she begins, and she is boiling with embarrassment, feeling that warmth everywhere, but she doesn't quite know why. She never realized how tall and thin he was, sitting there in his softly lighted office as she went on and on about the litany of discontents that had marked her life. And there's something different, something alluring, about seeing him, talking with him, outside his office, out here under the fluorescent lights of the supermarket where he's not her shrink but, instead, just a man she enjoys looking at.

"Julia," he's saying to her now. "Hi there."

"Hi." There is sweat at the back of her neck, in the crook of her arms, and even behind her knees. Who knows the source of this heat she's feeling here this chilly afternoon.

It's just the two of them loitering at the counter, Julia suddenly imagining Charlie's mouth at the back of her sweaty knee, tasting the salt as she stands here in the middle of her mindless workday, charged with the mundane task of bringing the Mishkins their groceries.

She can see that he hasn't shaved in a few days, and that, under the blazing commercial lighting, his eyes are vividly blue. She comes from a family of brown-eyed people, and the exceptional blue of his eyes charms her. There's something seductive about all that stubble ornamenting his jaw and chin that makes her feel a little unsteady there at the deli counter. She thinks about running her fingers along the fine line of his jaw, feeling its stubbled woolliness against her skin.

"I've been working on my thesis," she hears herself telling him, though this is a lie and she could kick herself for even raising the subject.

"Your old friend Flannery O'Connor, right?" he says.

"The spectacular, one and only Flannery O'Connor." *As in "A Good Man is Hard to Find" and "The Life You Save May Be Your Own."*

"I should add, by the way, that my wife, who's a writer, is a big fan of hers."

"Your wife's a writer? Really?" Interesting, she thinks, that he's never mentioned this before; she's flattered that he's finally, after a half-dozen appointments, sharing with her something personal about his own life.

"Yup, but she's home sick from work today," Charlie is saying, "so I'm just here to get some lunch for her before I get back to the office."

"You're totally breaking my heart, Dad," Julia hears the psychiatrist who's not a neurosurgeon say from somewhere behind her. "So what kind of writer?" she asks Charlie, anything to avoid talking about the thesis she feels so guilty about, the work she was planning to start months ago, before the shit hit the fan and living with Daniel began to feel close to intolerable. Just when she had to endure the loss of her teaching job, that job that made her feel like an accomplished person of a sort, not some underperforming doctoral student approaching her mid-thirties and going nowhere except to the supermarket and the podiatrist and the optometrist and audiologist, sitting there in one waiting room or another alongside those poor worn-out Mishkins, Julia herself waiting so impatiently, early on a weekday afternoon, to kick-start her own life.

The counterman hands over the Mishkins' food to her, and she places, uncertainly, the thin packages wrapped in waxy paper into the green-and-black plastic shopping basket at her feet. She's studying the contents of Charlie's basket—a jar of artichokes; a box of taco shells; a Styrofoam package of ground beef; a bottle of expensive-looking ginger salad dressing with Japanese lettering on the front label; a small cardboard tub of chow mein noodles.

Weird combination of ingredients, Julia thinks; she's still waiting to hear more about his wife and her writing. "Making tacos tonight?" she says. "Or is it Chinese food?"

Charlie laughs. "Actually, my wife's not much of a cook, so I'm the one who hangs out in the kitchen. Just ask my very grateful wife. Who, by the way, has a story in *The New Yorker* this week," he reports and after giving his order to the counterman, goes on—for just a bit too long, Julia notices—about how proud he is of his wife, the writer.

"I can just imagine," Julia says.

Now they're heading toward the line of cashiers at the front of the store, she and Charlie walking side by side, he with his shopping basket, she without the Mishkins' turkey breast and havarti, nonfat milk, and extra-soft toilet paper, because she's forgotten her basket over at the deli counter. Because let's face it, it's hard to focus on the Mishkins' shopping list and why she's here in the first place.

She wants to savor the weightlessness, the joyousness she feels floating out the door in Charlie's company. She wishes she had a camera with her so she might snap a photo of the two of them; she would love to have that picture, just one shot of the two of them, of her and Charlie, the first time they really talked together away from his office, out in the world, a snapshot she can look at anytime she pleases. A picture that will make her forget what it was like to have been the loneliest of wives, someone who, from the very first night of her marriage, had slept apart from her husband.

She senses Charlie doesn't want to prolong this impromptu meeting of theirs and so she lets him go, saying goodbye with a brisk wave of her open palm from right to left like a windshield wiper—nothing more than *adiós, amigo*—watching as he strides past the Ninety-Second Street Y, a Mediterranean restaurant, a street vendor on a corner selling fat red peppers, impressively long cucumbers, blue boxes of white mushrooms.

She's right behind him, every step of the way.

She watches him go into his building on a side street between Lex and Third, just an undistinguished postwar, white brick building, maybe fifteen stories high. She stands outside in front of the building, lingering there, unable to move forward or back, left or right, knowing she'll have to make another trip to the supermarket to get the Mishkins their groceries, but not caring, caring only that the fog of loneliness that's plagued her for so long—even beyond the long days and longer nights of her marriage—seems, at last, to have lifted.

It's the awakening of fresh desire and there's real joy in that, isn't there?

And too, she's just realized, this is the very first time Charlie has engaged in conversation with her without being paid for it.

She's not stupid: she's fully aware that falling for your

therapist is a "thing," that it's something that happens all the time, every day of the week. But that doesn't render what she feels for Charlie any less meaningful, any less potent, does it?

17
Mel

Her period is four days late—which has never happened before—then five days, then six, then seven, and then it's time for a frantic visit to the drugstore for one of those early pregnancy tests she saw advertised in *Mademoiselle*; all she gets for her ten bucks is a test tube, a vial of purified water, a medicine dropper, and bizarrely, some red blood cells fished out of a sheep. That same ten dollars, she reminds herself, was enough money for a favorite blouse of hers at Bloomingdale's last month.

They're eating dinner when she delivers the news to Charlie, who already knows her period is later than it's ever been. "I bought the pregnancy test," she tells him, "and I'm feeling a little sick even thinking about what the results might be." The food in front of her is a Chinese dish called "Ants Climbing a Tree"; Charlie has made it with mung bean vermicelli and minced beef, and normally it's one of Mel's favorites, but tonight even just the name of the dish sounds nauseating to her.

"Well, stating the obvious, we're in this together, babe," he says; it's what she wants to hear—except for the sound of the word *babe*. He's stroking her hair now and telling her, quietly, what they both know, which is that it's just the wrong time for them to go forward with this pregnancy, not to mention the simple fact that they can't afford it.

Charlie tells her not to cry, but she weeps in their bathroom anyway after a drop of urine proves what they've already feared. She's even more unnerved the next morning, after a phone call to her doctor, who describes himself as a practicing Catholic and says that in all good conscience, not only can he not perform the abortion she wants, he can't recommend a single doctor who will. Because, he explains, *it just doesn't feel right* to him.

It may not feel right to Dr. DeVivo, but what is Mel going to do, beg him for help because she and her husband are both just launching their careers and are nowhere near ready to even contemplate starting a family? The thought of becoming parents eight months from now feels as wrong as can be to her and her husband—is that what she's going to tell Dr. DeVivo?

She thanks him as politely as she can before she hangs up the phone, but nearly laughs when she hears him say, "You have a good day now."

Today is Wednesday; Mel's procedure is scheduled for Friday morning at a clinic on Long Island which was recommended to her by her childhood friend, Lisa, who's about to get her PhD in epidemiology at Berkeley and has already had more than one procedure herself. Mel has told Austin she's having several wisdom teeth extracted Friday morning—actually, that's three wisdom teeth and one supernumerary, in the anterior maxillary region of her mouth. All of this dental surgery had, in truth, taken place last summer, just before she began working at the magazine, but she can guess how convincing she sounds after she reports these very specific details to Austin and hears him say, "Well, wish you the best, dear heart. Don't know how we'll do it, but I feel confident we'll survive without you for a day."

During her free time at the office, she has been working hard on a revision of her story for Elizabeth Greenwell, doing everything she can to bring her characters more vividly to life, continuing to sharpen some of their already fiercely angry dialogue, and adding emotional heft to even the smallest quiet moments in the narrative. Thankfully, there's been more than enough downtime this week, when the slush pile is only moderately high and all there is for her to do, other than read manuscripts and answer Austin's phone when he's unavailable, is read aloud, slowly and meticulously, every word, every semicolon, of the galleys of the magazine's forthcoming issue that will arrive on the newsstand three months from now. It's occasionally her job to read those galleys to Rebecca, one of the two proofreaders in Editorial. Rebecca is Canadian and says "zed" for the letter "Z" and "washroom" instead of "ladies' room" and "a-boat" instead of "about" and sits next to Mel's desk talking a-boat her boyfriend, who is in his last year in medical school in Guadalajara, thank God, and will, if Rebecca is lucky, secure an internship for himself here in New York. Otherwise . . . well, Rebecca doesn't want to think a-boat that and of course Mel says she understands completely. *She who doesn't want to think about the miserable "procedure" she's facing just a couple of days from now.*

On Thursday night, she and Charlie lounge on their bed with their shoulders touching and watch *Barney Miller* and *Mork and Mindy* on their small black-and-white TV and try their best not to talk about her impending procedure. Mel, in particular, finds ugliness in the very sound of the word *abortion* and has asked Charlie not to say it out loud.

But he just did, instantly apologizing afterward. "Sorry sorry sorry, sweetheart," he says. "My mistake."

Though he and Mel almost always have a bowl of coffee Häagen-Dazs while they watch television together every night, Mel has been instructed in a phone call from the clinic not to eat after nine o'clock the night before the procedure. She knows Charlie wants his ice cream now and so she tells him to go ahead and take some from the freezer.

"No way, Mel, I would never do that to you," he says a

moment before a commercial comes on for a doll called Love 'n Touch Baby. On the screen, a woman is handing a doll to her little girl, and in the background a gentle voice is saying, "A brand-new mother has a lot to learn from a tiny newborn baby, and that's why Mattel created Love 'n Touch Baby."

"Jesus Christ," Charlie says, and rushes over to the television set to change the channel.

"Just eat your ice cream," Mel says. "Please." Even though the TV is on a different channel now, she keeps hearing the background singers in the commercial crooning the words *Love 'n Touch Baby.*

If only she could unhear it.

"So . . . how was work today? What's going on? How are those two new patients you were telling me about last week?" she asks Charlie, listening now to the sound of his spoon clicking against the small glass bowl filled with two perfectly shaped scoops of ice cream. She loves it when he's in the mood to share stories about those patients of his, leaving out their last names so he won't have to feel guilty about violating their privacy when he talks to her. "That straight-A high school student who was suffering from clinical depression? And that girl, the thirteen-year-old with acute suicidal ideation?" Mel shivers. "Just imagine her poor parents, having to deal with the knowledge that their child is so desperately unhappy at thirteen . . ."

"Hmm, sounds like you just might have a close relationship with a shrink or two," Charlie says.

"Oh, I do. So close, in fact, that I can do this"—she takes Charlie's paper napkin from his hand and brings it to his philtrum, the groove just beneath his nose, where a tiny splash of coffee ice cream has landed—"and no one can stop me." She smiles at him, and then she sighs. She wipes away the ice cream.

"Don't worry, by tomorrow afternoon you'll be eating Häagen-Dazs again, and everything else, too," he reminds her.

"And let's not talk about my patients, not tonight, okay? I'm just not in the mood."

"You know what, I wish I were a man," Mel hears herself say. "And then *I'd* be the one with the ice cream on my face, and *you'd* be the one lying on your back tomorrow with your feet in stirrups, counting backward from ten before the anesthesia kicks in."

"You don't think I'd trade places with you if I could?" Charlie says. "You don't think I feel bad that you're the one who's going to . . . well, I guess the operative word here would be *suffer* tomorrow?"

"Okay, good, you're saying all the right things, Charlie," she says, "all the things I needed to hear."

"And that's why you married me, because I say all the right things," he reminds her, and rolls his eyes.

"If you say so, buddy."

She and Charlie get into bed early tonight, right after the eleven o'clock news; Charlie is comatose within a minute or two, it seems, his arms locked possessively around her waist. It's Mel who can't sleep, not because she's unsure about the decision she and Charlie have made—there hadn't been a great deal to think about, really, the decision was effortless, they agreed—but because she wishes she didn't have to wait until morning to have the whole disturbing, frightening, lamentable business over with. When, finally, she falls asleep, it's well after 2 a.m. and then suddenly she's awakened by an all-too-familiar sound; it's Birkin, the cat, retching, a fur ball making its way through his stomach and out his tiny mouth. She switches on the lamp next to her and it's painful to watch as Birkin jerks backward on the parquet floor beside the bed, his whole body heaving, the puking noise sounding almost human. Leaping from the bed now in a vain attempt to get Birkin into the bathroom and onto its easy-to-clean tile floor, she lifts him into her arms, murmuring *my poor, poor baby doll*—the ordinary sweet talk she unthinkingly soothes him with—and runs toward the bathroom. But of course she's too late, of course the vomit shoots from Birkin's mouth onto the wood floor just outside the bathroom and of course Charlie sleeps through it all, because, Mel thinks, perhaps unfairly, it's just what husbands do.

Driving to the clinic in their boxy red Rabbit along the Cross Island Parkway, Charlie plays cassettes he made of their favorite Beatles songs; he's memorized the order of the songs, and when Mel asks for "While My Guitar Gently Weeps," he immediately fast-forwards the cassette until he finds it. She knows he would do anything for her; in just a couple of hours, after the procedure is over and she is so woozy she can't even leave the waiting room of the clinic or open her eyes, he will sit with her patiently, alternating between holding her hand and stroking her arm, assuring her, *we know you're going to be fine, sweetheart,* until finally she has to ask him to please stop—the hand-holding and everything else, too. Later, when they're home and the wooziness is finally beginning to lift, she will hear him running out the door of their apartment in search of just the right chicken noodle soup for her; the one that comes in an envelope, not the one in the can, which she thinks is just too salty and slimy.

But now, as they're settling into their seats at the clinic, waiting for Mel's name to be called, her eyes are wide open, and she stares across the room—no larger than Dr. DeVivo's small office—at a tiny woman in dirty red sneakers who's wearing a T-shirt that says,

LOVE IS BLIND, DEAF, AND RETARDED

Unbelievably, she's brought her two children with her, both of them, Mel realizes, still in their pajamas—one Wonder Woman, the other Superman, a cape drooping behind his elfin shoulders. The little girl, who's about five, and the older of the two, says, "No, I was very grumpy at the birthday party. I told you, I *hate* parties."

"Shut it, Nicole," her mother says. "Just shut it."

The little boy sitting in between Nicole and their mother is resting his head against the mother's shoulder. There's a Donny & Marie coloring book in his lap, and a blot of what looks like cream cheese at the corner of his mouth. A small, familiar green-and-yellow box of crayons is on the floor at his feet. "I'm tired and I wanna go to McNuggets or Kentucky Fried," he says. He's maybe four years old.

A woman in pink scrubs approaches the mother now. "Barbara?" she says. Then she looks at the children and says, "This is problematic," her voice a mixture of pity and annoyance.

"Yeah, apologies," Barbara says. "But they've got a coloring book and crayons and they'll just sit here quietly until my boyfriend gets here."

"Which will be when?" the woman in pink scrubs says.

Though Barbara says nothing, the look on her face says *how the hell do I know*?

"I'm very sorry, but this isn't a day care center," the woman says, clipboard and pen in hand. "It looks like I'm going to have to cross your name off the list and reschedule you," she threatens Barbara, but calmly.

Like Mel and Charlie, the half-dozen or so other women in the waiting room are all staring at Barbara, and then their attention shifts to little Wonder Woman, who's nonchalantly running her tongue up and down the full length of her bare arm.

"Will you STOP that!" Barbara says. "What's so delicious about that stupid arm of yours?"

"I hate you," Wonder Woman tells her. "I hate parties but

I hate you even more." She's crying now, but her mother is unmoved.

"Just shut it, Nicole."

Charlie puts his hand on Mel's wrist. "I'll watch the kids," he offers. Observing the facial expression on every woman in the room shift to one of relief, Mel sees Charlie for what he clearly appears to be—a mensch, one of those good guys who can always be counted on to do the right thing.

When she awakens from the anesthesia, she's hit with dizziness and nausea, and the dream she was in the middle of is still there floating in her memory: a family of roosters navigating the crosswalk to enter a supermarket in Honolulu, where she and Charlie had gone on their honeymoon . . . how many years ago? *Five?* she says uncertainly to a nice woman in scrubs who's helping her out of her surgical gown now and back into the sweatpants she was told to wear this morning. *Four and a half? How is it possible she can't remember how long she's been married?*

Not to worry, the woman in the pink scrubs is telling her benevolently, *not to worry about anything.*

Though Mel, at twenty-five, has never changed a baby's diaper and isn't quite able to imagine herself doing so, some years from now, in the middle of the next decade, her phone will begin to ring while she's washing a poop-stained, three-month-size onesie embellished with a green-faced Frankenstein and the words *I'm A Little Monster* across the front. The phone will continue to ring while Mel washes, by hand, in her bathroom sink, the sickeningly scented stains from her baby's tiny terrycloth bodysuit. As she runs to answer the phone in the bedroom, forgetting to turn off the faucet, soapsuds will drift over the edge of the sink and down to the bathroom floor; the bottoms of Mel's bare feet will turn damp and sticky. Only half-listening as Elizabeth Greenwell, who has called to report that one of Mel's *New Yorker* stories has been chosen, along with one of John Updike's, for the new edition of *The Best American Short Stories*, Mel will forget to thank her and will only think to say, "I can't—gotta go—so sorry." But then, to herself and to Jack, her mostly naked, exhausted, howling baby who's waiting in his crib for clean clothes and a soothing dose of maternal comfort, "Hold it—*what?* What did Elizabeth just say?"

Hey, hey, Mommy's going to have a story in Best American Stories! she will tell her eight-week-old baby, plucking him from his crib, rocking him in her folded arms. *Yes,* your *Mommy,* she will say, turning it into a song whose dopey, joyous lyrics she will sing again and again, until she finally believes them, and the baby, will, at last, miraculously stop crying.

18
Julia

Gently, she takes both of Charlie's hands and arranges them over her breasts and he seems to like what he's feeling; smiling at her, he bends his head and rests his cool lips on first one nipple and then the other.

"Come in and talk to me while I pee," Molly is saying.

"Pardon?"

"It's only pee," Molly reassures her. "Come. We'll talk."

This is not the first time Molly has extended this invitation, and Julia wonders if there's something going on here, something she needs to be paying closer attention to, which is the sad though not implausible possibility that both Walter *and* Molly are suffering from a touch of dementia. What if they start sliding steeply downhill while in her care—then what? Where would she turn to get help for them? She's not a social worker or gerontologist or geriatrician. All she is, at this particular moment, is an unskilled caregiver who should be spending every minute of free time on her PhD dissertation. As for the Mishkins, she'll just have to pray that nothing disrupts the status quo; who knows, maybe she'll get lucky.

"I won't bite," Molly promises her now.

Julia moves toward her, stepping over the granite saddle between the bedroom and the bathroom, where Molly is engaged in pulling down her stretchy black pants.

"Do you need help sitting down? And do you want me to close the door?" Julia asks.

"*No thank you* to the help sitting down, and *yes please* to the closing of the door."

For the two hundred dollars a week they're paying her, surely she can hang out in close quarters with an old woman who's hunched over a toilet.

"I've been thinking about you and how I only wish I had a young man to introduce you to. Unfortunately, all my friends are either old or six feet under. Or suffering from the D-word. I'll give you a clue—it starts with a D and ends with TIA."

Shutting her eyes, her hands fall to Charlie's shoulders. She examines the top of his head, the slightest thinning of his crazy blondish hair, and traces the smooth surface of the rims of his ears; they're velvety and close to his head, dainty as a woman's, she thinks. Her hands slide effortlessly down the length of his torso, from his chest to his hips, and now both hands are meeting at his silvery belt buckle, where she knows they don't belong.

Her mouth is where it doesn't belong, but she can hear him moaning, telling her not to stop.

He's probably the kindest, most empathetic man she's ever known and that's why she can do these things with such ease. And why the switch that normally controls her conscience has been shut off, maybe even permanently impaired.

He's a married guy but she just doesn't care.

"Miss, did I ever tell you what my mother's last words to me were?" It's Molly's voice, but Julia can't figure out where it's coming from. Now there's the familiar, ugly sound of a toilet flushing, followed by water hitting the basin of the sink.

Charlie is thanking her, murmuring his gratitude into her forehead as she pulls up and away from him. He's tired all of a sudden and wants to lie down but he doesn't say where.

"My mother was what you'd call a piece of work," Molly reports. "I don't think she ever really loved me. You hear people say things like that, but they don't really mean it. But I *do*. And you want to know what those last words to me were? 'You need to fix yourself—your slip is showing.'"

Why can't they just lie down in Julia's bed? She has plenty of room for him right here. He's welcome to spend the night, but his answer is no.

A very polite No thank you.

Molly wants to wash her hands now but can't see where the soap is. Julia puts a wafer of Irish Spring into Molly's hands and stands by with a towel thrown over her forearm, like an old-fashioned servant, faithful and obedient.

Drying her hands, Molly informs her that life isn't fair. "So if you're looking for fair, you can forget it, darling."

It feels good to be called *darling*, a word Julia can't recall either of her parents ever bestowing upon her. But maybe she's wrong about this; maybe her memory is faulty and while she was in the ER having her broken wrist X-rayed a quarter of a century ago, her father stood at her side with his thick, adult arm around her small shoulders, whispering, *Don't worry, darling. I mean, I can promise you that you're never going to remember any of this, okay?*

Yeah, right.

She wasn't even given prescription painkillers at the hospital to take the edge off. Just a couple of plain old children's Tylenol that didn't do it for her, mashed up and marinating in a teaspoon of orange juice. Tylenol and some ice cream from the family freezer when they got home from the hospital, her father's secret still perfectly safe. He'd fractured his little girl's wrist but the oblivious doctor in the ER swallowed whole her father's ridiculous story about how Julia had tripped and fallen down the basement stairs. Never mind that they were imaginary stairs leading to an imaginary basement. That night she'd desperately wanted a cone from Carvel, always her favorite, but it must have been 5 a.m. by the time they got back, and everything in town was closed except their freezer. There was an earnest, late-night promise from her father to get that chocolate-covered chocolate cone for her the following day, though this promise was soon forgotten. Disappointingly, after a night where she felt a little like an attention-getting VIP, things seemed to return to normal by morning; when she awoke, she was just Julia, but with a plaster cast that reached her elbow and had to be covered with a double layer of plastic bags from the supermarket when she went into the shower. There was also the issue of temporarily having only the use of her left hand, which was tricky business for a righty, and one that required help from her mother. Who, Julia noticed, was being especially kind to her, addressing her as *precious doll* from the moment Julia went to her, weeping quietly—after her father left her and Andrew lying on their bedroom floor where he'd thrown them and then retreated into the den to watch TV, which generally seemed to have a calming effect on him.

Let's wait till Daddy calms down, her mother would always say in a whisper, stroking Julia's hair or massaging her shoulder.

Too little, Mom, too fucking late.

On the fifteen-minute drive to the hospital, three-year-old Andrew asleep next to her in the back seat of their Ford Falcon in his pajamas and red ski jacket, Julia could hear the brief but furious whispering up front, and then nothing at all. Her jacket had been silently positioned over her shoulders by her father; her arm was in a sling fashioned by her mother from a pillowcase, and it didn't hurt much as long as she didn't move it. But it had turned a horrible, deep blackish-blue, ugly as a monster's arm and frightening to look at. Neither of her parents swiveled around for a peek at her from the front seat, and it was lonely back there with Andrew snoozing and her mother and father saying not a word to her. She moved closer to Andrew and rested her head against his diminutive shoulder, hoping he would wake up and talk to her, but he slept soundly. It was, after all, two in the morning.

It would take a long while before she understood that they were nowhere near an ordinary family. They were so far from ordinary, it was kind of a sick joke, she told several of her shrinks over the years. The shrinks nodded in agreement, but none of them had much to say that was helpful. Mostly they left the talking to *her*, and she grew tired of the sound of her own voice blaming her father, and her mother, too, for having been far less than exemplary parents.

When she went back to school after New Year's, the cast on her arm was, at first, of great interest to everyone in her class, and even to her thirtyish teacher, who signed it "Good luck from Mrs. Longmeadow!" as if it were a high school yearbook she'd been asked to autograph. Julia was thrilled to have Mrs. Longmeadow's signature on her arm, and when, six weeks later, the cast was removed, it was carefully laid to rest in the pajama drawer of her dresser, where it stayed for several years, chiefly because of that signature, which, to Julia, had the value of a celebrity's. (A lifetime later, she would come to realize that she'd had a crush on Mrs. Longmeadow, who was vivacious and pretty, and knew how to talk to children in just the right way—never could Julia imagine her saying *you kids are driving me fucking insane.*) Mrs. Longmeadow lived just a few blocks from the school, and right before the holidays she'd walked the class to her small house and seated everyone on the floor of her den in front of a shiny silver Christmas tree. They sang holiday songs and then Mrs. Longmeadow handed out stockings filled with iridescent pencils, animal-shaped erasers, and colorful plastic paperclips.

Mrs. Longmeadow was her favorite teacher (later that year she would show up at school on St. Patrick's Day in a mint-green wig) and it had crossed Julia's mind now and again to tell her how, exactly, her wrist had been broken. Her friends from school knew there was no basement in Julia's house—she had to tell them something that would make sense to them, and so she came up with the idea that she'd tripped over the cat's food bowl in the kitchen on her way to answer the telephone. Her friends seemed to think this was funny, and so she wrote and illustrated a story about it in her weekly art class. The story she told in those few pages seemed to possess the satisfying ring of truth; for years she kept it buried in her pajama drawer next to the plaster cast, never showing it to her mother or father.

Sometimes, when it was hard to fall asleep because of all the things that worried her, she would lie in bed and fantasize about Mrs. Longmeadow inviting her to come and live with her and her husband; of course she would be allowed to bring Andrew along with her. Mr. Longmeadow owned a drugstore in town and stood behind the counter in a white uniform complemented by a nice-guy smile. He wore an orange, bar-shaped plastic pin that said *George* on it, and underneath his name were the words *Licensed Pharmacist*. He and Mrs. Longmeadow had no children of their own, and that was one of the reasons Julia could so easily imagine moving in with them, Andrew in tow. In her fantasy, which she kept revisiting—always at night, never in daylight in her classroom at school—she and Andrew had bunk beds in the Longmeadows' home, and they slept through the night uninterrupted until Mrs. Longmeadow came into their room in her bathrobe to wake them for school, perky even in the early morning as she lifted the shades in their bedroom and told them, cheerfully, to rise and shine. She might have assured them, as their mother could not, that no one was ever going to barge unceremoniously into their room at night and slug them. But there was no need for that assurance, really, because in Julia's imaginings, she and Andrew already knew, already understood they were safe in the Longmeadows' little house on Arbor Lane, a house even smaller than their own.

Years later, turning the construction-paper pages of the crudely written and illustrated story of her broken arm, Julia wept for her younger self, the eight-year-old who'd been just young enough to believe the stupid lies she herself had been so eager to tell.

"I *said*, if you're looking for fair, you can forget it, Miss," Molly is saying, and Julia nods her head.

19
Mel

Her lucky twenty-nine-cent Bic pen has done it again; she's just sold "Autumn," her second story—after three wearying rewrites trying to darken her character's family history—to Elizabeth Greenwell, who calls Mel at work to report, in her understated way, "We're taking it."

YesyesYES! Mel would like to cheer, but she keeps it to herself for the moment; certainly she knows not to say a word to Austin, and offers only a happy thank-you in response to Elizabeth's news. But is there something else she should be saying? A smarter, more articulate way for her to express her gratitude? She doesn't know what's expected of her here, and wishes she and Elizabeth could do this the simplest way possible—through the good old US mail. She would love to have been able to put the key in her mailbox after arriving home from work today and pull out that mini 4 x 5 envelope that cost thirteen cents in postage to send her—and with her name typed on the front by Elizabeth's typewriter as she sat at her desk at *The New Yorker* thinking of Mel and her story.

But those days are permanently gone; from now on, all good news from Elizabeth Greenwell will come to Mel over the phone.

It will be the bad news that will make its way to her mailbox, the letters from Elizabeth saying, *I'm sorry. I know that after a couple of rewrites for us you're disappointed in this news. But I'm confident you'll place this story elsewhere.*

And Mel will, nearly every time, publish the story in some

other glossy magazine that will pay her generously, though never as generously as *The New Yorker*. And she will never forget to be thankful to Elizabeth.

She lights up a True Blue at her desk, inhaling so deeply that somewhere in her chest she feels a jolt of pain.

"No no no," Elizabeth is saying, and it's as if Mel is in Elizabeth's office at *The New Yorker* and has fired up a forbidden cigarette. Or, perhaps, has said something profoundly wrong. "No, no, thank *you*," Elizabeth says. "Do you know how difficult it is for us to find a hundred good stories a year to publish? Can you imagine what hard work that is?"

Oh, Mel can imagine it; she who reads the slush pile hour after hour, Monday through Friday, unfailingly sanguine, but never once having found even a single story that has interested Austin for more than the first couple of paragraphs.

We always hope for another story from you, she hears Elizabeth saying to her now, and it strikes Mel as utterly, laughably, wildly improbable that all of this is happening to her.

Oh, what a lucky, lucky duck she is.

20
JULIA

Julia is out walking a chubby Dalmatian named Romeo who's giving her a hard time. He has some arthritis in his knees and has to be dragged out the door of his Ninety-Third Street apartment, into and out of the elevator, out the side door of the building, and then down the five broad stone steps leading to the street. Nancy, his owner, a lawyer who helped one of Julia's friends through a particularly venomous divorce, has asked Julia to stay over in her apartment with Romeo for the weekend until she's back from a wedding in New Orleans. She's left a folder full of alphabetized take-out menus for Julia, along with instructions to order whatever she likes. Beef lo mein and a spring roll sound tempting, or maybe a lobster roll from the steakhouse across the street, a restaurant she could never afford to frequent, not when she was married to Daniel, and certainly not since she's been on her own. But with Nancy's blessing and the tidy, very generous pile of dollar bills that have been left on the kitchen counter for Julia's dinners this weekend, she can treat herself to that lobster roll. This is what she is contemplating as she coaxes Romeo along tonight. He's not her favorite "client"—as she likes to think of the dogs and cats she cares for—but who wouldn't sympathize with a dog plagued by arthritic knees?

The sun is on its way down and Julia's stomach is making noises about dinner. Romeo, however, isn't going anywhere. He's sitting in the middle of the sidewalk in front of the steakhouse, head resting languidly on his front paws.

"Come on, move it, kiddo!" Julia says. Even though the

dog is ignoring her, Julia looks down in his direction and tells him that he needs an attitude adjustment. "Come on, Romeo, please don't do this to me," she says, embarrassed to be stuck here on the street blocking pedestrian traffic with a big ungainly dog who just won't cooperate.

"Need some help?" she hears Charlie Fleischer say. He saw her as he was leaving the drugstore across the street, he tells her, and puts down the plastic bags he's carrying, and then kneels on the sidewalk.

"We have to stop meeting like this!" she teases him. "First the supermarket and now here we are again." Of course he doesn't know about the first time, when she was guiding the Mishkins across the street and Charlie didn't even notice her.

Maybe he can help her get the dog off the sidewalk and back home to Nancy's apartment, where Romeo himself lives the good life.

But Romeo, it turns out, cannot be persuaded to move even one of his four paws in the right direction.

"I'm going to have to go back to the apartment to get his wagon," Julia says. "Can you possibly stay here with him for three minutes while I'm gone?" she says to Charlie, immediately wondering if this is a wacky request to ask of her therapist. They're both squatting on the sidewalk now; Charlie is petting Romeo's smooth coat.

"Wait, how was your week?" he asks. "You've been doing well?"

"Pretty productive," Julia says, and this is the second time she's lied to him about this.

"So you've had a chance to work on your thesis? Terrific!"

"Well . . . I haven't had time to really flesh things out yet . . . But here's the official title: 'An Examination of Violence in the Fiction of Flannery O'Connor, Carson McCullers, and Eudora Welty.'"

Charlie nods—approvingly, she thinks.

"Oh, and by the way, I read your wife's story in *The New Yorker*."

No comment from Charlie, who is still petting Romeo, stroking his chin now.

"I especially liked the last sentence," Julia says. "Do you remember it?"

"I'm ashamed to say I don't," Charlie says as Romeo begins to lick his face vigorously.

"'And that's all I know, for she will always be careful with her confidences,'" Julia recites. "Sound familiar?" She doesn't tell him how many times she's read the story, searching for hints about their marriage but, to her disappointment, finding none. "Romeo, stop!" she says now. "You're getting all that disgusting saliva on my distinguished therapist!"

"It's fine," Charlie says, and laughs.

A tiny girl in pearls and a tiara, accompanied by a sobbing, very pregnant woman wearing her coat open on this surprisingly mild winter evening, walks past, the two of them holding hands. "Your father's a pig," the woman tells the little girl loudly. Dangling from the gold chain around her neck is a gold cross ornamented with a crucified Jesus, the Savior all in glistery diamonds.

"Poor thing," Julia says softly, and wishes she had something of substance to offer the weeping mother—maybe some useful advice about how to leave the pig.

"So what about that wagon for your friend Romeo?" Charlie is saying. "Why don't I just carry the big guy home for you?"

"We'll carry Romeo together," she says, and winds up, instead, in charge of Charlie's plastic bags from Rite Aid that happen to hold a couple of bright pink boxes of tampons. What would his wife think if she knew that one of his patients was toting those feminine hygiene products of hers, she wonders.

Romeo is drooping from Charlie's arms now as they cross

the lobby of Nancy's building and head for the elevator, which is scented with the salmon someone must have cooked for dinner tonight.

Julia rubs the dog's soft belly as they slowly rise to the twenty-fifth floor. "Hey, did you know that Dalmatians are born pure white and don't develop their spots until they're about two weeks old?" Her voice sounds a little trembly; she hopes Charlie doesn't take note of it.

"Did not know that," Charlie says. Then the two of them fall silent because they can feel the heat rising, Julia thinks. They exit the elevator and Charlie lowers the dog to the carpeted floor of the hallway. Once again, Romeo shows little interest in getting a move on.

"Not that I'm making excuses for him," Julia begins, "but he's got some arthritis in his knees . . ."

"Well, then he and my mother have something in common," Charlie says, smiling. "Though I think my mother's in better shape than your pal here."

This time he and Julia work together to entice Romeo to his front door. Fumbling with her keys, even though the one she needs is easily identifiable with a purple plastic sheath at the top, Julia can feel her breathing turn slightly ragged. "Come on in," she says, as if this were her home and it were only natural for her to extend the invitation.

She needs something to drink and so does he, she tells Charlie. Water? OJ? A beer?

He says no thank you, that he has to get home, but there's something she has to show him, she insists, and leads him from the foyer into the living room, to a built-in bookcase lined with books bound in faux leather—books that, she happens to know, are for decorative purposes only and can be purchased by the yard or by the foot.

Decorative purposes only? "Unbelievable!" Charlie says, and Julia points out volumes by Socrates, Plato, Aristotle, and everyone's favorite, Machiavelli. Opening a couple, she shows him that they're in German—not that Nancy, the divorce lawyer, bought them expecting to read them, she says, and winces a little at the thought of all those unread books.

She puts Plato and Socrates back on the shelf next to St. Augustine and Spinoza, and then she turns to Charlie and he is so close, she can feel his breath. They've known each other for three and a half long months now, she tells herself, and then she collapses against him and soon both of them are moving purposefully down the varnished hallway, his hand warm in her even warmer one.

21
Charlie

Nope nope nope, absolutely not, he is *not* doing this. But Julia is telling Charlie she wants him, her voice soft but her intent loud and clear. He needs to tell her in a louder voice, that, guess what, since he became a husband, he has come to understand the importance of loyalty and protecting the love of your life, at all cost, from anything that might threaten her or cause her even the slightest hint of pain—physical or the other kind, the kind that strikes squarely and powerfully through the heart. But now, mystifyingly, Julia is telling him—her voice nervous, he thinks—about "A Good Man Is Hard to Find," one of the Flannery O'Connor stories she's considering focusing on in her dissertation . . . but why is she talking about this now, about a cat in the story, a cat called Pitty Sing, named after a character in *The Mikado*—why is she talking about a cat when he needs to go home to his wife to cook dinner, tacos made with ground turkey, and cheddar and cilantro, and just a couple of dashes of salsa because Mel hates it when her lips burn from any kind of spicy food.

What hurts, Charlie wants to tell this sweet but confused patient of his who's now going on so earnestly about this fictional cat— a creature who ends up inadvertently causing the deaths of a family of six, she says—what hurts is the thought that Julia wants to be something more than his patient, as though not understanding he has a wife waiting for him at home, hungry for the tacos he promised to make when he left for work this morning, brushing his lips across his wife's, kind of a dry, soulless kiss that didn't take him, or his wife, anywhere. Mel would never tell him this, but he *knows* it nonetheless. The truth is, they haven't had spectacularly good sex, not recently anyway. Not that it was impossible to love someone deeply and still have mediocre sex.

Please, I want you to, Julia is saying, sounding less tentative, more determined, and he puts his arms around her. And this is the beginning of the end, the two of them now without their clothes on in the king-size bed of that woman who owns lazy dog Romeo and who buys, by the yard, books she has no interest in reading.

Tell me you love me, he thinks he hears Julia say, but how can that be? Ah, he was mistaken, he realizes: what she actually said was *Tell me you love me just a little*, the hopefulness in her voice kind of heartbreaking.

Not now—but soon—he will come to realize that Julia's need for him is a turn-on, that it has aroused something in him, something he just can't live without.

With the tip of his finger, he traces the constellation of beauty marks spouting from the outer corner of one dark-brown eye, marks that look, to him, like sooty tears. There's something sexy about them, but he can't say precisely why.

I love my wife, he would like to tell Julia, but the words, though true, suddenly seem altogether irrelevant and are nowhere to be found, just like the sentiment that should be behind those words. Even now, before he really transgresses, he wants to be forgiven for being the married man who craves Julia's flattened stomach, the breasts that stay impressively upright when she kneels in front of him, her mouth where it doesn't belong. There's a word for what he is feeling, and he suspects it isn't love—it's lust, which, like love when requited, is one of life's great, intoxicating pleasures.

His saliva is on her nipples; he likes the way it makes them gleam in the glow of the floor lamp at the window. He's intoxicated by that gleam.

He's a good person and so is she, he tells her.

I have to go, he says, but he doesn't sound very convincing, not even to his own ears. There are things of paramount importance he should be thinking about and they come to him one after the other, a parade of reminders marching on little flat-footed cartoon feet: *wifedinnermarriage* and *neverever-sleepwithapatientyouidiot*. Somehow they come and go in a heartbeat and leave no lasting impression; they're completely beside the point.

I have to go, he says again, because isn't this what he's supposed to say? But Julia's mouth is on his now; he can no longer speak.

You want to stay, I know you do, she is saying, her wet mouth pressed against his ear, and it feels so fucking good, he can hardly breathe.

She's on to him; she really does understand his weakness.

Now his life, on automatic pilot a bit this past year, is secretly headed somewhere else. Someplace touched with excitement. And all of a sudden he finds himself thinking *but really, what's wrong with adding a little something into the mix, enhancing your life instead of seeing the same old same old ahead of you?*

This is the sort of thinking that makes him believe no one is going to get hurt—he'll make certain of that.

After all, he's a mensch, isn't he?

Though, in a way, it makes him vaguely melancholy to acknowledge it, this rekindling of desire reminds him of what had been ignited in them when he and Mel were in college, reminds him of how much he's missed that rapturous feeling sparked simply by being in the presence of someone new, attractive, and available.

But the thing is, we have no future together, you and I, he wants to say to Julia. It's important, he knows, that he tell her this, that she understand that because of his love for his wife, this relationship isn't going anywhere except the bedroom.

If only Julia could read his mind, he wouldn't have to say the words out loud.

22
JULIA

She watches as Charlie gets dressed, watches as he zips up his jeans, yanks over his head a T-shirt emblazoned with John Lennon's self-portrait, and shoves his feet into his unlaced Nikes, forgetting all about his socks. He seems tense, exasperated, even, and offers not a word to her.

"You said I'm a good person," she reminds him. "You said we're both good people, and we know that's true, okay?"

"Let's not talk about it."

"You're not sounding very friendly," she says, and hands him his socks, which he stuffs into the back pockets of his jeans, one thick black sock in each.

"I'm sorry, Julia, it's just that I want you to understand," he says. He's heading to the small foyer with a closet on either side.

"Understand what?"

At the front door, he turns to face her, to tell her something that isn't as bad as she feared, only that he won't be able to see her as a patient anymore, now that they've slept together.

"It just wouldn't be ethical," he explains, "and I don't want you to ever feel shame about anything, about any of this."

He bends forward, slips his tongue inside her mouth gently, playing with the tip of hers, and she knows that he would never be the kind of husband who would insist on separate beds, separate bedrooms. He would be an exemplary husband, the kind who would, someday, have the words *devoted* and *loving* etched into his gravestone alongside the word *husband.*

Before too long, given enough time, he will fall in love

with her—and that's when she will ask him to marry her, she decides.

She thinks of the little girl out on the street in her plastic pearls and tiara, and her weepy, pregnant mother. *Your father's a pig!* she can hear the woman shouting.

It occurs to her, again, that what she longs for is relief from loneliness, and instead, in its place, intimacy, along with a small helping of the simple, uncomplicated happiness that she just knows will flow from it—from intimacy, both emotional and sexual, the kind Charlie probably once had with his wife, she bets.

It's clear to her in this moment that his marriage is dead. She's certain of it, and certain, too, that he's a good man who will never reduce her to tears or threats.

If asked, she will admit she's never truly believed in God, but that she does have a strong belief in love and that she's sick of living without it. When Charlie kisses her goodbye, this time it's just a touch of his lips to hers, but she'll take it, no complaints.

The complaints will come later. And there will be so many of them, Charlie will be swallowing down Valium, .5 milligrams, twice a day.

Julia will apologize, numerous times, because really, she'll tell him, she wants nothing more than to bring pleasure to both her life and his. His life and hers.

23
Mel

Not long after the sale of Mel's new story, after it has been set in type, she receives a check from *The New Yorker* for two thousand six hundred and twenty-five dollars, and realizes, amazed, that she can use that single check to pay the rent on their apartment for nearly a year. When she points this out to Charlie, they agree, buoyantly, that, even if—worst-case scenario—she were never to sell another story, it's time for them to move to a larger space. Lucky duck that she is these days, she and Charlie are told by their super that a large one-bedroom in their building here on the Upper East Side is available for them. All they need to do, the super casually informs them in his poorly lit basement office, is fork over a gift to him of three hundred bucks and the apartment is theirs. His name is Roland; he's small and dark-haired, and his mustache is the thickest Mel's ever seen and reminds her of some famous porn star whose name she doesn't care to recall.

A hefty bribe, that three hundred dollars Roland has requested, but one, Mel and Charlie instantly decide, worth paying. And they will close off the dining room in the new apartment and convert it into a mini-office for Mel so she can work on her stories in the evenings and on weekends without ever having to kick Charlie out into the unfriendly streets of the city on a polar winter night or a sweltering August afternoon.

A new apartment and another story coming out; she's the happiest she's ever been, she whispers into Charlie's ear the night before the move, but, no surprise, he's already fallen asleep after a long day spent packing up their books and clothing and a couple of hundred LPs and their turntable and receiver and speakers and cassette deck, their pots and pans and dishes and linens and their wedding album, even though their journey is only as far as the seventeenth floor.

She kisses the back of his neck, the side of his face, letting her mouth linger against the lovely warmth of his skin as he sleeps. This is home to her, under the covers, beneath the sturdy cage of his arms settled around her; this, to her, is the safest place on earth.

24
JULIA

Charlie has given her a Xerox of a photo of himself and his brother in their Cub Scout uniforms from long ago, a picture, he says, that took second prize in some Boy Scout–sponsored photography contest his mother had entered in the early sixties. He and Jeff were awarded a five-dollar gift certificate from their local Carvel; those were the days when a small cone would set you back fifteen cents. It was a prize he and his brother went crazy over, and which had their parents chauffeuring them back and forth to Carvel through a spring and a summer for their weekly fix.

Mostly it's Julia who has the opportunity to look, at her leisure, and with such longing, at the handful of snapshots she and Charlie have exchanged. Though occasionally, Charlie has told her, he gets to sneak a look as well. In his office; while he's riding home on the crosstown bus; sometimes even when he's at his apartment and in the bathroom with the door locked securely behind him, he takes delight, he says, in old pictures of her in a bikini in Fort Lauderdale; in a strikingly short skirt, waiting in line with her friends at the Pepsi-Cola Pavilion at the 1964 World's Fair; in a turquoise one-piece bathing suit, her pretty legs dangling off the side of a diving board at a friend's house in Woodcliff Lake, New Jersey.

It's so easy—and so gratifying—for Julia to see how much he savors this secret life of his. Of theirs.

25
Mel

Elizabeth Greenwell has invited Mel and Charlie to a cocktail party at her apartment on Fifth Avenue, across from the Park. Mel hasn't a clue what to wear, but is too shy to ask Elizabeth any questions when the invitation comes to her over the phone at work. Never would she want Elizabeth to know that this is, in truth, the first cocktail party at which her presence has ever been requested. She'll dress herself all in black, and hope for the best.

The day before the party, Mel finds a business-size envelope from *The New Yorker* in her mailbox. She's received these envelopes several times before; either there was a check in it or, amazingly, a couple of pieces of fan mail from people who'd read her story "Untroubled Lives" and had something flattering to say about it. The first time she was sent a letter from a fan, she found it so thrilling, she had to stop herself from sprinting to the phone to call her mother—gone three years now—and share the handwritten note on that piece of lavender stationery from a stranger who had been sufficiently moved to correspond with her. She opens this most recent letter when she gets upstairs to her new apartment, and is utterly unprepared for what she sees.

Ms. Fleischer:

I would like to take this opportunity to let you know how much your recent story in the NYer sucked. I find it unbelievable that a magazine of such distinction would lower their standards so dramatically that they were willing to publish your piece of shit.

Cheever and Updike, yes—Melissa Fleischer, an emphatic NO!

Sincerely,

SERIOUSLY PISSED OFF READER

No signature, no return address, just a thirteen-cent postmark from Poughkeepsie, New York.

Good thing Mel's married to a shrink; waiting for Charlie to come home, she rereads the letter just once.

Melissa Fleischer, an emphatic NO!

Charlie offers her an especially long, drawn-out hug and all the right words: *Rip up the stupid letter and forget you ever saw it,* but she suspects forgetting won't be that easy.

She calls Elizabeth Greenwell the next day as soon as she gets to her desk. She has the letter with her, which she reads aloud to Elizabeth, from start to finish, in a voice that's a little unsteady.

"Oh dear," Elizabeth says sympathetically. "No doubt from someone whose work has been rejected by us over and over again. We've seen this sort of thing before, but you can't take it personally, Mel."

She can't? How *else* is she supposed to take it?

"The receptionist on our floor knows she has to open all those letters and go through each one before forwarding them to our writers; clearly she wasn't doing her job properly. But I know you'll be smart and tear up that ridiculous letter into a thousand and one tiny, tiny pieces and throw it into the trash. And we'll see you and your husband at the party tonight, yes?"

Mel finds herself nodding her head obediently, as if Elizabeth could see her.

Then, against her better judgment, she shows the letter to Austin as he sits at his desk drinking coffee from a red-and-white ceramic cup, a True Blue in hand. She wants—inappropriately—she knows, to lean against his narrow shoulder, as if he were her father and given to affectionate pats on the back every now and then. But Austin is not her father, and even more significant, he clearly doesn't hold her writing—the work she lives for—in anything close to high esteem; if she's looking for another dose of sympathy, she should be looking elsewhere.

She shows him the letter, and hears him say *asshole*, and now he's grabbing a book of matches, holding the letter over the empty metal garbage pail at the side of his desk and setting it on fire. Together, neither of them saying a word, they watch as the letter is incinerated.

"Okay, feeling better, dear heart?" Austin says, and takes a noisy sip from his ceramic mug. "And by the way: if, in fact, you can't stand the heat, it would be wise to get the fuck out of the kitchen. Posthaste."

Wise counsel, as it turns out.

Mel and Austin will, a half-dozen years from now, each have a black-and-orange ceramic coffee cup shipped to them by their distinguished book publisher, the surface of the cup embellished with the last names, in alphabetical order, of the seventy fiction writers in their stable. Leading the second row of authors, Mel will see, is Austin's name; bringing up the rear of the fourth row will be her own.

An elderly, unsmiling doorman buzzes Mel and Charlie up and gestures toward the elevator down the endless, polished marble hallway, where another elderly, humorless guy in a dark blue uniform opens and closes a creaky gate, treating his passengers to a bit of a bumpy ride nineteen stories upward, where, they are surprised to see, there's only a single apartment occupying the entire floor. When Charlie rings the bell, another uniformed person, this time a middle-aged woman in a black dress, a ruffled white apron tied around her waist, welcomes them. There are twenty-five or thirty people standing around the enormous, high-ceilinged living room, which overlooks the Park and the shimmery lights of the Upper West Side; in the far distance, Charlie whispers to Mel, you can see New Jersey. None of the guests, an even mix of women in skirts or dresses and men in jackets and ties, drinks in hand, looks familiar, but then Mel sees Nina Levinthal, whose novel won the Pulitzer a decade ago, and whom Austin had cruelly described as *not the comeliest of women*. Mel recognizes her from her author photo on the back of her most recent story collection. She has short gray hair and thick bangs cut in a very straight line across her forehead so that they cover her brow; she's dressed in a plain white blouse, a denim skirt, and those comfortable shoes with laces and heavy rubber soles that Mel and her friends wouldn't be caught dead wearing. But she's a dazzling writer, Mel knows, and can wear whatever the hell she likes, fashionable or not. Her heart begins to thump a little faster just at the sight of Nina Levinthal standing there and talking to a patrician-looking guy in well-polished Weejuns and a tweedy jacket.

Elizabeth is nowhere in sight. Searching for someone to talk to besides Charlie, Mel approaches Nina and introduces herself, Charlie trailing behind her.

"So nice to meet you and would you like part of this *amuse-bouche*?" Nina says. She is fifty years old, but her voice is still sweet as a young child's; Mel is seduced by it, as she always is when she hears it over the phone.

"Pardon me?" Mel says, when what she'd intended to say was, *I'm the greatest admirer of your fiction. Oh, and also your poetry and those ultra-smart essays.*

"Well, I suppose it's more of an hors d'oeuvre than an appetizer," Nina is saying. "It's just that it's shrimp wrapped in bacon and I'm one of those who was raised in a kosher home and so it just doesn't seem right to me. But when it was offered to me, it seemed just, I don't know, rude to turn it down, and now I'm stuck with it. Unless, of course, you'd like to take it from me. It's untouched, I assure you. I—"

"I'm Scott McCreanor, Elizabeth's husband," the guy in the tweedy jacket interrupts, and Mel watches as he neatly extracts the bacon-wrapped shrimp on a toothpick from between Nina Levinthal's thumb and index finger and tosses it onto a nearby doily-covered silver tray of tiny egg rolls. "Enough about the damn shrimp and bacon," he says cheerfully. "We're done with it." He shakes Charlie's hand, and then Mel's. "So you're one of Lizzie's new finds?"

Lizzie? Really? This isn't the Elizabeth whom Mel knows. Or could ever imagine knowing. This is way too informal for *her* Elizabeth.

"*Mamaleh!* Please don't!" she hears a woman's voice say, and Mel is, in an instant, reminded of her own beloved and sorely missed mother, who so often, and so tenderly, used that identical Yiddish endearment to refer to Mel herself. She misses her mother more than she's ever missed anyone; she longs to somehow see her again, as if, in some other galaxy, that were even a possibility.

"*Mamaleh*—I said *don't!* Do *not* tell that story to anyone, ever! It's mortifying!" she hears once more, and wants to cast her arms around the gray-haired woman across the room who's dressed in a floor-length peasant skirt and leather sandals, and whose arm is looped, Mel now sees, around Elizabeth's waist. It hits her—and apparently Charlie at the same moment—that this must be Elizabeth's mother, and Mel and Charlie shoot each other one of those looks of theirs, sharing their astonishment at what simply can't be true, which is that the supremely WASPy Elizabeth Greenwell McCreanor is the daughter of a Jewish mother. *NOT* possible, they tell each other silently; if they were seated at a table now, Mel and Charlie would be surreptitiously kicking each other under that table and relishing it.

She's surprised Elizabeth has never told her this, and fascinated by how ever-mysterious her fellow humans continue to reveal themselves to be.

She will saunter over to Elizabeth now, leaving Charlie behind with Nina and Scott, and let that mother named Judy Weitzman—in that turquoise-and-yellow peasant skirt and the blouse with all those little tassels hanging jauntily from the neckline—know that Mel herself is a member of the clan.

She and Elizabeth are about to discover that Judy, along with Mel's mother, attended, in the late 1930s, the very same James Monroe High School on Boynton Avenue in the Bronx.

Mel loves this connection between them, this surprising connection between their two mothers, but isn't sure that Elizabeth loves it, too. Hard to tell from the small, enigmatic smile on her editor's face now. But Judy Weitzman herself is clearly feeling it, her arms around Mel in a distinctly warm embrace as Mel reveals that her own mother was someone who must have used that word *mamaleh* a million and one times, her voice brimming with affection for her only daughter, her only child.

Maybe being raised by a Jewish mother isn't regarded by Elizabeth as any sort of defining marker for herself; maybe all of this just looms larger in Mel's head than it should, but for Mel it will always remain something that links her to Elizabeth in a way that she treasures.

26
Julia

In the many months since her divorce, she still hasn't become happily accustomed to sitting around her apartment at night watching TV alone. Tonight, after an infinitely long day escorting the Mishkins in cabs to and from midtown doctor appointments, she's watching one of those documentaries on WNET which she already knows isn't going to end well. Armed with a lime-flavored lollipop on which she could so easily crack a tooth or two, she watches the story of a tigress who is billed as "The World's Most Famous Tiger." This celebrity tigress has one milky blue eye veiled by a cataract, and on one cheek, a pattern of fur that closely resembles a salad fork and makes her immediately identifiable to her many thousands of admirers in India, where she has spent all nineteen years of her long and adventurous life. She is dying now of old age and starvation, and Julia is already choking back tears. Soon enough, the tigress has taken her very last breath; a state funeral of sorts follows, with uniformed Indian guards standing at attention in her honor as workers ready her for cremation, laying wreaths of orange carnations across her body. Sobbing, Julia pulls the lollipop from her mouth and wishes she could call Charlie, even though it's already after ten and a phone call to him at home is out of the question no matter *what* time it is.

On her TV screen, radiant orange flames from the funeral pyre rise toward the sky, matching the orange carnations that are now little more than ash. Julia absently slides the lollipop back into her mouth, wipes her tears with the fingertips of both hands. She falls asleep sitting upright on the love seat in her studio apartment, and then, leaning against the hard wood of an armrest, she dreams that Charlie has sent her a letter: *There's nothing wrong with you, Julia! You're a good sensitive soup, trust me.*

When she awakens, a few hours later, she remembers the letter perfectly and struggles to make sense of it. Then it comes to her: "You're a good, sensitive *soul* indeed," she says out loud, and smiles, because it's always nice to get a compliment from your boyfriend, even if it's only in a dream and even when your face is gluey with dried-up tears and stale, lime-scented saliva.

She contemplates calling Charlie from Sarasota, where she's spending the weekend visiting her friend Emily, who has recently moved from a scruffy neighborhood in Brooklyn to a small rented house on Florida's Gulf Coast. It's been something like fifteen years, she thinks, since that Columbus Day weekend one-night stand of theirs; the one neither of them cares to talk about. They talk, instead, about Emily's two brief marriages, and about Daniel, Julia's underwhelming ex. And then, finally, about Charlie, who Julia fails to mention is married.

They drink a little too much white wine from a jug of Inglenook before, during, and after dinner, dozing off in front of the television set following what they agree is a noticeably unfunny *Saturday Night Live* skit; in it, Al Franken is dressed as a sumo wrestler and is outed by his wrestling partner, a tall thin guy who, in the skit, is also his lover. Julia and Emily listen as Franken's character fatally shoots himself offstage after being outed. The TV audience, despite a few scattered giggles, doesn't seem to know what to make of the suicide; after all, what is the show meant to offer its viewers every weekend except reason to laugh?

Bummer, Julia says, and the next morning she wakes up

with a mild hangover. She calls Charlie at his office, where he promised he would be catching up on some paperwork over the weekend. She says her flight gets in at ten at LaGuardia tonight, and asks if he can please pick her up since a cab is so expensive, but his answer is an immediate and resolute *no*. There's no chance at all, he explains, that he can possibly come up with a convincing excuse to leave home tonight—and what?—not return until well after midnight? What's he going to tell his wife? he asks Julia, as if it's *her* responsibility to provide him with just the right excuse.

He sounds remorseful, but who cares? Why can't he just tell his wife the truth? Julia says.

"What?" Charlie says. "Why would I ever want to do *that*?"

This is when Julia hears herself say, "You know, if I were a different kind of person, I might think about calling your wife and telling her you're picking me up tonight, and then, very casually—"

"You know I love you," Charlie interrupts. "And *I* know you would never do anything so cruel."

"Well, you *say* you love me, but not picking me up at the airport tells me that obviously you don't," Julia explains. "And that makes me really angry, *Honey Pie*."

She hears a string of love-you's meant to appease her, meant to avert the flame of rage that can sometimes overtake her in a split second.

It makes her sick to think of these angry, destructive impulses she possesses to say and do the wrong thing when all she wants is to do the right thing.

"Fine fine fine," she tells Charlie. "Just forget it!"

On the subway home from the Mishkins' apartment now this Monday evening, jammed awkwardly between two chunky passengers but thankful for this narrow slice of seat on a downtown express train, she stares across the aisle at a bosomy woman in a T-shirt that boasts ONLY GOD CAN JUDGE ME.

Julia thinks now of her father and of that indelible, uncontrollable fury of his that she witnessed all too many times during her childhood, and she allows herself to wonder if there's something in her that, disastrously, is in some way connected to the very worst part of him. But this can't be true—can it?—and she has to dismiss the possibility only an instant later. Because she knows who she is, and knows who her father is, and there just can't be that connection between them. This father she hasn't seen in months. And months. And perhaps, may choose to never see again.

A family of four blonds—two parents and a pair of twin boys, no older than six or seven—each of them wearing black pants, white T-shirts, and blue suede sneakers with thin white laces, have settled all in a row directly opposite Julia. They've linked their hands and are praying lustily out loud right before they're about to chow down on their red-and-yellow paper containers of Egg McMuffins arranged on napkins in their laps.

God is great, God is good, and we thank him for our food. By his hands we all are fed. Give us, Lord, our daily —

McMuffins, Julia murmurs, and has to acknowledge there's a part of her, maybe more than a small part of her, that envies the family she sees seated so contentedly before her.

27
Mel

Nothing makes her feel like her truest, best self more than when, on a Sunday morning or after work on a Thursday night, she's sitting here at home writing stories in her miniature office in a cushiony armchair from Charlie's childhood den, her feet propped up on a small, tiled table, spiral notebook in her lap, a cigarette in her right hand, Bic pen in her left—stories mostly in the present tense, mostly about the infinite ways, large and small, in which her characters manage to disappoint one another. Typing up those handwritten pages on her Olivetti when she's finished for the day, she savors the lovely weight of them gathered in her hands or resting in her lap.

She isn't happy when the editor-in-chief, with his ever-present unlit cigar protruding from a corner of his mouth, approaches her, along with Daphne and a couple of other editorial assistants, and asks them to please show up at the office tomorrow at the unspeakably early hour of 6 a.m. Actually, Mel realizes, he didn't use the word *please*; she only imagined it.

What's the big emergency? The celebrated Lincoln Pastorelli, that sometimes-brilliant writer with the unmistakable whiny drawl—not to mention well-known substance abuser and notoriously bad driver who, apparently drunk, ran one of Mel's friends off the road in the Hamptons late one summer night—has some chapters of a new novel, and if the magazine is going to feature them in the next issue, Mel and her fellow flunkies will have to be at their typewriters by sunrise. Oh, and they won't be getting anything extra in their paycheck, but they can take a cab to work tomorrow morning and be reimbursed for the fare, and too, *maybe* can leave a bit earlier in the afternoon than usual instead of hanging around until five o'clock.

"Of course, this is merely a *favor* I'm asking of you," the editor-in-chief explains. "Feel free to say no if it's just too much of an imposition for you to arrive at six tomorrow morning. Of course if you *do* show up, you'll have earned Lincoln's gratitude. And Austin's." He smiles vaguely; like Daphne, he's not the squishy type. "And mine, too," he finishes.

How can Mel say no? How can she not show up when she knows the boss wants her there typing away madly like some . . .well, typist for hire?

Afterward, when the editor-in-chief returns to his office with his comically duckfooted gait, the assistants bitch quietly behind his back, but it's clear that none of them will fail to show up tomorrow morning.

Mel's thinking about how much she hates going to bed early—which she'll certainly have to do tonight if she's getting up before 5 a.m. and doesn't want to fall asleep tomorrow morning typing Lincoln's pages—when she looks up to see the editor-in-chief standing over her.

"Where's Austin?" he says. "It's after three o'clock, Goddamnit. Where the hell is he?"

There's something about his pissed-off demeanor that makes her think he *knows.*

"I honestly don't know," Mel says.

And honestly, she doesn't.

Not for sure, anyway.

And she just doesn't want to think about it, Goddamnit.

In the morning, she kisses her conked-out husband goodbye, hails a cab for herself on Lex, and arrives at the office at precisely six o'clock. She and Daphne and the other couple of editorial assistants, their desks all in a vertical row, remove the gray plastic covers from their typewriters in unison, and the sighs of their discontent echo down the linoleum hallway. Except for the editor-in-chief, there's no one else in the office, and why would there be? Who would be crazy enough to show up at sunrise except a quartet of underpaid assistants afraid of losing their jobs?

The boss hands out their assigned chapters and of course Mel takes a look before she begins to type. There's something thrilling, she concedes, about the prospect of typing up the work of an acclaimed writer like Lincoln. But as she reads through his chapter, she is stunned to see that these pages are disappointingly mediocre. Maybe even less than mediocre—the more she reads, the more it becomes clear that some of this is seriously soapy and over-the-top. So this is what happens when a writer becomes famous, she wonders. So famous that even Austin is afraid to edit him? If even remarkably talented writers like Lincoln can produce such disheartening stuff, does this mean that, even years from now, *she* will struggle to get her own stories exactly right, but sometimes will fail catastrophically, as well?

Absolutely.

She begins to type up Lincoln's chapter, and the distinctive sound, here in the office, of those five electric typewriters all going at once punctures the early-morning hush now; the truth is, the monotony of it is almost enough to put Mel to sleep right here at her desk.

Years later, when she has locked herself away in her bedroom to work on her novel, she will hear the greatly loved, high-pitched voice of her four-year-old son, just beyond the door, answering a preschool pal's urgent question: *But what does your mom* do *in there?*

Oh, my mom's job is called a typer. All she does in there is type.

28
Julia

She's waited a few months to summon up the courage—though not in person, only in a phone call—to get a definitive answer from Charlie about whether or not he actually loves his wife. When he hesitates, for only a moment, one afternoon in his office, and then says *yes, I do*, in a voice emptied of all uncertainty, Julia ends the conversation right there, slamming the Mishkins' phone back into place against the kitchen wall. Seething, she silently dictates to herself, while leftovers for lunch are heating up in the toaster oven, the letter she's going to send to Charlie.

So you think you're going to get away with this, think you're going to get a free pass, honey pie?

Well, think again. You have exactly 24 hours from the time you get this to tell your wife about us. If you don't, well, who knows what could happen. Not a joke, honey pie. Seriously, 24 hours.

P.S. I love you.

"You know we're part Italian, don't you?" Walter is telling her as she gets down on all fours to look for one of his hearing aids. She finds it under the couch, as usual, trimmed with a light coating of dust. "We're related to Leonardo da Vinci, who was born in 1452 and was a vegetarian," Walter continues.

"Part Italian? No we're not, we're Ashkenazi Jews," Molly says.

"Wrong! I was brought up in the Catholic Church."

"Oh, Walter. Walter Walter Walter. What are you *talking* about, my handsome hero?"

Angry though she is with Charlie, Julia has to smile: how deeply Molly loves this old, old man, who, with his long, broken-but-never-fixed nose and sharp chin, is anything but handsome. Handsome? That's Julia's newly disappointing boyfriend, the one who loves his wife, maybe even more than he loves *her*.

"They say Leonardo was like a god. More god than human," Walter reports.

"Really?" Julia says, and announces, "Lunch is served," after taking the dish of lasagna from the toaster oven.

So he loves her . . . but he loves his wife as well.

She has to face it: there's just too much love in this guy's heart. Now the sweetish smell of tomato sauce and onions and ricotta is making her sick, or maybe it's the ease with which she can imagine the sound of Charlie's kisses falling so lightly against his wife's sullen, downturned mouth every night just before they hop into bed together and turn off the lights. (In truth, she has no idea *what* his wife's mouth looks like, but takes pleasure in imagining its sulkiness and the wife's irritable, unpleasant nature.) It kills her that she and her boyfriend have never, not even once, had the opportunity to shut off the lights in her bedroom and fall asleep together for the night. He can't afford to drift off to sleep in her bed even for twenty minutes, he's explained to Julia, generally in a hurry to get home, no matter what the day or hour. *Stay*, she's said to him so many times after they've made love. *Stay here naked in my bed and fall asleep with your hand resting warm and cozy between my thighs.*

"I'm really angry my name isn't engraved on the Statue of Liberty," she hears Walter saying.

She pours herself a Pepsi and stands at the kitchen counter sipping it, watching over the Mishkins from a safe distance, enjoying the silence, and considering whether she should actually send a threatening letter to Charlie. She's contemplated a letter like this once or twice before, when Charlie had disappointed her at the last minute because his wife unexpectedly made plans for them that, he claimed, just couldn't be avoided.

Bull . . . shit!

"You know, my wife's not as sexy as she looks," she hears Walter saying indifferently.

"Thanks for the insult, Handsome Hero," Molly says, but she doesn't sound insulted.

Walter takes his wife's hand and lifts it to his mouth. His lips are coated in tomato sauce; there's a translucent sliver of onion pasted to his upper lip. He kisses the back of Molly's hand and leaves the onion and an orangey, mouth-shaped print across the branches of rubbery-looking veins that lie so close to the surface of her skin. Old-lady hands. A little unsightly, even with a wedding band and engagement ring on her finger.

Don't look at the wedding band, Julia tells herself. *Don't look. Do. Not. Look.*

She writes the letter—mostly the same one she'd dictated to herself—on a piece of note paper she finds in a drawer in the Mishkins' kitchen cabinet, and then, in another drawer, finds an envelope and a fifteen-cent stamp portraying a grim-looking, big-eared John Steinbeck. Addressing the envelope with a freshly sharpened No. 2 pencil embossed with the words B*oard of Education—City of New York*, she drops it decisively into a mailbox along Third Avenue on her way home.

You have exactly 24 hours from the time you get this to tell your wife about us. If you don't, then good luck, honey pie. . .

Sorry sorry sorry, of course she didn't mean it, she tells Charlie over the phone two days later.

Of course, he says, of course he understands. After all, he's a shrink; he understands everything.

After they've had sex in Julia's apartment early one evening, she plays idly with Charlie's wedding ring, sliding it off his finger, slipping it on and off her own.

"Whatcha doin'?" Charlie says.

As if he doesn't know.

"It hurts me to see you wearing this," she says. "You understand what I'm saying, right?"

She asks if he could please not wear it when they're together.

It doesn't seem like a lot to ask of him, but he makes a face, one that seems to suggest that what she wants is evidently just too much. "Come on, Honey Pie," she says, "don't you get that it kind of kills me to see it on your finger?"

"Of course I get it," he says, "and I'm sorry. I'll try and remember next time, okay?"

It fits comfortably on her index finger, and they both forget all about it as she goes down on him now, pleasing him just the way he's so patiently instructed her.

She finds the ring on the laminated counter in the bathroom after he leaves, but doesn't know how it got there. She considers tossing it down the toilet and why shouldn't she? Why should she have to be reminded, each time they see each other, that Charlie inhabits another life, one where she's plainly irrelevant? Now she's envisioning herself both a tenured professor with a PhD and a cool young mother to her and Charlie's imaginary son and daughter, hosting their birthday parties at Playland, attending their silly/sweet fifth- and sixth-grade plays, and years later, graduations, their children's names embellished with asterisks on the commencement programs, denoting "Summa Cum Laude" and "Phi Beta Kappa." And why not? Why shouldn't this life be Julia's? A life so much more satisfying than the one she has now; a life more crowded with people and obligations, noisier and busier.

And God knows, happier.

Holding his wedding ring between her middle finger and her thumb, she drops it into the toilet now, where it sits quietly, uttering not a single sound of protest. She puts her palm on the handle of the toilet and rests it there, unable to press down. She feels nothing, neither excitement nor regret, and that, in itself, is dispiriting.

Eventually, wearing an elbow-length pink rubber glove, she reaches into the water and fishes out the ring. Washing it off with a more-than-generous squirt of dish detergent, she dries it thoroughly with some sheets of toilet paper, and deposits it into the blond-wood jewelry box that sits on top of her dresser. She forbids herself to look at it over the next few days, but who says she has to listen? One night when she's feeling particularly desolate, she takes the ring from the jewelry box and goes to sleep with it on her finger, rubbing the gold against her cheek and along her mouth, caressing it.

Charlie knows she has it, and they've already made plans to meet so she can return it.

When she hands it over to him in a Chinese restaurant on the Upper West Side, not far from his office, it feels like one of the most painful things she's ever had to do.

An act of true generosity, offered because, well, she loves him.

"Oh, yeah, thanks," Charlie says casually, and this licensed psychologist doesn't even have the emotional intelligence to wait until after dinner—the dinner his wife believes is a meeting with some shrinks from the Manhattan Psychoanalytic Society—before sliding it back over his ring finger. "Should we order scallion pancakes for an appetizer?" he says, but Julia is so angry, she leaves him sitting there in the maroon faux-leather booth patched with masking tape along the back, and heads for the door. He hurries after her, but it's too late; she's on her way back to the subway and has nothing more to say to him tonight.

He follows her down the steps and into the subway station, and she lets him put his arm around her when they get to the bottom of the stairs.

"You know *me*, I'm a homeless romantic," he says, and kisses her ear.

"What?"

"Oops, sorry, I meant *hopeless* romantic."

"You're hopeless all right," Julia agrees, but he's got her laughing, and that's worth something, isn't it?

But when she is feeling her worst, or maybe her loneliest, a day or a week or a month from now, she will imagine herself with his wedding ring in hand, imagine herself sending it straight down the toilet with a single empowering flush.

29
Mel

Mel's second story, "Autumn," appears in *The New Yorker*, and she starts to get letters from editors in the city, all of whom say they would be delighted to take her to lunch to discuss the possibility of publishing a novel of hers. But what are they talking about? *What* novel? She writes stories—she's never written anything that's continued beyond page seventeen and guess what, has no desire to do so. None! She's always happy to be treated to an elegant lunch where there are immaculate white tablecloths draped over the tables and waiters who speak with continental accents—especially at the Algonquin, where she's had lunch more than once with Elizabeth Greenwell—but she has no intention of deceiving those editors, all of them women, who work at companies called Random House and Doubleday and Simon & Schuster and who seem so enthusiastic about this hypothetical, unwritten novel of hers. Sorry to disappoint them, but she's just a short-story writer and that's just the way she likes it. She wishes she could discuss this with Austin, but every morning when she comes to work, he makes her feel as if this part of her life, the part that truly defines her place in the universe, that offers her pretty much the greatest fulfillment and excitement, simply doesn't exist. To him, Mel understands, she's nothing more than someone who performs the lowliest of tasks—scouring so efficiently through the slush pile; using the phone to check in with Richard, his fellow adulterer, in search of a conveniently empty bed; using that same phone to engage Austin's wife in lengthy conversation in the middle of the afternoon so that all three of them—the wildly unfaithful womanizer, the uneasy wife, the resentful young assistant—can steer clear of what lies at the dark, dark center of his life.

You know what? Sometimes that resentful young assistant just feels like giving him a good smack.

30
Julia

As Walter disappears into the bedroom to hunt for his checkbook one afternoon—of course he won't let Julia help him look for it (*it's MY money, mine and my wife's and nobody else's!*)—she goes to the refrigerator for the glass of orange juice Molly's requested. Pouring her some from a carton of Tropicana, Julia is confused, at first, about why the container is filled with apple juice. And then she sniffs it.

"MOLLY! Can I ask you a question?"

"You certainly may," Molly says from her seat at the dining-room table. "But please don't raise your voice like that, Miss."

Before Julia hears her explanation, she carefully transports the glass of "apple juice" into the bathroom and pours it down the toilet. Then she washes her hands three times.

What she wants to know is why there's a half-gallon of pee in the Tropicana container.

"Oh, *that*," Molly says. "Not to worry. It's good for that eczema I have on my elbow. It's very helpful for your skin in general, you can even use it to wash your hands. It's sterile, don't worry. We saw it on WNET, Channel 13, I can't remember. But we would never drink it, Miss. We're old, but we're not crazy!" Molly says, and laughs. "Feel free to try some on your hands, or anyplace else. I heard that it helps clear up athlete's foot, too. Oh, and by the way, the orange juice is in—"

Walter is shambling down the hallway now in the slippers Julia ordered for him from their Lands' End catalogue. They're a half size too small, and his bare feet are hanging out over the back, but he's grown fond of them and doesn't care. "Come over here, I have to ask you something, Miss," he says. His checkbook is tucked under one arm.

Julia is by his side now, and she rests her hand on his rounded shoulder. "What can I do for you, Walter?"

"Let me ask you, Miss, when did the insanity start?" he says in a whisper.

"Pardon me?"

"Let me put it this way: I'm afraid one of us is insane but I don't know who." He's whispering in her ear, blowing warm air inside it.

She doesn't want to be here anymore. Doesn't want this job where the Tropicana carton standing so innocently in the refrigerator next to the fat-free milk holds sixty-four ounces of piss instead of orange juice. She wants to go home and bang her head against something hard. And then collapse on the floor and remain there for a good twenty-four hours or so.

And *then* wake up to a brand-new life.

Just in case you ever foolishly forget; I'm never not thinking of you—this is the message she leaves for Charlie several times a week, the message she calls in to his answering service and knows will be delivered when he checks in with them, as he does at least twice a day. She knows the voices of the operators; she hears their exasperation, their pity, their boredom, but still she continues to call in to the service, knowing her messages will, without fail, be read aloud to Charlie, who needs to hear them, who needs, she believes, to be reminded.

31
Charlie

On a Wednesday night after work, in bed with Julia—her head on his bare chest, listening, she says, to the beating of his heart—Charlie is aware, as always when he's here with her, that he needs to be home soon, less than an hour from now, as it happens. He needs to make a stop in SoHo first, at Dean & DeLuca, to pick up some gourmet chestnut bread he and Mel have decided is their new favorite, and he's looking forward to making French toast with it, maybe adding just a teaspoon of cognac and some orange zest, from a recipe Mel found in a magazine at work.

Julia has moved off him and rolled onto her side now, and he buries his nose in her dark hair, sniffing the coconut scent of her conditioner. "I've got to get going," he tells her with a sigh.

"Hey, Honey Pie?" she says, and there's a sigh from her, too. "Can I ask you something? We've never talked about this, but it's been on my mind even though I wish it weren't . . . so listen, I'm sure you understand how creepy and unnerving this is for me, but do you and your wife ever sleep together?" he hears her say.

He lifts his face from her hair and says, "Excuse me?" As if he has no idea what it is she's asking.

"Please don't insult me, Charlie," she says, though she doesn't sound hostile, just uneasy.

He doesn't want to hurt her, but doesn't want to lie, either. He's told dozens of lies to Mel over these weeks and months, particularly when, driven by lust, he's stopped off at Julia's apartment for an unscheduled quickie on his way home from work; lying to Julia, as well, would just be too much.

"Actually . . . we do," he tells her.

"Do what? Finish the sentence, Honey Pie."

"We do sleep together," he says.

"Define 'we'. . ."

"My wife and I," he whispers, having learned it's best not to say Mel's name aloud when he's in Julia's presence. The mere sound of his wife's name makes his girlfriend's stomach hurt, he knows. And another fleeting thought of her, of Mel, causes him a pinprick of regret, which he consciously chooses to disregard here in Julia's bed.

"Say the whole sentence to me," she urges him.

"But why are you doing this?" he wants to know. "Why do you want me to hurt you like this?"

"Just say it." Her voice is muffled, her mouth pressed against the inside of her arm.

"Okay, my wife and I do sleep together. From time to time," he confesses softly, and Julia's immediate response is to turn away from him and over onto her other side.

"Go away," she orders him. "Go away and don't come back. EVER, do you hear me?"

"Come on, Honey Pie." He's getting into his boxers now, and looking around for a missing sock. This isn't the first time he's left here without a sock or a belt; once he even left his wristwatch, and sometimes he thinks Julia is keeping souvenirs of his visits, claiming she doesn't know where this or that disappeared to. "Come on, Honey Pie," he repeats. "Just don't let yourself think about it, all right?"

Do what I do: Just. Don't. Let. Yourself. Think. About. It.

"Whatever," she says. Out of bed, barefoot, and naked except for her lilac-colored panties, she walks him to the front door of her apartment. "I need you to tell me that you love me."

"Love you," he says obediently. He rubs his open palm

gently against her nipple, enjoying the feel of it stiffening against his hand.

"Tell me again," she says, and with two fingers, shifts the pair of gleaming silver hearts back and forth along the necklace he gave her for Valentine's Day.

"Love you," he says again, because he always, always tells the truth, at least to *her*.

At least most of the time.

Until tonight, he would have said he's done a pretty good job, so far, in keeping both his wife and his girlfriend happy—both these women who occupy front-row seats at the very center of his life.

Not that he's congratulating himself.

Well, maybe just a little.

But only for a split second.

Going downstairs for the mail at noon on Saturday, he grabs an unsatisfying handful of bills, a copy of *The Atlantic Monthly*, and a birthday card from his parents, which has arrived three days early from the suburbs of Westchester, as usual. And as usual, that early arrival annoys him, even though he knows his parents mean well and that, neurotically, they just can't endure the possibility of his birthday card arriving even a day late.

Mel is still in the shower when he gets back upstairs and goes into the bedroom, where he tosses the mail onto his nightstand, unread, and is briefly transfixed by a documentary on TV starring a chimpanzee who has been trained as a lab assistant.

Now he is opening an envelope inside of which is an awkwardly folded, handwritten letter from Julia on a piece of typing paper; somehow it slipped between the pages of *The Atlantic Monthly* and the sight of it is alarming enough to dampen Charlie's palms with perspiration and raise a field of goosebumps along all four of his limbs.

HONEY PIE: You have to go to your bank and withdraw $1,000 for me. I need to start seeing my new therapist twice a week from now on and you're the one who has to pay for that extra weekly session, understood? Because, big surprise, YOU'RE THE ONE WHO'S RUINING MY LIFE!

I thought your love for me was something special, but I realize now I'm just an idiot and it's all your fault. So screw you, honey pie.
Oh, and p.s. you have no choice but to hand over that $1,000. No joke. JUST REMEMBER: I KNOW WHERE YOUR WIFE LIVES! (And also where she works!) And both her phone numbers!

Charlie feels his mouth go dry; he feels his heart thumping in what he recognizes is genuine terror.

Staring at the TV now, he sees that the chimp in the documentary is dressed in a long white coat and white sneakers, and is feeding cages of animals in the lab; small cages holding white rats and mice, and a couple of cinnamon-colored hamsters.

He knows Mel is the sort of wife—not like other, more freewheeling women, a couple of whom are married to college friends of his—who would be devastated by a phone call from Julia. There is something so vulnerable about this wife of his, so small and modest and often self-effacing; someone who has to hoist herself up onto shelves in the supermarket to reach what she wants; who needs help getting the big bag of dirty clothes down to the laundry room twice a week; who almost let her driver's license expire when they first moved to the city, and whom he can scarcely recall behind the wheel of their car over the past couple of years. He instinctively knows he is willing to do anything at all to spare her the pain of discovering what he and Julia have been up to. Distraught, shredding Julia's letter into the smallest pieces, he considers withdrawing the thousand bucks from his savings account at Citibank.

He considers it even though he's just a young middle-class guy with plenty of monthly bills, including hefty student loans on both his end and Mel's—and even though he's aware that despite Julia's troubled relationship with her father and mother, her parents have been paying for her health insurance for years and would probably spring for the cost of her extra therapy, too. He understands she is blackmailing him as punishment for continuing to sleep with his wife, and that perhaps if Julia didn't love him so deeply, as she claims to, her anger wouldn't be nearly so toxic.

Thinking about this, he feels a brief flood of remorse for the pain he's caused Julia.

He watches, in a daze now, as the chimpanzee finishes up his chores. The chimp, whose name is Ziggy, is mopping the floor of the lab, swabbing down the same area a half-dozen times, his back bent in hard labor.

"What a cute little guy," Mel says, after she emerges from the shower. There she is in the doorway, a small figure in a velour bathrobe and bright yellow flip-flops, smiling at Ziggy.

It occurs to Charlie, in another vaguely sickening minute, that the sort of husband he's already proven himself to be is the sort who won't be winning medals for meritorious conduct anytime soon. But then, as Mel dips into the walk-in closet in the bedroom in search of a pair of jeans, he's already contemplating what to say to his pissed-off girlfriend. *May I remind you that blackmail is a criminal offense? Come on, don't act like a Looney Tune, Honey Pie!*

As Mel comes out of their closet, barefoot and in bell-bottoms that sweep along the bedroom floor, Charlie arranges his arms around her in an unmistakably heartfelt embrace, something neither of them, after more than five years of marriage, has been offering the other lately, he realizes.

"What?" Mel says. "Why are you looking at me like that?" Her head is tilted against his shoulder. Ziggy, the simian lab assistant, has a banana peeking out of each pocket of his lab coat, and a pair of sunglasses fixed on top of his head.

"Do you love me?" Charlie says.

If asked, he would have to admit he probably no longer deserves Mel's love. But thankfully, no one's asking, and Mel, in her innocence, her blind faithfulness, offers him precisely what he wants to hear.

"What kind of a question is that? *Of course* I do, you idiot!" she says breezily. He's so grateful, he thinks he may feel a tear starting to form in one eye. "Why would you even *ask* me a question like that?" Mel is saying. "Everything okay?"

"Oh, you know me, I'm just a sentimental asshole," he jokes.

"Hey, if there's one word I would never use to describe you, buddy, it's 'sentimental,'" Mel says, and now they're laughing together, and it's a moment he prizes.

When Julia phones him at his office on Monday afternoon, he's in between patients and eating lunch on a flimsy paper plate at his desk—limp leftovers from the eggplant parmesan he made from scratch last night—and reading the automobile section of the Sunday *Times*. She's calling to offer an apology, it seems. *Of course* he doesn't have to give her that thousand bucks! *Of course* he isn't ruining her life; in fact, she says, he's enriching every single day of it.

Later in the week, she sends a card to his office decorated with a sad-eyed kitten dressed in a glittery pink tutu. Printed inside are the words "Love you with all my heart"; directly beneath them, Julia had written, *P.S. To quote the incomparable Virginia Woolf: "Just in case you ever foolishly forget; I'm NEVER not thinking of you."*

It's the sight of that NEVER that gives him pause, a frisson of panic he'll just have to ignore.

32
Julia

Walking along Lexington Avenue a month before the official first night of spring, not plugged into the music on her transistor radio, just minding her own business after a long day with the Mishkins, Julia trips on a piece of buckled sidewalk and falls flat on her face. *Literally* flat on her face, except at the very last moment, she manages to swivel her head slightly to the side, sparing her nose and front teeth. Of course it's rush hour when she lands on the pavement, and she is mortified at the way foot traffic stalls around her; a half-dozen or so do-gooders on their way to the subway come to a stop and offer their help. Shifting over onto her back, she shows her face to horrified spectators, all of whom seem to respond in unison with a noisy intake of breath and cries of *Oy!* or *Christ!* or *Jesus!*

"Can I see what I look like?" Julia asks anyone at all, and when a woman her own age bends down with a plastic Covergirl compact and snaps it open so Julia can get a view of her face in the small round mirror, a few of the other good Samaritans shout, "Stop, are you crazy? Don't let her see!"

"Don't let me see *what*?" Astonishingly, she isn't in much pain—it's really just her self-esteem that feels injured—and when it's suggested that someone needs to call an ambulance from the pay phone right there on the corner, Julia doesn't understand why. She tries to sit up, but one of the good Samaritans says this isn't a smart idea and asks if anyone can volunteer a blazer or a jacket to put under Julia's head as she lies there on the sidewalk on the west side of Lex waiting for the ambulance to arrive. A dark cotton suit jacket materializes a moment later, and is folded and tucked under her by a sweet-faced, preppy-looking woman with a tortoiseshell headband in place in her hair.

"Is there anyone you'd like us to call?" another good Samaritan asks. "Friends? A brother or a sister? Parents? Husband? Boyfriend? Anyone who can go to the hospital with you?"

Friends? A brother or sister? She's not going to bother her friend Rachel in the Jersey suburbs who has recently, painfully, been divorced, or her brother, Andrew, who's in grad school studying cultural anthropology at the University of Oregon . . . And her parents? Not going to disturb their homemade chicken potpie dinner filled with slippery, dirty-white mushrooms and crumbled, bacon-flavored chips in their little kitchen on the South Shore of Long Island. What would they offer to do, anyway, those seriously disappointing parents of hers? Drive all the way into the city, kill themselves looking for a parking space, and then sit around engaged in some hand-holding while waiting to hear the news from the doctor in the emergency room about their klutzy daughter's prognosis following her humiliating fall? They're the antithesis of the hand-holding type, always were and always will be . . . As for that husband, he's merely an ex and very much into preserving and protecting his all-important privacy. And that leaves . . . the boyfriend. Who she thinks loves her, but only when he can find the time and the means to elude that other life of his, the one busy enough with his therapy practice and all those needy patients he claims he doesn't feel comfortable talking about; a wife; his parents in Westchester; and oh yeah, occasional sex with that aforementioned wife. Of course he's the one Julia wants to call—her guess is Charlie's heading homeward now on the crosstown bus back from the West Side, and then stopping off at the A&P to shop for dinner.

"Thank you all, but no thanks, not necessary to call anyone," Julia tells the assembled good Samaritans, most of whom are beginning to move on.

She tries to sit up again, and this time it's a paramedic who is advising her otherwise, asking if she'd lost consciousness for even a split second before or after she fell, or if she feels faint now.

No. And no. She's fine and just wants to go home.

The paramedic looks at her as if she's nuts. "Sorry, *not* a good idea," he says. He tells her she's definitely going to need to be examined in the ER by an intern or resident from the departments of internal medicine or general surgery. His partner, a woman named Mychelle, is helping him lift Julia onto a stretcher as the kind owner of the suit jacket reclaims it and wishes her the best. It's less than a five-minute drive to the hospital, where Julia is pretty much ignored for over half an hour as she lies there on the stretcher, her right eye hideously swollen, as is her brow itself. A male nurse has brought her a hand mirror to hold up to her frightening face, but when Julia asks for an ice pack to help reduce the swelling in her cheek—the cheek that will, in time, turn a deep fuchsia, then black, blue, and green, and finally, days later, yellow—the only response she gets is a shrug before the nurse hurries away, presumably to attend to someone in far worse shape. One by one, Julia asks three other uniformed employees biding their time in the vicinity if they can please get an ice pack for her as the swelling on and around her eye grows even worse. But only one of the three responds.

"I don't work here," he says; this is when Julia begin to weep.

A woman on a gurney is wheeled next to her, accompanied by a guy in a soiled gray sweat suit who is saying, "I've got five syllables for you, angel baby: "Roll. With. The. Pun ches. All right?"

"Is that so?" the woman says. There's blood encrusted around the curve of her ear and leaking from one nostril. "Well, I've got four syllables for *you*: Screw. You. Jay. Son. How's that?" She looks over at Julia. "What the hell happened to *you*?"

"Nothing much," Julia says, and the woman turns away, satisfied.

Julia has her tears under control by the time a doctor not much older than herself stops by to examine her. "Look at YOU!" the doctor says, her enthusiasm accompanied by what appears to be an approving smile. "Hard day at the office?"

"Or something."

The doctor, whose name, spelled out on her badge, is S. Silverstein-Diamondstein, cleans off the dried blood above and beneath Julia's eye with cotton balls dipped in antiseptic. In a tired voice, she asks if Julia's vision is okay and whether her head hurts.

"I'm fine," Julia assures her. The woman on the gurney next door is arguing with the guy who had five syllables for her. They're both drunk, Julia realizes.

"Hey, you're crying," Dr. Silverstein-Diamondstein says. "Here, have a tissue." She checks Julia's vitals, takes down her history, then reports that she needs to have a "skull series"—several X-rays of her skull—before being released back into the wild.

And how long is this going to take?

"Well, since it's not an emergency, and there's a pretty long list of patients ahead of you, your wait could be . . . who knows? An hour or two?" Dr. Silverstein-Diamondstein reports.

Great.

Julia carries a book with her, as always; today it's a three-decades-old, yellowing paperback of F. Scott Fitzgerald stories. But because one eye is swollen shut, she can barely make her way through a single paragraph. She thinks of the last time she was a patient in the ER; it must have been over twenty-five years ago when she fell down those imaginary stairs in that imaginary basement of hers.

Waiting for the skull series and with nothing better to do, she fantasizes about what Charlie would say if she could send him a picture of how appalling she looks right now—the purple bruising is already beginning to migrate down below her eye and beneath her cheek—and she wonders if he would even contemplate excusing himself from the dinner table, disappearing out the front door of his apartment with some mumbled explanation to his wife and then hightailing it over to the ER to sit beside her and hold her hand in his as she waits to be wheeled away for her skull series. She would even let him keep his wedding ring in place and wouldn't say a word about it or eye it resentfully, as she sometimes can't stop herself from doing.

If only she could call him and say, *I need you, Honey Pie. Right now. Please! I'm in the ER at Lenox Hill and seriously need you to come over here and keep me company.*

Really? Would he really blow off dinner with his wife and make his way to her side? So what if her face looks like it's been steamrollered; she's guessing even a close-up snapshot of her injuries wouldn't be enough to get Charlie away from his wife and over to the ER. Because what spur-of-the-moment lie could he possibly invent that would entitle him to come to her?

"Truthfully, I'm feeling a lot better since I gave up all hope," she hears a patient in a neck brace say as he's wheeled past her.

What's that *all about*? she'd like to ask the guy, but he's already gone.

She knows what she can't expect from Charlie, and yet she expects it nonetheless. And feels betrayed yet again by his love for his wife, by his failure to give *her* what she wants, what she knows she *deserves*. Now it's a guy in a wheelchair who occupies the space next door. "So I was in sales, then the Heavenly Father told me to quit, and become a pastor . . . and that's how I ended up buying the Porsche nine-eleven," the man's voice says.

"Wait, so the Heavenly Father told you to buy a Porsche? Is that what you're saying, Pastor Johnson?" a female voice asks.

Julia leans forward on her gurney, but all she can see is a pair of bare feet on the wheelchair's footrest.

"Correct," the pastor says. "He did indeed."

"That's fabulous!" the woman's voice says.

The skull series will show Julia that her brain is perfectly normal; that's the good news. The bad news is that by tomorrow, the whole right side of her face will have turned a deep magenta, as if attacked by some out-of-control maniac wielding a can of spray paint.

33
Mel

In stolen bits of free time at her desk at the magazine, and then as home after work, Mel is busy revising a new story for Elizabeth Greenwell—one that Elizabeth says she is strongly intrigued by but evidently hasn't yet fallen in love with madly enough to want to publish. Her editor thinks Mel's characters still need *a little more flesh on their bones.* She's written to her more than once, *You're just not digging deep enough*. And she has reminded Mel, in her most recent letter, that it's conflict that has to be the fulcrum of her narrative. *Fulcrum*, a Latin word that meant "bedpost" and which, humiliatingly, Mel had never heard of—just like steak tartare.

Her job, as Mel sees it, is to win Elizabeth over so that she tumbles headlong into love.

Mel will give Elizabeth more of herself, reveal more of her own life in this new story. She thinks of that first semester when she was a freshman in Providence, and the October afternoon in 1970 when she tripped and fell near campus, right in front of the First Unitarian Church on the corner of Benevolent and Benefit Streets, twisting her ankle so viciously on the eighteenth-century red-brick sidewalk, she had to clench her teeth to keep from crying out against the surprising intensity of the pain. Riding by on his bicycle, a stranger—a senior psych major named Charlie—stopped to help her, and gave her a lift on the back of his bike to the university health service, where he would stay by her side until her ankle was X-rayed, and then afterward, as she hung around for the radiologist's report. While they were seated in the waiting room in uncomfortable chairs, Mel's leg fully stretched out and her ankle throbbing, this stranger who had so generously rescued her listened as Mel told what she saw then as the coolest story of her childhood. The story of how, not long after she'd taught herself to read the summer she turned four, she grabbed her copy of *The Cat in the Hat,* and without her parents noticing her absence, slipped away to bang on the doors of some of the seven or eight suburban homes in their cul-de-sac, boasting to her neighbors as they stepped outside for a better look at her, *I can read!* Then opening up her Dr. Seuss book and demonstrating her newly discovered talent to those amused neighbors, some of whom invited her in for cookies and juice or orange soda, and none of whom bothered to call Mel's parents. She must have been gone for an hour or so in that leafy little Long Island suburb, and her parents were frantic with worry until she finally showed up on their front lawn, *The Cat in the Hat* tucked under her arm, its pages disheveled and stained. She was too young to understand exactly what she had done wrong; all she understood was that *The Cat in the Hat* was her most beloved possession, and for weeks afterward she would insist on sleeping with it under her pillow. It was this story—Charlie told her—and the thought of this four-year-old pipsqueak swaggering around her neighborhood crowing exultantly about being able to read *The Cat in the Hat* that made him fall in love with her, months after her sprained ankle had healed and they'd been going out together for most of the fall semester.

She will, this instant, incorporate this story from her childhood into her new manuscript for Elizabeth Greenwell, "On the Corner of Benevolent and Benefit Streets." Both the childhood story and Charlie's reaction to it will add a little more flesh to Mel's fictional characters—and will render things all the more poignant when one of those characters so heartlessly betrays the other.

34
Mel

Austin is sending her downstairs to the lobby to pick up a copy of *The Times* at the newsstand; apparently his pal Richard wrote a blistering review of a new novel Austin has read and admired. He's heard about the review from the young novelist, who went berserk when he read it this morning, but Austin wants to see it for himself. He gives Mel a buck and asks her to bring back a pack of True Blues along with the paper. Martin Glass emerges now from his office next to Austin's and says, "Oh, you're going down, Melissa? Can you get me a pack of Marlboros while you're there . . . and also . . . a Three Musketeers? Or if they don't have it, I'll take a Milky Way. Here's a dollar for you."

"Hey, what is she, your errand boy?" Austin says, but he winks at Mel as if he's said something funny.

She *does* feel like an errand boy, but she does as she's told.

Years from now—on a perfectly cloudless weekend morning in the 1980s—Mel, the former errand boy, will grab a copy of the paper of record from a pile at her neighborhood newsstand, and turn, as she always does first, to the arts section. She will discover, in the two minutes it takes her to scan the startling, completely unexpected review of her first novel, precisely what it's like to be shamed, oh so publicly, by a stranger who seems to wield all the power in the world, at least to Mel. There will be phrases like "nearly perfect pitch" to describe Mel's dialogue; her "carefully crafted language" and a flattering sentence about how she uses "her gift" to portray the world; at the very end of the review, Mel will see the words *abundant talent*, but hardly any of this will stay with her permanently, and none of it will serve as much of a consolation. Instead, she will focus on the words *seriously flawed* and will go home and hide in her empty bathtub, yanking the colorful polyester curtain across the tub, enclosing herself in that uncomfortable place and ignoring her husband's pleas to act like a grown-up and come to the phone and talk to the friends and family calling to congratulate her. Those well-meaning callers will not, of course, see what *she* will see, will not understand why she will continue to characterize this day as the second most disastrous day of her still-young life.

What kind of writer, she will ask herself, sheds tears over the word *maudlin*; what sort of writer fails to focus on phrases like "abundant talent"?

Happily, she will redeem herself just a year later, when this very same terrifyingly powerful and fearless critic will heap praise upon her new collection of short stories. And yet Mel won't ever be able to dismiss those words "seriously flawed" from her memory.

Never.

But lesson learned: never will she allow a critic's words to wound her like this again.

35
Mel

Mel, along with the Canadian proofreader, Rebecca, is proofing the centerfold of the magazine where, in three months, there will be a special feature entitled "Who's Who in the Literary Cosmos." There's a "Red Hot Center" in this particular cosmos, along with many planets surrounding that orangey sun. Included among the eleven names inscribed across the sun in yellowish print are Wayne's and also Nina Levinthal's, along with the critic who will deem Mel's first novel so disastrously flawed. At the very bottom of the centerfold, miles beneath the heavenly bodies fixed in the blue-black sky embellished here and there with the names of literary stars, is the category labeled "On the Horizon." Mel's envy of those young writers, as she spells their names aloud to Rebecca slowly and deliberately, stings a little; though really, how can she not be jealous of those who are already being recognized there on the horizon.

But in the next decade, in the same year when Mel will suffer the indignity of what she will always regard as being "trashed" by *The New York Times*, she will also be lucky enough to have her name included in the magazine's centerfold.

It will be Wayne's good fortune to again be fixed at the glowing center of everything, while Mel will be officially consigned to the very bottom of the cosmos, though it will feel, to her, like an honor, just to have her name linked, however tenuously, to Wayne's in the pages of the magazine—years after she will have abandoned her desk and her IBM Selectric out there in that dulled linoleum hallway high above Madison Avenue.

36
Julia

She wants to be recognized, Julia tells him. She and Charlie are both on their knees on her kitchen floor; he's helping with a couple of messed-up tiles that need regrouting. Her short, dyed-black hair has some dust in it, and he brushes it away with a delicate swipe of his knuckles. Except for a faint crescent of yellowish-green under one eye, all evidence of her fall onto the pavement has vanished.

Charlie says he doesn't quite know what she means by "recognized."

"I guess I mean . . . I want you to introduce me as your girlfriend to some of your friends. I want our *relationship* to be recognized." Julia fools with the thin green rubber band around her left wrist, snaps it against her skin with two fingers from her other hand.

She is trying to look at him so beseechingly that he will discard the words *No can do, Honey Pie* and offer her another question instead.

"How many is 'some'? Do you mean two or three?" he asks her.

"Really, a couple would be fine . . . Or maybe even just one friend, if that's all you feel comfortable with." Now she's snapping the rubber band so vehemently against her wrist, Charlie puts his hand out to stop her from hurting herself.

Introducing her to even one friend is too much, he starts to tell her, then says that surely she has to understand—as someone who inhabits a secret life together with him—that there are rules that must be followed, chief among them that no one can know even a single detail about the intimacy they share.

"But look, okay, give me a little time to think about it," Charlie says, and puts his hands on his thighs to steady himself while he leans over the newly grouted tiles to kiss her.

"Love you," Julia says. And then, very matter-of-factly, "Oh, and I want you to fuck me. Right. Now."

He tells her he's never had a woman talk to him this way, ever, and that he has to admit it's a turn-on.

"As it was obviously *meant* to be!" Julia says, and she smiles.

The two of them don't even make it back to her bed, but end up on the floor, a few feet away from it, twisting around in just their underwear on a velvety, well-worn oriental rug until she asks him, in a whispery voice, to take off her bra, and below, a brand-new pair of underwear made of the thinnest black lace, and which she bought just for him. He says he's never been with a woman who wore such seductive underwear; this, too, is a turn-on, he tells her.

Afterward, they talk about the oriental rug, the one Julia inherited from her parents following her divorce and her move from the apartment she shared with that nutjob husband of hers who refused to let her sleep in his bed.

Charlie would, he concedes, like to slug the guy.

What kind of a husband doesn't want to share a bed with his wife? he says, and adds, "It kills me to think of the way you've been mistreated by the men in your life. *Kills* me."

"I do love you, H.P.," he tells her now as they're getting back into their clothes, and she wonders if he knows how much she needs to hear this, and also if it's the simple, unvarnished truth.

A few minutes later he confesses that there's no way he will be introducing her to even a single friend of his. It's just too risky, he insists. And doesn't she know he's always been a pretty risk-averse kind of guy?

"Why do you do this to me?" she says. "First you say the right things and then you say the wrong things and then I just don't even want to look at you anymore. So go away, please. Go. Away!" She points to the front door, and her hand is shaking, and when he stops to kiss the side of her face on his way out, she says *I hate you.*

In the morning she calls his answering service and leaves her favorite message: *Just in case you ever foolishly forget; I'm never not thinking of you, H.P.*

37
Mel

The first thing Mel sees when she gets up each morning is the 9 x 12 photograph of her mother and father on their twenty-fifth wedding anniversary, which is set on the night table on her side of the bed and which she continues to find enthralling. In the picture, taken by an amateur photographer at the party her parents threw themselves at a French restaurant in midtown just a few years before her mother died, Mel's generous-hearted mother is in a silken, royal blue dress, looking off sweetly into the distance. Her father has a satiny black bow tie at his throat, a white carnation pinned to the shoulder of his suit jacket, his hand on her mother's shoulder. His head is tilted slightly downward as he looks at her adoringly, a serene smile fixed on his face. A supremely confident guy when he's treating his orthodontic patients in his operatory, and someone who possesses, Mel believes, an excellent sense of the driest humor, he is not what anyone would regard as a particularly gentle guy. But that is what Mel savors most in the photograph, the tender look on her father's face.

She still needs to get over her mother's death, and she knows it; it's been three years, and she needs to figure out how to stop missing her day in, day out, unremittingly, like some obsessed, heartbroken teenager. Enough, after all, is enough.

She's smiling now, noticing, for the first time, the way the tips of her parents' noses are gleaming in the light of their happiness. She'll point this out to Charlie when he comes home tonight, and she can already feel the weight of his arm across her shoulder as he looks at the photograph of his in-laws, trying to see what it is *she* sees in the faces of her mother and father. What she sees there is the very incarnation of domestic tranquility—*sholom byiss,* as her grandmother had called it, in Yiddish. According to her grandmother, there was nothing more essential than that; it was where the best, and the most important, sort of fulfillment lay—in a peaceful home, among those you loved. And this is what Mel herself has always believed, that it was pretty much everything she wanted.

Well, not *quite* everything.

38
JULIA

A few weeks ago, after Julia asked him to (well, *begged* him to), Charlie told his wife that he and some other shrinks who were members of the Manhattan Psychoanalytic Society would be going on an overnight retreat to a hotel upstate, near Woodstock. This was a lie told to his wife strictly on Julia's behalf because Julia had long been bugging him to figure out a way for the two of them to have a vacation together. What she had fantasized about was a week in Acapulco or the Caribbean, but Ulster County was the best he could do, and hey, she'll take it.

The plan for today is to drive up to somewhere called the Dreamcatcher Cottage, which Julia found for them ("Ideal for your romantic weekends!" the ad in the travel section of *The Times* promised jauntily) and which looked bright and welcoming, she thought, for the forty-five dollars Charlie is paying for a single night. More than anything, she finds the name "Dreamcatcher" alluring, and it's only five minutes from downtown Woodstock, which she has never visited.

She's washed and conditioned her hair with some absurdly expensive stuff she first discovered in the shower in the apartment where Toby, the Pomeranian, lives, and packed her one and only sexy nightgown, which is pink, ankle-length, and low-cut, and looks and feels like satin, and which she wore a couple of times on her honeymoon—a brief, uneventful trip to Maine and Nova Scotia she and Daniel had taken five years ago.

She heard from Daniel not long ago, but it was something

about tax returns and she hasn't gotten back to him yet with the paperwork he wanted.

He can wait. Forever, for all she cares.

The big leather shoulder bag she's packed holds, among other things, a pair of flip-flops, an extra bra, two different flavors of deodorant, and a couple of Flannery O'Connor books, including *The Complete Stories,* which she's reading for the third time, in high hopes it will inspire her to get busy on her dissertation.

She will sit here on her corduroy love seat waiting for the call that will let her know Charlie is downstairs in his Rabbit; never mind that it's only 9 a.m. and that he told her not to expect him till noon. Just the opportunity to spend two hours in the car with him feels like something worthy of celebration, something she's earned.

39
Mel

Mel is busy making brownies for them at the kitchen counter, tossing some multicolor M&M's into the batter just for fun.

She has no idea her husband isn't going where he says he is going—on a retreat with some fellow shrinks from that psychoanalytic society he belongs to—and that he is, instead, heading off to an overnight with his girlfriend. They love each other far too much for either of them to ever violate the sanctity of those wedding vows she and Charlie repeated out loud on a sultry summer evening in 1974, her own voice quivery and unnaturally high-pitched but Charlie's sounding proud and perfectly steady.

Here he is now, coming in to say goodbye to her, depositing a single kiss at the top of her head.

"That's *some* kiss," Mel starts to half-tease/half-complain, but then Charlie is pitching a couple of exuberant handfuls of M&M's into the brownie mix and she says, "Jesus, enough!"

"You'll be okay alone here, right?" Charlie says. This will be only the third or fourth night he and Mel have spent apart since their wedding.

"No problem at all," Mel says. "I'm cool." He kisses her again, on the cheek this time, and she can smell the pleasing scent of toothpaste on his breath; it makes her want to give him a real kiss and then he's sticking his pinkie into the raw brownie mix and licking it from his fingertip. "There's raw egg in there, don't do that!" she yells.

He dips his pinkie one more time into the batter. "Call you tonight after I get there, okay, honey?"

"Enjoy yourself!" Mel yells after him, but she's too late; he's already out the door.

She's back to work revising "On the Corner of Benevolent and Benefit Streets" as soon as the brownies are in the oven and she's set the kitchen timer. Though she will probably miss Charlie for the day and a half he'll be away, she will make good use of her time alone. She fixes herself a quick dinner, just one of her cream-cheese-and-olive sandwiches, and struggles with her story for much of the night, smoking so many True Blues that she finds herself light-headed by the time she begins laboring over the scene of one of the cruelest betrayals she can imagine—a woman casually sleeping with her best friend's husband and feeling not even the slightest stirrings of regret.

Never in her life has she wanted to please anyone as passionately as she wants to please Elizabeth Greenwell. So she will do her best to give her editor everything she wants—beautifully shaped characters inhabiting what she hopes will be one witty, elegant story after another that will compel Elizabeth to keep making those phone calls to her, each time uttering that trio of ordinary words that Mel lives for: *We're taking it!*

Later, when there will be nothing much to look forward to on television except Johnny Carson, she will grow tired of waiting for Charlie's call; he will have been gone for almost nine hours, and she will be feeling anxious. He's a confident driver and an excellent one, but what if he's been in an accident somewhere along the Thruway, she will ask herself. She'd forgotten to ask the name of the hotel where he'll be bunking with another shrink, splitting the cost of the room with someone named Logan, whom she's never met. It's weird to think of Charlie sleeping in a room with someone she doesn't even know. And though she will hate to admit it to herself, she will feel surprisingly lonely attempting to fall asleep in their double bed here at home with only Birkin, the cat, to keep her company. His long gray fur will ornament the front of Mel's black T-shirt as he lies nestled in her arms; she will welcome the soothing hum of his contentment, but it will not be enough to keep her from worrying about where her husband is.

When, at last, she will finally hear the sound of his voice again tonight over the phone, her sense of relief will be so profound, she will not even bother to ask the question that will have been on her mind all night: *What the hell took you so long?*

40
Charlie

Driving to Julia's building downtown, Charlie is beginning to feel the slightest bit guilty, a discomforting twinge of remorse. At a stoplight he idly watches the pedestrians passing in front of him; one particularly tall woman reminds him of his patient Francine, who's confessed that monogamy is too much, really, to ask of a person. This skinny, six-foot-tall daughter of Holocaust survivors told him she had been raised to believe that, above all, she had to learn to depend on herself, and only herself. In fact, Francine isn't his only patient who has confided to him that not everyone needs the certainty of knowing they will be sharing their beds with the same person night after endless night, three hundred and sixty-five nights times twenty, thirty, forty years. But she's the one he knows he will never forget; he can see her now, talking to him at her weekly appointment, sprawled carelessly on the Ultrasuede couch in his office, unable to control her impulse to pull out one eyelash after another right there in front of him, no matter how gently he tries to draw her attention to what she is doing.

The things he knows about his patients!

It even feels as if he already knows too much about Mel, and sometimes he wishes he knew less. Like the day before her period arrives, she turns sullen and even unfriendly, and complains bitterly about the disorganized way he unloads the dishwasher; that when obsessed with reworking one of her stories for her editor, she turns into a chain-smoker who hides herself away in her mini-office for hours at a time—and then when she finally joins him in bed after a long shower, her skin still scented with cigarette smoke, she is so mortified that she feels compelled to turn away from him. Even after he assures her she doesn't have to. Indeed, he knows this is what she will be doing all day today and tonight, smoking away in her office, thinking about the characters in her story.

He loves her and would never want to hurt her—never—but as he heard Francine inform him only last week, *life is short and then you die.*

An excuse that can be used to rationalize just about anything, he suspects.

But here is Julia, an expectant look on her face as she opens the passenger-side door of the Rabbit and places her big leather bag inside. And he is blinded by lust and knows it.

41
Julia

As she slides into the passenger seat next to Charlie, it hits her all at once that this is the seat where his wife parks herself whenever they're driving off together somewhere.

She wishes her mind didn't operate this way, wishes she could be the sort of person who instinctively makes the best of things and could just be grateful for this sleepover date of theirs.

"Everything okay?" Charlie asks her, and they French-kiss for a minute before he pulls out into traffic; she loves the way the tips of their tongues engage in little games with each other.

"Nice car," she offers, though really, she thinks, it's nothing special, just one more econobox on the road. When she pushes back the seat and stretches out her legs to get comfortable, she discovers there's some toy abandoned on the rubber mat at her feet. A couple of metal toy cars, it turns out: a two-inch red Mazda shoved nose-first into the interior of a bigger, heavier, yellow sports car that she can't identify.

She's rolling the Mazda's tires up and down her wide-open palm when Charlie says, "Oh, sorry, those are Sam's, my little cousin, actually, I mean Sam, my wife's little cousin; we babysat for him last weekend." Immediately Julia blushes, as if she has embarrassed herself.

"No need to apologize," she tells Charlie. The yellow car, about six inches long, is a Lotus, Charlie says; it has doors that open and a dusty plastic windshield with a wiper half the thickness of a blade of grass that she moves back and forth with her fingertip. Thinking too hard of the little boy the cars belong to and his connection to Charlie's wife, she's opening and closing the doors of the Lotus nervously, and it's no surprise when Charlie reaches over, puts his hand across hers, and says, "Please don't, you're going to break it."

Maybe that was her intent, and maybe they both know it, and now she feels ashamed.

"Don't think about any of that," Charlie says. "It's just us for the next thirty-six hours, H.P."

She leans her head against his shoulder, the Lotus in her lap now, her finger manipulating its gear shift, which is half the width, and half the height, of a straight pin.

She just can't stop herself.

Of course, that minuscule gear shift breaks off and lands under the steering wheel of the Lotus. Using a fingertip, she's able to extract it, and slips it into the pocket of her jeans, wondering if Cousin Sam is ever going to get his cars back and notice that one gear shift is missing.

Sorry, little guy.

The Dreamcatcher Cottage is about the size of Julia's studio apartment, but it's immaculate, and on the table as you come in, there's a plate of four shrink-wrapped muffins, and a steel bowl filled with green and red grapes, a shining pear, two mandarin oranges, and one firm banana without even a single brown spot. The bed is queen-size, and pretty soon they've peeled back the patchwork quilt and gotten themselves out of their clothes and between some very soft sheets. It makes her happy hearing Charlie whisper that she's beautiful—something her ex never once bothered to tell her—and that he loves the feel of her warm damp body collapsed on top of his after they've both come.

Everything is sweet and good, and after making love a second time they decide to skip dinner in favor of two cinnamon muffins and whatever is in the fruit bowl. There's also a coffee maker, ceramic mugs, and packets of Maxwell House, and fresh milk in the minifridge.

They're sitting up in bed, naked, sipping their coffee contentedly, and then Charlie happens to glance at his watch.

"Shit!" He tells Julia he forgot to call his wife, and would she mind getting dressed and maybe taking the car for a spin while he makes the call?

It's a surprisingly warmish night in early March, and the Rabbit is parked right beyond the Dreamcatcher, but no, she's not getting back into her clothes and going out there and into the car just to make it easier for Charlie to talk to his wife.

Paging through a paperback collection of interviews with Flannery O'Connor that she's brought along with her, Julia is trying hard to ignore the one-way conversation as Charlie talks on the phone planted right here on the nightstand next to his side of the bed. He's trying now to walk away from her, naked, as he talks, but the phone cord is just too short, and Julia is staying put in this cottage that measures a mere four hundred square feet and where she can hear every word he voices to his wife. The paperback rests against her pillow; Julia is lying on her side, reading about violence and how, Flannery O'Connor believed, it could prepare her characters to accept their moment of grace.

Julia wonders when *her* moment of grace is destined to arrive. *Sorry*, Charlie mouths to her as he listens to his wife talking about something or other.

What does he think—that Julia can't hear him offering his wife the words "Okay, baby, okay, love you" not once, but twice, just before he hangs up the phone?

When he and his wife are finally disconnected, he gives Julia an enthusiastic kiss, one that misses her mouth and lands, instead, on the tip of her nose.

"Great," she says.

"What?"

"You're a shrink—don't you understand *anything*?" Now she's off and running; this is the way she gets when she's hurt.

"You think I'm deaf? You think I can't hear you when you say 'I love you, baby' to your wife? Don't you realize how insulting that is?"

He stares at her, looking bewildered. "Insulting?"

"Insulting to *me*!" she has to explain. "You have a PhD in psychology—what is WRONG with you?"

Charlie is shrugging his shoulders, saying he's truly sorry she feels insulted, but that there are certain things he doesn't really see a need to apologize for, and saying *I love you* to his wife is one of them.

Hearing this, Julia feels sick, and tells him she wants to go home. She puts her clothes back on, and in the bathroom, she gathers up her things; her makeup bag and flip-flops, and the moisturizer that has a scent like cotton candy and is way too expensive for a person with her kind of shaky finances.

"Please just go away," she says when he follows her into the bathroom and tries to put his arms around her. "Please." He has hinted, over these many months of their affair, that the two of them have no real future together, that he will never leave his wife. Maybe Julia is imagining it, but she would swear he's told her this—though not in so many words—almost as many times as he's told her he loves her. But smart as she is, this is all very confusing. If they have no future together, why are they here in this sweet little Dreamcatcher Cottage with the queen-size bed, and the extra-soft sheets, and no reason to hurry back to the city until tomorrow? If he loves his wife so damn much, why has he continued to betray her? And why is she, Julia, so baffled by all of this? Why isn't she paying attention to the flashing neon sign warning her to proceed at her own risk? It's so brightly illuminated and it's right there in front of her, but she simply chooses to ignore it.

She's feeling very stupid now, very unsure of herself. She is overcome with remorse, though she's not sure what it is she wants to apologize for.

I give up, she tells Charlie now, and allows him to steer her from the bathroom back into bed. She flings her clothes onto the nicely varnished wood floor, and she and Charlie rest in each other's arms all night. No more arguing, no more disappointing each other, just the two of them pretending they have all the time in the world to lie here together, undisturbed; two people so clearly in what anyone, Julia knows, would call love.

They never do make it into town to check out the pleasures of Woodstock.

42
Charlie

So how did everything go with his buds from the Manhattan Psychoanalytic Society? Remind her again which of them were the guys from grad school? And did they all have dinner together in town in Woodstock and what kind of restaurant was it and how was the food?

And why is Mel asking so many questions, not a single one of which he feels like answering, now or ever.

She's seated at the edge of their bed, rubbing the tip of Birkin's chin until he purrs and watching as Charlie empties his canvas overnight bag, tossing his plaid pajamas and his boxers and socks from yesterday onto the floor.

"Pizza," he says, though he hasn't an inkling where this response is coming from. "Hawaiian pizza with pineapple and ham. That was our dinner, no big deal."

Ugh, he hears Mel say, and he cringes.

"Glad I wasn't there with you guys. I mean, you know how I hate even the *thought* of pineapple on pizza. Ugh," she says again.

On his knees, he continues going through the bag, taking out his zippered dopp kit bulging with a tube of toothpaste, dental floss, deodorant, and a hairbrush. And then he's looking at an unfamiliar plastic bottle, very small and pale blue and he's reading the words *Personal Lubricant* and under that, in small print, *For Enhanced Intimacy* and his stupid heart begins to thump so frantically, he's afraid Mel will hear it. He shoves the bottle—which belongs to Julia and somehow mistakenly ended up in his bag, sticky and ornamented with a couple of hairs—into the back pocket of his jeans and hopes and prays he doesn't forget to dump it into the compactor out in the hallway past the elevator when he goes to throw the garbage out later.

"I missed you," Mel is saying as she bends down to pick up the laundry he's thrown onto the floor. "I was busy working all night yesterday, and today, too, but I missed you, Charlie."

"Missed you, too," he says, and at least his heart has quieted down and he can lean toward her and offer his wife a kiss.

43
Mel

Mel will, when Charlie returns to their bed tonight, feel his breath, even and soundless, through the thin fabric of her nightgown against her back; she will wonder why he is too tired to touch her, even if only for a moment. Instead of asking, she will arrange his arms soothingly around her, listening for his grunt of approval, and the mumbled words "love you" that will accompany it, as they always do.

44
Julia

I would like to ask you to marry me, Julia has told Charlie more than once, and his answer is always the same, *Maybe in another lifetime, but I'm sorry, not in this one, H.P.*

Why *can't* he? Because he's strongly hinted that he has a perfectly good marriage, with a wife he loves, and no desire to give it up. According to him, he never will. Julia knows this; they've been over this many times, and yet she can't stop wanting more than he can give her.

Or is willing to give her.

A couple of times when she proposed marriage to him in this new decade, they were seated upright and fully dressed in Charlie's office or on the love seat in her studio apartment; one time they were naked, lying in her bed after sex, Julia idly dipping her fingertip into the pool of cum that had settled in the hollow of his navel, finger-painting his stomach with a narrow streak of what eventually dried sticky as glue.

Tonight, when they are again undressed in her bed, she says she understands, rotating, with her thumb, his wedding ring, which sits a bit loosely on the fourth finger of Charlie's left hand. Her face is canted downward as she works the ring; when he tries to tilt up her chin so he can kiss her, she swipes at his hand in annoyance.

"Don't," she says, and now it's Charlie who says he understands.

So much understanding, so much disappointment.

So where is the happiness that's supposed to accompany all that love they're both feeling? At the moment, it's nowhere to be found.

"I'd be such a good wife to you," she says earnestly, her fingers now at the underside of Charlie's wrist, as if she were taking his pulse. "I'll work on getting my dissertation done, no more dragging my feet, and that's a promise to myself, okay? I'll find a tenure-track job in the English Department of someplace stellar, maybe Columbia or Barnard or even Yale . . . And you know what, we'd have such a good life together, trust me."

He asked her, as always, to set her kitchen timer, just in case they lost track of time and fell asleep after sex, which has never happened yet but which, Julia senses, he always lives in dread of; when it goes off now, she can see something like relief in his face.

Gotta go, gotta get home, H.P.

They offer each other goodbye kisses, but as he's heading toward the elevator, Julia stationed at the front door of her apartment, she wonders if he hears a whispery *fuck you* in his wake.

Whispery, but oh so very very angry.

45
Julia

So she's done with his ridiculous answering service; a couple of the operators delivering her messages to Charlie have, in fact, asked him, half-jokingly, if she's his craziest patient. Hearing this insulting piece of news from Charlie made her so angry, she broke up with him for almost a week until, once again, she called his office to apologize, and he picked up the phone himself.

Apology accepted, once again.

Just in case you ever foolishly forget; I'm never not thinking of you: she will send her message to Charlie's office again and again, now scribbled on cards ornamented with a small fleet of pastel hearts or with a pair of smiling squirrels in a rowboat, their noses touching, or with two black-and-white birds nuzzling each other with bright orange beaks.

Charlie has asked her, kindly, not to do this; he knows she is thinking of him, he says, and doesn't need the reminder, and so she cuts back from three or four times a week to just two, mailing her cards on Fridays and Saturdays, the loneliest days of her week. She would like to do as Charlie has asked—really she would—and cut back all the way to zero. But why can't he understand that she needs this, needs to let him know that he is center stage, right there in the very spotlight of her life, she thinks now, as she heads toward her neighborhood post office on Tenth Street to mail her April Fool's Day card.

PART TWO
APRIL 14, 1980

46
Mel

What Mel inadvertently discovers in Charlie's backpack after suddenly getting up to pee—at 4:27 a.m. on this Sunday night in the middle of April, the hundred-and-fifth day of the year—will alter their life together in ways so large and small that she cannot now, in the instant of her discovery, even begin to imagine or enumerate them. As she crouches next to the backpack on the floor, in the foyer of their apartment, examining the single sheet of bright white 8½ x 11 typing paper that will spell the end of their old life and the beginning of their new one, her left hand, the one holding the paper, begins to tremble. Until this moment, she recognizes, the word *betrayal* had no meaning in her life with Charlie, or so she would have sworn less than an instant ago.

There's no signature on the sheet of paper she's still holding in that unsteady hand of hers, no evidence announcing *who what where*, or when it was sent to Charlie. One hundred and forty words, no more or less—she counts them several times just to make sure she's made no mistake. As if the number of words makes one bit of difference.

I thought you loved me in a way that was worth everything, Honey Pie. Funny, right? I'm such an idiot. Okay, so you loved me—I get that—but not in the way I needed. Even so, I wish I could wrap my arms so tight around you and touch your face again with the tips of my fingers and talk to you about everything in the world. You'll never understand how much I adore you and for that I'll never forgive you, Charlie.

Please don't respond to this letter. I just want you to go away and pretend none of this ever happened. GO AWAY! PERMANENTLY, you asshole! And remember, no matter what happens between us, I always have your wife's phone numbers. MEMORIZED! PERMANENTLY!

I thought you loved me in a way that was worth everything, Charlie.

In the long moment Mel spends reading that single sentence typed by a stranger's hand, all the happiness she has felt in this life seems to have evaporated, and she will soon swear she's forgotten its taste, and wonder if she will ever savor it again.

Still crouched beside Charlie's backpack, unable to move, Mel reads the letter over and over again, until she knows every word of it. Though it's a warm night, there are goosebumps all along her bare arms, and along the length of her legs under her favorite drawstring pajamas. Beneath her gauzy camisole, beneath her skin, her heart is banging like crazy, like madness itself, letting her know that her life, and their life together—hers and Charlie's—is in serious jeopardy.

You'll never understand how much I adore you, some other woman has written to Charlie. Finally Mel gets it through her head that someone out there, some nameless human being, wants to use her fingertips to delicately explore the landscape of Charlie's face, one that Mel would like to smash, this very moment, with, let's see . . . one of her Cuisinart sauce pans or fry pans, or maybe just her own clenched fist, whatever's easiest, whatever's within reach. She would like to see some distinctly red blood spurting from Charlie's freshly flattened nose, see an eye or two swollen shut under a black-and-blue brow, a busted lip coated in a slimy amalgam of blood and saliva.

I. Am. Married. To. A. Lyingcheatingadulterer.

This is what she will tell herself, sometimes in the smallest whisper when she's lounging in bed with Charlie, her currently dead-to-the-world husband, sometimes slightly louder as she's cleaning the bathroom sink with Ajax while Charlie's still at his office with a patient, sometimes louder than that while she's taking a leisurely shower late in the evening.

I am married to a lyingcheatingadulterer.

Even as she says the words aloud tonight standing there with the original letter creased in her hand, she knows that she loves him—i.e., this man to whom she's been married for nearly six years, and with whom, she believes, she's meant to spend the rest of her life.

But she who has never had a murderous thought in her head would, in truth, like to tear him apart with her small, thin-fingered hands that look so much like her mother's.

She hopes this girlfriend is a nothing-much-to-look-at who will never be able to make Charlie happy. She hopes this homely lovesick girl she's conjured will die unexpectedly tonight, perhaps with bricks falling on her from a great height, or a bicycle running her over in the middle of a busy street uptown, downtown, midtown, wherever. Or maybe she'll trip and take a nosedive into the subway tracks just before an express or a local comes roaring into the station at rush hour. Mel doesn't wish her an agonizing death, not really, she just wants her gone from the universe. Gone yesterday.

So who is this lovesick girl? Who IS she? And how can she do this to somebody else's marriage?

She's probably one of Charlie's patients, someone who fell promptly and effortlessly for Charlie and his sweet face, the one that showed, so naturally, the empathy he was always feeling for those anxious, depressed, conflicted patients of his. Mel had fallen for that face herself, and has loved him ever since that first semester of her freshman year. But today, at the advanced age of twenty-seven, she has, at last, come to understand, so intimately, what the simple word *shattered* is all about.

Crushed/smashed/reduced to the messiest human pulp . . . by the one person she'd known for certain would have done absolutely anything and everything to keep her safe in this world.

She may have had a couple of her stories published in *The New Yorker*, but that doesn't preclude her being strikingly stupid in other areas of her life, does it? Hey, maybe she shouldn't be beating herself up; after all, isn't the loving wife always the very, very last to know?

Ah, the wisdom in those seriously tiresome clichés.

Well, you know what, Charlie: *Heaven has no rage like love to hatred turned.*

And thank you, William Congreve, dead these past two hundred and fifty years but still smart as a whip when it comes to love, hatred, and women.

She's back in the bedroom looking at Charlie now, that lyingcheatingadulterer sleeping there so peacefully in their bed, flat on his back, dressed in plaid boxers and a white T-shirt, one long bare arm flung across his brow, the other resting along a stomach bisected by a line of unruly dirty-blond hair, the gold on his ring finger visible in the lights of the city streaming through the venetian blinds that he neglected to close properly before they went to bed tonight. There'd been no sex tonight, as it happened, just his arms wrapped cozily around Mel as the two of them exchanged their second "love you's" of the day before falling silent and turning away from each other and toward sleep.

It's 4:57 on a Sunday night/Monday morning, and in a couple of hours the alarm on their clock radio will go off, and both of them will be forced to get a move on—to get ready for breakfast, ready for work, ready for the busy life they have adapted to so well, they're pretty much on autopilot. Butbutbut . . . surprise, surprise: this guy taking up valuable space in her bed is a lyingcheatingadulterer with a moral compass that has, alas, been disabled. Or so it seems.

She's still dry-eyed, which strikes her now, at 5:03 a.m., as bizarre and improbable, given that, for the very first time in her life, Mel would describe herself, with all accuracy and no exaggeration whatsoever, as utterly heartsick. Dizzy with the pain of knowing she's been the target of a conspiracy against her and her happiness.

She wonders if Charlie and his girlfriend have a secret handshake. A special wink or nod that signifies their love for one another, even if that love wasn't enough to suit the girlfriend's fancy.

Problem is, Mel can't get back into bed beside him, because even the mere thought of sharing space with him and his splayed arms and capricious heart sickens her. As much as she wants to awaken him with the news that he's been busted, the very best part of her demands that she permit him to sleep until their alarm gets him up and out. Because, she knows, she's a good wife with a pure soul and an equally pure heart, unlike him, that lyingcheatingadulterer in his red plaid boxers still sprawled on his back, his nose straight up in the air, his deceitful heart ticking away.

If only she hadn't had too many cans of Tab to drink last night and then gotten up to pee; if only, after leaving the bathroom, she hadn't slipped some health insurance forms into Charlie's backpack so he could take care of them at his office in the morning and send them off to their insurer. If only she hadn't stuck her hand in the backpack and come away with the letter from that pathetic dimwit who wanted to touch Charlie's face again with the tips of her fingers.

So many, many questions Mel has yet to ask him.

She takes the letter fired off by the angry girlfriend who mistakenly thought Charlie had loved her in a way that was worth everything, and she tapes all four corners to the mirror in their bathroom; across that 8½ x 11 sheet of typing paper, she writes, in all caps, with a purple Sharpie:

YOU LEFT THIS IN YOUR BACKBACK—AND I'M GUESSING THAT, SUBCONSCIOUSLY, YOU WANTED ME TO FIND IT.

She's meticulous about her commas even at 5 a.m. when her heart is sick and her eyes burn painfully, even though a single tear has yet to form. She arranges herself cautiously on her side of the bed, as close to the edge as she can get without falling off, careful not to allow even an inch of herself to make contact with her husband, that lyingcheatingadulterer who is still—and always will be, she suspects—the goddamn love of her life.

47
Charlie

He's dreaming about his adored grandfather, Morris—that seventy-year-old guy dressed in khaki Bermuda shorts and a straw baseball cap running alongside Charlie's buoyantly happy five-year-old self as he learned to ride his two-wheeler on a summery day—when he hears his name being called.

"Grandpa?" he says.

"Charlie! You need to get up and check something in the bathroom," Mel is telling him. There's an urgency in her voice that worries him, and he fumbles with his eyeglasses on the nightstand next to him, knocking them over onto the carpet. The room itself is still half-dark behind the pale wooden slats of the blinds covering the long rectangle of window that looks north toward the farthest reaches of the city's East Side.

"Crap," he says, and feels around with his hands until he finds his glasses, without which the world, for him, is a blurred, smeary mess. Yawning, he's aware that he needs to brush his teeth immediately—his breath is still garlicky from last night's take-out dinner of chicken-and-broccoli from Chef Wang's—but first he's got to pee.

"I'm tired," he reports to Mel, "and so lazy, I can hardly summon up the energy to get up and go to the bathroom." He squeezes her bare shoulder under the thin strap of her camisole, and is startled when she knocks his hand away. This isn't what she does, what either of them does; they're nearly always good-humored and gentle with one another, two people grateful to share a life.

"Go into the bathroom," Mel says. "Will you please just go?"

"Is something wrong?"

Mel gives him a shove, and it isn't a half-hearted one. "Just go in there!"

"You don't have to be nasty about it," he mumbles.

"Nasty?" she says. "I'm sorry, did you say 'nasty'?"

He has no idea what's up with her. The day has scarcely begun; why does she sound so bitter? So unlike herself.

Fine, he'll go into the damn bathroom. It's only six steps from the edge of the bed until he hits the marble saddle at the entrance and almost trips over it with the big toe of his left foot. Then he sees it, the sheet of typing paper taped to the slightly cloudy mirror above the sink, and the words in large purple print. He blinks in the bright fluorescent light of the bathroom, trying to understand what it is his wife is telling him. Now he sees that the sheet of paper is a letter from Julia. That old letter from last month where she specifically told him to disappear from her life. Though of course she didn't mean it—she never really meant any of the angry words she sent him—because the following day, as was her habit, she called with an apology. He took out the letter last night, planning to show it to Julia the next time he saw her; show it to her as a reminder of her venomous anger that has, periodically, been driving him a little crazy for months now. Every so often, usually when she was at her most forlorn, she would leave an angry message with his answering service, and the operator, most often a woman, would read the message to him in a voice so impassive, it was almost laughable: *You're useless to me. Useless. So, we're done. Finished, okay? We're over! Don't call me ever again, understood?* After that, Julia would disappear for a couple of weeks, and for Charlie, there was always a sense of loss mixed with relief. Later he would wonder, as they were enjoying five-star makeup sex yet again, if, all along, he might have been confusing lust with love.

"This . . . is . . . *exactly* what I didn't want to happen!" he hears himself saying now in a voice that sounds both aggrieved and plaintive. Then, more quietly, "Shit!" He tears the sheet of typing paper off the mirror, crumples it fiercely in one hand, and tosses it into the small plastic garbage pail next to the sink.

When he comes back into the bedroom, Mel is slumped against the headboard, staring into the small bowl she's made of her linked hands. She's talking to him quietly, refusing to look at him. "Who *is* she?" she says. "Who's this person who thought you loved her in a way that was worth everything, *Honey Pie?* A patient?"

"Uh . . . former patient," he says, because what's the point in lying now? But he answers as softly as he can. He's back on their bed, seated upright next to Mel and wondering if she will order him to get the hell out—of their bed, their room, their apartment, her life. *Their* life.

He hopes to God he's safe, that things will go well enough. What he needs to do is focus on damage control here.

"Do you love her?" Mel wants to know. Her voice is so quiet, and so trembly, Charlie can barely endure listening to it.

He thinks for a moment or two, and comes up with something he believes is both honest and yet not excessively painful for Mel to hear.

"It's complicated," he says carefully.

But even the word *complicated* makes her wince, he sees. "And do you love *me*?" she asks him.

Instead of offering a simple "yes," he chooses, instead, to say, "Put it this way: you're the one I'd give my life for if a truck were suddenly to come barreling down the street heading in our direction and I could only save one of us. But you already knew that, right?"

She's still refusing to look at him. "What I don't know is what the word 'complicated' means . . . So when did you and your"—she pauses—"girl . . . friend, or whatever she might be, last sleep together?"

He will soon learn that Mel will never again use the word *girlfriend;* from now on, she will say *your bitch* whenever she and Charlie happen to turn to the subject of Julia. But she will say it casually, without malice, as casually as anyone else might say "your wallet" or "your keys." For her, Charlie will come to understand, it will be a kind of shorthand, the most satisfying way of referring to the woman with whom her husband had been having an affair. Soon enough, the crudeness of the word itself will cease to bother him. And Mel will, forever after, once it's been established whom they're talking about, refer to Julia as "she" or "her"; no further identification required.

Charlie's instincts, for the first time since the beginning of the affair, lead him in the direction of honesty now. "We were together, um . . . a couple of weeks ago," he says. He stares straight ahead at the vertically aligned rectangles of color of the Rothko poster framed above Mel's dresser. What he remembers of that final evening with Julia was that it was one of those infrequent encounters when he'd taken off his wedding ring and placed it on Julia's night table, a gesture meant as a gift to her. Although he resented the numerous requests from her (and experienced fleeting spasms of guilt whenever he removed his ring), he understood that the sight of it was, to her, unnerving, reminding Julia of what it was she wanted to forget—that he was, unequivocally, someone's husband. Instead of waving his left hand in front of her that last time, showing off his ring-less finger, he let her discover for herself that the ring was gone. Raising his hand to her mouth, Julia had kissed his knuckles one by one.

"*A couple of weeks ago*," Mel repeats, and breathes in sharply, with her mouth open. It's impossible now to ignore the undeniable evidence right here in their bedroom that what he's done has brought a heavy weight of grief upon his wife. He doesn't know what he's meant to do here, though most likely he would if she were a patient of his; in his office, thankfully, the right answers generally come to him. But here in his bedroom, dressed in his pajamas, they elude him. The words *damage control* return to him, but he doesn't know what, precisely, this entails. And when Mel asks how long the affair has been going on and hears his mumbled response, *uh, something like fourteen months, maybe*, her body collapses on itself over their bed; her face touches her knees, her hands clasp her ankles. Her breathing turns into a kind of wet, noisy howl, and when Charlie begins stroking her hair, her howling only grows louder.

"Never tell me her name," she says. "If you tell me her name, I will kill you."

"Understood," he says and, with infinite regret, removes his ice-cold hand from her lovely soft hair.

48
Mel

Sitting here on their bed with her husband beside her, Mel has never in all her life felt as lonely as she does now.

She doesn't need a seismometer to tell her that on the Richter scale, the earthquake that has capsized that fortunate life of hers can be quantified as an unequivocal ten.

Now she listens closely as Charlie is explaining it all to her. "She tried to blackmail me, Mel," she hears him say. "She sent me letters and left crazy messages with my answering service, messages threatening to spill the poisonous beans to you. Honestly? I'm actually relieved now that it's over and out in the open. I mean, she rattled me with those insane, excessively angry messages, so much so, I'm kind of embarrassed to say, that I occasionally had to rely on Valium to help me through it."

Instead of being horrified by the notion of what Mel perceives to be this blackmailing psycho, she finds herself somewhat amused, amused enough to laugh out loud on this day that she will always refer to as the most wretched of her life. The truth is, she gets a kick from hearing her psychologist husband use the words *crazy* and *insane* to describe his girlfriend/blackmailer.

"Something funny?" Charlie says.

She's rather enjoying the thought of him being blackmailed by the bitch he was sleeping with, Mel tells him, and then is surprised at how injured he looks.

"Forgive me, did I hurt your feelings?" she says. "I mean, if you're looking for sympathy, Charlie, you'll have to look elsewhere."

"I really wouldn't have minded if she'd disappeared from my life," he tells her. "I want you to understand that. I mean, I think that if I could have ended the relationship, I would have."

"You would have if you could have? Sorry, but was she holding a loaded gun to your head? A sword?"

Charlie tries to put his arm around her, but she doesn't want it. "Please don't touch me," she says, and moves farther toward the edge of the bed. "Do not." Who knows, it's possible she may never let him touch her ever again.

"Mel, she *was* holding a gun to my head, obviously not literally, but it was almost as if I could feel the cold muzzle of a nine-millimeter Glock at the side of my head. She was going to tell you, and seriously, it killed me to think of how devastated you'd be, so of course I had to do whatever it took to prevent you from finding out."

"So . . . correct me if I'm wrong, but what I'm understanding here," Mel says, "is that you were in thrall to a blackmailer who threatened you multiple times throughout your sordid little affair?"

Unashamed, apparently, of the words *sordid* and *affair*, Charlie turns his face in her direction as he insists, "I'm telling you, Mel, I had no choice but to keep the affair going in order to preserve our marriage."

"Let me get this straight: you have the gall to tell me this bullshit about *having no choice* but to sleep with her? Is this a joke?"

"It's just that I kept thinking she would get sick of the whole thing, you know, all the ways in which I continued to disappoint her, and then she'd disappear from my life and you'd never know and never suffer even a moment's pain over any of this. But it didn't turn out that way; she just wouldn't let go . . . She . . . These last months were pretty not-great, believe me. I told you, I actually had to take Valium because of her nuttiness."

Pretty not-great. Is that something close to bad? Awful?

Mel loves the word *nuttiness*; would that be a scientific term among Charlie and his buddies at the Manhattan Psychoanalytic Society?

He's gazing at Mel now, plainly looking for sympathy again.

"Cry me a river, babe," she says. She admires the momentary chilliness in her own voice, but then her hostility gives way to more tears.

Over the next few months, Mel, who was never really one to turn on the waterworks, will shed more tears than she has in a lifetime, and will continue to be astounded by what sometimes feels like her husband's endless capacity to cause her pain.

"I need you to explain this *thing* you two had going," she hears herself instructing Charlie. Her face is no longer resting flat against her bare knees; somehow she's found the strength to sit up again and has drawn her knees to her chin.

"What?"

"I mean this thing the two of you had with each other." She and Charlie are talking in near whispers.

"*What*?" he repeats.

If only she could look at him, maybe she'd be able to recognize something in his face, his eyes, the set of his mouth, that will give her a clue about what he's feeling at this very moment. But she cannot bear to look at him.

What if she can never bear to look at him ever again?

"Was it a fling?" she asks him. "A passionate love affair? A passionate fling? Or was it just *you* thinking with your dick? Tell me." It occurs to her now that she's never once heard anyone say of a woman, "*Oh, you know, it wasn't really much of anything, she was just thinking with her pussy, that's all.*"

"It's complicated," Charlie says again, the reply that makes Mel want to punch him.

Maybe in the face.

Maybe in the nuts.

Or maybe directly over the place where his heart continues to beat.

He tells her, stammering only a bit, that probably the easiest way to explain it is that he just "kinda" fell for someone who'd fallen for *him*.

This is the way a shrink with a PhD from Columbia talks? He just "kinda" fell for someone?

"She loved you, so you felt an obligation to return the favor, to love her back?"

"I don't know . . . I find it hard to talk about these things with you. I don't *want* to discuss these things with you."

"You're a psychologist—what are you *talking* about? What is your *problem*?"

Mel remembers a T-shirt she saw a neighbor wearing in the laundry room the other night when she went down to claim a load of towels from the dryer.

MEN ARE REALLY STUPID;
LET'S THROW ROCKS AT THEM!

She feels dizzy now.

Maybe it's vertigo.

Maybe a decrease in the blood flow to her brain.

Improbably, she thinks, the earth is still spinning on its axis.

Maybe it's the earth's spinning that's causing her dizziness.

Or maybe it's just that she no longer understands the most fundamental facts of her own life.

"Who *are* you?" she asks her husband, finally able to take a peek at his now-unfamiliar face. "Who. The hell. *Are* you?"

He looks up at her, puzzled. "What do you mean? I'm me," he says. "Who else would I be?"

He's telling her again now, with an earnestness and gravity she hasn't often seen in him, that as far as *he's* concerned, the affair is over, *finito, finis,* that he will contact the nameless blackmailer and end it immediately.

Mel believes him, but why, she asks herself, should she? Why, in the wake of his harrowing betrayal, should she ever again believe anything he tells her? Because he tells her that she has absolutely no reason whatsoever *not* to believe him?

She's deeply nostalgic for the good old days (was that just yesterday?) when she could so effortlessly swallow whole every word he fed her.

Later, a few days from now, when she's feeling a little stronger, Mel will allow herself to think of all the ways in which he has betrayed her—every loving word spoken aloud to the blackmailer, every kiss so lovingly delivered to the blackmailer's mouth, her collarbone, the crook of her arm, the underside of her knee. And perhaps cruelest of all, the sexual intimacies he shared with this blackmailer of his; Mel will, surprising herself, be able to imagine it all. The tip of her husband's tongue fluttering against the blackmailer's inner thigh, first the right and then the left, then drawing closer and closer to the star of the show, bestowing upon his blackmailer's clitoris the very same loving attention he'd given *her,* his wife. The thought of this will bring Mel to tears of both rage and sorrow, and once again, she will want to punch this immensely disappointing husband she can't seem to stop herself from loving.

But what Mel has to do now is navigate the rest of this singularly miserable day—the very worst day of her life.

Now she has to call the office to say she won't be in today. Austin answers the phone himself, as he usually does, and as soon as he says, "What's up, dear heart?" Mel realizes she'd like to punch *this* lyingcheatingadulterer, as well.

A migraine, she tells him, the first she's ever had.

49
Mel

Charlie, she's aware, thinks the word *adultery* smacks of all things religious, of a biblical lexicon, and he just can't connect to its meaning, just isn't moved by it. But—and who can dispute this?—cheating is cheating, whether you believe in Ye Olde Ten Commandments or not, Mel advises him on this immeasurably long and shitty day. Parked on the Naugahyde couch in their living room with his bare feet crossed on the parquet coffee table he built with his own hands before their wedding, Charlie tells her to stop lecturing him. He tells her that her tears only serve to irritate him, reminding him, as they do, that he's caused her pain—and what husband wants to be reminded of the hurt he's inflicted upon his wife?

Yeah, yeah, Mel gets it, but still, she can't stop shedding those tears.

Now he's accusing her of self-pity as she stands across from him, weeping, no tissues available to her, just the convenient back of her hand.

"Self-pity?" she says. "I haven't even known about this for twelve hours! Don't you understand *anything,* Dr. Fleischer?" She says that it feels as if, in one fell swoop, he's wiped away her happiness, her sense of security, firebombed the very center of her life, of *their* life together. It astounds her that he doesn't know this, that he, a fucking therapist, hasn't figured this out on his own.

Whipping out their Merriam-Webster dictionary from the bookcase that occupies an entire wall of the living room, he looks up the definition of "self-pity" and reads the words aloud to her: "'a self-indulgent dwelling on one's own sorrows or misfortunes.'" For a millisecond, Charlie's face is contorted by his contempt for her; she could never have imagined him looking so ugly, and the sight of him now sickens her.

She's stunned by the outright cruelty of what he's just done with that dictionary of theirs.

"Honestly, what is WRONG with you?" Mel asks him. "You're a *therapist!* Where's your damn empathy?" Woozy, she grips with both perspiring hands the top of the couch in front of her. "You're a stranger to me, okay? I don't know you and I don't wanna know you, understood?"

"Do you want me to leave?" he asks her, his voice suddenly softer, his face softer, too. Shoving the dictionary back in the bookcase, he says, "Look, I'm sorry, babe. Truly."

"You need to go," she says, "and I mean right now." But as he heads for the coat closet in the foyer, she hears herself say, "Waitwaitwait, where are you going?"

"Honestly, I don't know," Charlie says, and then he's out the door, and suddenly Mel is terrified of what might be irretrievable, afraid that she and Charlie will never talk lovingly to one another again; clasp each other's hands again; sleep in the same bed together again; or even see one another again. She is entirely unaccustomed to the feel of this profound misery and just doesn't know what to do with it, how to handle it, how to vanquish it. Slumped on the floor now with her back pressed against the front door, her face in her hands, she thinks of her grandmother and those Yiddish words *sholom byiss*—and what a gift it had been to inhabit a peaceful home among those she loved best. It was a gift Mel had been fortunate enough to possess, and so it's just impossible—*impossible*—to accept that her luck has finally run out.

Somehow she makes her way to the bathroom, where she arranges herself on the cool ceramic floor, uncertain of what she is meant to do this minute and the next.

She lifts up her tank top and puts a hand over her soft pale tummy and massages it tenderly. Now she hauls herself up off the floor and goes to the refrigerator for something, though she's forgotten, the instant she gets there, what that might be.

When Charlie slinks through the front door less than fifteen minutes later, a complicated apology already on his lips, Mel shushes him: *I don't want to hear it.*

Though she may be a weepy failure as a betrayed spouse, it seems—she reminds herself now—that she may be en route to some success as a writer.

Certainly she's a huge success as an utterly, unconditionally, hopelessly faithful wife.

50
MEL

Mel slips back into the office in the morning, and is thankful to be confronted with a slush pile of real substance, rising almost a foot above the top of her desk, where it sits. The last time she was in this office, seated at this desk—was it only last Friday?— she was, for all she knew then, a faithful young wife married to her faithful young husband, a twenty-seven-year-old babe in the woods who had never had a personal connection to the brutal word *betrayal*. Today, despite her best efforts to look like someone who's been through nothing more than the ordinary wear and tear of daily life here in the biggest, noisiest city in America, she isn't surprised when her older and infinitely wiser colleague, Daphne, says softly but accusingly, "You look like shit."

"Sunglasses," Mel says.

"What?"

"If I'd worn sunglasses, you wouldn't have noticed." Mel knows her eyes are still puffy from all those self-indulgent tears of hers, and orders herself to stop tearing up again.

"Any desire to talk?" Daphne says.

Thanks but no thanks. "I appreciate it, but to be honest, I'm fine."

"*To be honest,* I can see that. But if you happen to change your mind," Daphne says, "and decide you're less than fine, I can—"

Turning her head, Mel sees Austin bent over his desk, pen in hand, deleting deleting deleting, sees the cigarette smoke from his True Blue rising, and that familiar aggressiveness with which he's disfiguring the typed pages of what she guesses is probably another of Wayne Morrissey's manuscripts, Austin in pursuit of whatever truly perverse pleasure this must bring him. And she knows what it's like to feel disfigured.

She knows, too, that she may never stop looking over her shoulder, examining and reexamining every word of her still-beloved husband's, every gesture, every sideways glance; she may never stop looking for warning signs that all is not what it seems.

Unexpectedly, her vision and hearing will sharpen; she will see and hear things that others will miss. Maybe, it hits her now, these are actually gifts that will, for the rest of her life, serve her well as a writer.

She hears Austin calling her name now. When she walks into his office and he says, "I need you to Xerox this for me, dear heart," she realizes that what *she* needs is to apologize to his wife, to tell Hillarie that she recognizes that she, the underappreciated underling, should have been distraught over how profoundly Austin had wounded and disappointed *her*, the loving wife. She recognizes that she, herself, should have been smarter and kinder in her understanding and for this, too, Mel will never forgive her oblivious old self, that idiot who understood nothing. She's getting all worked up now, and she imagines slugging Austin, hard, on the chin.

Or maybe in the solar plexus, at the pit of his stomach.

Whichever would be more painful.

Closing her eyes for a moment, she can see her left hand folding itself confidently into a fist and heading straight for Austin's gut.

Instead, she takes Wayne's manuscript from her boss and swings by the Xerox machine, where she starts to do exactly as she's been asked, slapping the first page of Wayne's story facedown on the machine.

But now she's enraged again.

She thinks of tramping back into Austin's office and accusing him of being a rapist of a sort—he has, after all, just finished raping Wayne's story— and she can see with her own eyes how he's deleted not just sentences here and there but whole paragraphs, one after the other, while adding a veneer of sentences of his own.

Whole fucking paragraphs.

Literary rapist—those are the words that come to her.

With Wayne's story and its Xeroxed copy under her arm, she goes back to her desk, resisting the impulse to have it out with Austin. She finds Wayne's number in her Rolodex, and dials it. But then chickens out and hangs up as soon as she hears his voice. She watches now as Austin leaves his office and swans down the hallway, his coffee mug in hand; this is what gives her the chutzpah to dial Wayne's number again. She can feel an artery in her temple pulsing vigorously, but this time, hearing his voice, she tells him that Austin has betrayed him. *Yet again*, she adds.

"Wha?" Wayne says. "Who is this?"

"It's Mel," she says, "at the magazine."

"Wha?"

He sounds a little smashed, a little intoxicated at ten in the morning, but at least she can say her piece and maybe, if she's lucky, still have a job to come back to tomorrow.

"Mel?" she hears him say. "Who's Mel?" or maybe "Whose Mel?"

"You know," she says, "Austin's Mel?"

"Ohhhhhh, right. The baby writer. You woke me up, Mel, by the way. And by the way, I'm not hung over, I'm just sleepy, okay?"

Empowered by her simmering outrage, she doesn't apologize for waking him, but only says, "Look, Wayne, you know you've got to rescue your stories from Austin, from all that surgery he does on your wonderful—"

"*Look*, baby writer, I'm not going to tell you to mind your own fucking business, because I can see that your heart's in the right place—it's definitely in the right place—but, well, will you *please* just mind your own fucking business?"

It seems everyone wants her to mind her own business, but how can she live with herself if that's all she does? And clearly, ironically, she's a failure when it comes to her *own* business, her own marriage, her own life—for which she has no gift at all. *Nada.*

"I'm going back to sleep now," Wayne is saying, "and I want to repeat that, contrary to what you may think, I'm not *hung over*."

"I believe you," Mel says. "I get it." She looks at the Xeroxed pages of his edited story on her desk, and her anger, which had been slowly evaporating, begins to boil again. She notices now that Austin has changed the name of one of Wayne's characters. And her age. And what she looks like.

Come on! Her own esteemed editor would never do something so appalling; Elizabeth Greenwell is nothing if not respectful of Mel's work. In fact, no one—not even her parents, who were so proud of Mel for being an Ivy Leaguer—has ever treated her with such regard, no one has made her feel quite like Elizabeth does, like someone of actual, genuine accomplishment.

Little does she know that Wayne's work will, eventually, beyond his sadly abbreviated lifetime, be restored to its former state; when she learns of this, years from this moment, tears will spring to her eyes. But now she's telling him, "Look at what he did to you, what he's doing to you, to your new story. Just look!"

As if Wayne had the Xerox in front of him, and could see what she sees—though, as it happens, he's already hung up on her.

51
Mel

Just two days later, when she and Charlie have their first session with Krystyna, their highly recommended marriage counselor who agreed to see them immediately, Krystyna will attempt to get Charlie to understand the obvious. But first this middle-aged woman with a master's degree in counseling makes sure to tell Mel and Charlie that although she was born in postwar Krakow and grew up in Tirana, the capital city of Albania, please not to worry, her English very good.

"Very good," Charlie and Mel agree—one of the few things they will ever agree on in Krystyna's office here on the ground floor of a prewar building right off East End Avenue.

Mel takes an instant, superficial dislike to Krystyna because, though the counselor's heart might very well be situated in the right place, at this first appointment she's wearing those clunky brown leather Earth Shoes that look ridiculous with her panty hose and short skirt. They're hideous, but Mel can't stop looking at them as Krystyna talks and talks and talks about compassion and compulsion, compulsion and compassion.

Whenever this hundred-dollar-an-hour, offensively expensive therapist uses the word "*compassion*," Mel and Charlie think she is saying *compulsion*; when Krystyna says *compulsion*, what they hear is *compassion*.

The compulsion, Melissa, that you husband feels for you, seems completely authentic, yes?

The compassion you husband felt to make love to his girlfriend is not something you had control over, Melissa, though of course it not hard to understand why you would have wanted to have that control.

It's confusing, this compulsion/compassion thing, just like their marriage, which has lasted, thus far, close to six years—nearly every day of which had been unmarked by anger, recriminations, or heartrending disappointment, Mel would have said. Until a few weeks ago, anyway. Then again, it's been proven, just recently, that she herself was a major fool, regarding the state of her marriage, certainly.

You're SUCH an idiot, she persists in telling herself three, four, five, six times a day.

"Come on, baby, don't call yourself that," Charlie pleads whenever he hears her berating herself, but why should she listen to him about this or anything else?

Her husband is kind of an idiot, too, but he's also an accomplished liar. He doesn't like being referred to as a piece of shit, a suitable metaphor which Mel can't help but find herself employing, given the circumstances that have led them to Krystyna's office today. Charlie has asked Mel, numerous times, to use the acronym "POS" instead, but she keeps forgetting, perhaps deliberately so, she would have to acknowledge.

She would still be insisting that this marriage of theirs had been a pretty stellar one—there had been plenty of openly loving moments, occasionally excellent sex, and not a single fiercely angry argument that she can recall—until, of course, she discovered Charlie and the blackmailer had been at it for months, something like fourteen, in fact.

There's no point in asking her to say the blackmailer's name aloud because she will never be able to do it, she says, explaining to Krystyna that this would confer on the blackmailer a dignity she doesn't deserve.

When pressed by Mel, Charlie reports that the blackmailer has very dark, very straight hair, and polished, almond-shaped nails. (Mel's own hair is an ordinary, unexceptional light brown and slightly wavy; her nails are permanently marred by vertical ridges caused by a thyroid deficiency now under control.)

Unlike some betrayed spouses, who want to know next to nothing about their competition, Mel wants to know absolutely everything about this dark-haired blackmailer with those polished nails.

Krystyna says, *Melissa, you killing youself,* referring to all that hurtful information Mel has compiled, and will continue to compile, day after day. But Mel doesn't care. Who the hell is Krystyna, anyway—is she Sigmund Freud? Is she Carl Jung? Nope, she is not. She has a master's degree, and a specialty in helping struggling couples keep their imperiled marriages in one piece. *So what?*

"Big deal," Mel says. "So what if I'm killing myself accumulating every bit of information I can on the complicated history of Charlie and his fucking blackmailer, so *what*?"

"Oh Melissa," Krystyna sighs, and wraps her silk shawl more firmly around her shoulders.

"Oh Melissa," Charlie sighs. He and Mel are settled on an espresso-colored love seat accented with brass nail heads.

Krystyna is in a matching armchair facing them. "You can't keep harming youself like this, dear. You pain will only get worse. And worse."

Now Krystyna is urging Mel to let go of her disappointment. When Mel tells her that unexpectedly she's come to realize it's far less painful to be disappointed in herself than in the so-called love of her life, Krystyna nods.

What have you done to my life? Mel asks Charlie, but he doesn't answer.

In the appointments that follow, Charlie will talk, in Krystyna's office, about his own disappointment in himself—how he always, going back to his childhood, needed validation, but continued to feel just a whit undervalued and underappreciated by his mother and father, even as his older brother forged ahead, quitting his job as a well-paid litigator and opening his restaurant on a cobblestoned street in the West Village by the time he hit thirty, having no such need for that parental pat on the back.

Validation? What better validation than another woman who wants to wrap her arms so tight around Mel's husband and touch his face with the tips of her fingers and talk to him about everything in the world.

Okay, Mel gets it; what's not to understand?

Let go of you disappointment, Krystyna will repeat during every one of their sessions.

Easy for *her* to offer advice.

"Charlie," Krystyna is saying now, "why you not understanding that by sharing all sorts of intimacies with you affair partner, you have devalued everything you had with Melissa over the course of you marriage? Why you being so stubborn? Why you keep saying that those love letters, those—"

"Those birthday gifts, Valentine's gifts, gifts of oral sex," Mel interrupts, "everything you and the blackmailer exchanged, EVERYTHING, how can you keep saying that those things did absolutely NOTHING to diminish what *we've* had together all these years since college? Seriously, Charlie, do you not understand the meaning of the word 'devalued'? What's wrong with you?"

"There's nothing wrong with me," Charlie says, and folds his arms across his chest.

Two words for you, buddy: magical thinking.

Ah, magical thinking: the same kind of thinking that seems to have led Charlie to believe that adultery could be classified a harmless, victimless activity.

"As long as you don't get caught," he explains earnestly to Mel and Krystyna.

Harmless? Victimless? This is the guy with degrees from two Ivy League schools, one of those degrees being a doctorate in psy-

chology? Come ON!

Stupidest smart guy I ever met, Mel tells her husband, making him flinch.

52
Julia

It's the day before Julia's thirty-fifth, a birthday she was planning to celebrate with no one in particular, though she's still hoping Charlie might be able to meet her even if only for an hour, bringing along a single pink orchid, as he has from time to time in the past. He's not the most romantic guy in the world, she's discovered, but there's that sweetness about him which she can't help but find irresistible. Often, after he's left her apartment and gone home to his wife, Julia finds handwritten notes waiting for her on the kitchen counter, under a magnet on the refrigerator door, or under her pillow, notes saying, "Love you, H.P." or "Already missing you" or just "Big hug." She's kept every one of these, Scotch-taping them to pages of the small, leather-bound notebook one of her students gave her as a gift at the end of the last semester she taught at Queensborough.

She left the Mishkins an hour early for an appointment today with the head of the English Department at a small Catholic college in the Bronx, and she's still preparing herself for the interview as she rides along on the subway now. A pair of youngish-looking—but gray-haired—nuns in navy blue habits, one wearing white canvas sneakers and sipping from a can of 7Up, the other red-cheeked and smiling, are sitting across from Julia, laughing and talking together like teenaged girls. They're probably in their early fifties; a box of Clairol Nice 'n Easy Hair Color would do it for them, though if vanity is a sin, the nuns wouldn't be permitted to use Clairol to cover up their gray, would they?

The nun sporting those pristine white sneakers sounds affronted as she says, "Today's my sister-in-law's birthday, and I sent her a beautiful card more than a week ago, but so far she hasn't called to thank me."

"That's plum rude," the other nun says. "I'd give her till tomorrow and then I'd send your sister-in-law a note telling her how disappointed you are in her neglecting to respond."

"Right on, sister!" says her pal, and winks at her. They're the coolest nuns Julia's encountered, and she takes their presence on the subway car with her as a clear sign that her interview at Saint Anthony's will go well.

Getting off the subway now, she climbs up the dirty, steeply pitched stairs to one flight below street level, where a little kid, probably younger than ten, is playing the theme song from *Love Story* on a portable keyboard. He's dressed in a black suit and a red bow tie, and is apparently some kind of prodigy, unaccompanied by a mother or father, or anyone at all. At his feet is a wicker basket half-filled with quarters and a scattering of paper money; he acknowledges Julia's dollar bill with a curt, efficient nod in her direction.

"You're very welcome," Julia says, and has to stop herself from patting the top of the kid's head.

She walks across the street to wait for the bus, which will take her almost directly to Saint Anthony's. Just as she's settling into her seat, a white-haired man next to her says, "My wife and I are meeting friends at a vaygan restaurant after the theater tomorrow."

"I'm sorry, what?" Julia says.

"A *vaygan* restaurant," the old man repeats. "No animal products at all, including eggs and cheese. It got four stars in *The Times* or, I don't know, maybe three. And did you know that Bronson Alcott, father of Louisa May Alcott, was a vaygan?"

Julia smiles, but only because *Little Women* was her favorite book when she was eight or nine; the very first book she received as a gift from her parents. She could care less about Bronson Alcott's dietary habits.

Looking outside the window of the bus, which is stopped at a red light now, Julia can see an ambulance, and an Orthodox Jewish guy on a stretcher, blood on his forehead, his suede yarmulke askew.

"Oh, for Christ's sake, it's *vegan*," a woman across the aisle says. "VEE gan! If you say *vaygan* one more time, I'm going to slit my throat."

"Suit yourself," the old man sitting next to Julia says.

The interview had gone well, Julia thinks. At the end, the chairman of the English Department, a large woman with a military bearing and a nearly indiscernible hint of a German accent, asked, from across her desk, "Myerson—would that be a Jewish name?"

"It would," Julia said, so quietly she wasn't even sure she'd spoken aloud. "Would that be a problem?"

"I can't imagine that it would," Professor Kohler said. She lit a cigarette, slipped it between two fingers of one hand and shook Julia's hand with the other, and then it was over. Julia had hoped for a smile, and though none was offered, she still, hours later, feels hopeful about this job which will, in fact, never be hers.

At home tonight, she's watching *The Rockford Files*, and suspects she will always be a little in love with James Garner, whom she's had a crush on since watching him Sunday nights on *Maverick* with her father years ago, the two of them seated side by side on the plaid couch in the den while her brother was asleep and her mother was in the kitchen washing the dishes after dinner.

Sometimes her father's arm was around her as they watched James Garner, that card sharp on *Maverick*, talk his way out of trouble.

Sometimes, when her father called her *pussycat* and deposited noisy kisses on her cheek or forehead, it was so very easy to believe he loved her.

The phone rings tonight just as Rockford is gathering together a couple of ex-cons to help an old friend of his deal with her belligerent pimp.

"Hey, H.P." Warmed by the sound of Charlie's voice and surprised that he's able to call so late, Julia assumes he's checking in to find out how the interview went at Saint Anthony's.

"Hey, listen, I'm calling from a phone booth," Charlie begins, and it isn't the interview he's calling about; it's something else entirely.

"Wait, WHAT?" she says. "I don't get it, what was your wife doing with that letter I sent you, what, like, a month ago?" She remembers the letter now, the one where she told Charlie she'd mistakenly thought he loved her in a way that was worth everything; and too, she remembers how it ended. *I just want you to go away and pretend none of this ever happened.* But she hadn't meant it, of course she hadn't. She doesn't remember his response to the letter, only that she called him to offer an apology and they were back where they were before, seeing each other whenever they could, most of the time in her apartment downtown, the two of them lying naked in her bed with the lights on so they could savor and admire and examine each other's bodies, her nipples stiffening between Charlie's splayed fingers, then his mouth on her there and everywhere else, too, and it was the best she'd ever had and she couldn't live without it, without him. And wouldn't. *Would not.* He was married, but she understood, no matter his words to the contrary, that his marriage was dead, and that rendered morally acceptable to her everything she and Charlie were as a couple; and she could live with herself and not think about his wife, a subject Julia hasn't ever wanted to contemplate these past fourteen months. Just like she's not going to think too much about what Charlie is telling her now.

"But I don't understand, didn't your wife mention the word 'divorce'?" she asks him. "Even once?"

He breaks the news quietly, and also with a sigh, one that makes Julia think he might be annoyed with her question. "No," he says. "She did not."

Julia is outraged; she wants to know why, after what Charlie's done to his wife, she wouldn't want to divorce him. "What's wrong with her? Why wouldn't she want to dump you? I just don't get it," Julia says, and her disappointment is blistering.

He assumes it's that his wife still loves him, Charlie murmurs. He sounds faintly embarrassed.

Julia suddenly feels nauseated; for an instant she worries she may lose every mouthful of her dinner directly on the floor next to her bed. "That's insane! I mean, *she's* insane!" Julia says. "How could she possibly continue to love you after what you've done?" Then, more softly, she adds, "What *you and I* have done."

Honey Pie, she hears him say, followed by another sigh.

"No offense, but wouldn't you think your wife would want to fucking kill you?" Julia says.

"That's very nice," Charlie says. "Thanks a lot."

"I'm just saying that from *her* perspective, from *any* wife's perspective, you're a seriously shitty husband." Julia is weeping now, and can't believe Charlie was careless enough to get caught, and that his wife is evidently just too dense to recognize the serious nature of his betrayal. "Can't we talk about this in person?" she asks him. "I can come uptown to your office tomorrow, and we can—"

"I don't think that's a very good idea," he says, interrupting her.

"But why not? Why *can't* we do this in person?"

"Well . . . maybe we'll talk later, okay?"

No, it's not okay, but she doesn't ever want to sound needy and petulant, and so she keeps her mouth shut.

"But listen . . . I think this is it, Julia," he's telling her. He's saying that now that his wife knows, he just can't hurt her even more than he already has.

This is it, she hears herself repeating. So he's going back to devoting himself to his wife, but where is *she*, Julia, going? Back to the Mishkins, who appreciate her like no one else ever has? And who might even admit to loving her?

"So . . . I hope the interview went well today," Charlie is saying.

"Like you care."

"You need this job, come on, you know you do."

"Really? I'm supposed to believe you actually care?" she says, and she knows her bitterness is unmistakable.

"Of course I care. You don't see that the idea of you spending your time with the Mishkins all day when you should be teaching and making some serious progress on your dissertation makes me feel like crap? Makes me sad?"

Really? What makes *her* immensely sad is the thought of him and his clueless wife arranging themselves in bed night after night, Charlie's arms tight around her waist as he whispers heartfelt apologies into her ear. *Sorry sorry sorry. Sorry I ever met her, sorry I divided myself so neatly in two and felt only the slightest sting of guilt.*

"You piece of shit," Julia says in a whisper, and hopes he hears her.

Though she has no idea where she is going, she gets herself out of the apartment and over to the subway at Union Square, where in place of a little boy playing the theme song to *Love Story*, there's an evangelical nut yelling, "Say NO to Satan! Say YES to Jesus!" over and over again. But instead of "Satan," she's pronouncing it "Sah-tahn."

"NO," Julia says, "no no no," and the woman smiles at her gratefully.

53
Julia

Hey, it's not as if guys haven't broken up with her once or twice before; they have, and Julia has survived. It's not as if she didn't take control and end her marriage when it became intolerable to her. It's just that she so wanted this, so wanted a full, expansive, all-out life with Charlie. A life where the two of them could fall into bed together at night and wake up as the alarm went off the next morning; where they could take turns leisurely brushing their teeth in front of the bathroom mirror; where they could joke around as one of them casually cleared the table after dinner and the other lined the dishwasher with their plates and glasses; where they could do weekly loads of laundry and her bras could tumble intimately with his boxers in the washer and then the dryer; where they could celebrate their birthdays and anniversaries on Saturday nights with friends whose company they relished; where they could go to movies, and concerts at Lincoln Center, and theater on and off Broadway, always arriving together and leaving together, their hands linked in public, and too, their lives, forever after.

And children? She's come to realize that she'd like to have at least one, which might be why she very clearly told Charlie there was no need for condoms, no need to worry, she'd take care of the birth control—and he smiled, happy, like any dude would be, not to have to use a condom.

Smart men are such idiots sometimes, you can hardly believe it.

He thinks he's in line for a free pass here, a free pass from her? *Well, sorry, Honey Pie, no, not happening.*

You've ruined my life, Honey Pie, and I'm going to get even.

She's addressing an envelope and rummaging around looking for a book of stamps in her dresser drawer.

Even though she hasn't the vaguest notion of what she could possibly mean by *getting even*.

She thinks that what she wants is compensation—for the enormous unhappiness he's caused her, and continues to cause her now. She doesn't know in what form, exactly, or how to get it, but compensation is what she's going to look for, because, one way or another, he's got to pay.

54
Charlie

As soon as he arrives at his office today, he sits down at his desk and writes, in black Magic Marker, a one-word letter to Mel, one that's deeply felt, and also happens to be the same one he's handed her four days running.

Then, after a few moments of contemplation, he takes out another sheet of typing paper and writes the same letter to Julia.

He hears from Julia in a couple of days; she's happy to get his apology, she says, and regrets the threatening letter she sent him. No, she's not going to get even; he doesn't need to worry, she assures him. No worries at all.

Mel has told him she's happy with his letter, too, even though she's now read it five days in a row, and suggests to him that there's no need to keep doing this.

Of course that's fine with Charlie. All he wants these days is to make Mel happy. To make everyone happy.

Wholehearted apologies all around.

SORRY

SORRY

SORRY

SORRY

SORRY

55
Mel

When she is in the worst of moods, drunk on self-pity and absolutely ashamed of it, she sees herself rewriting recent history; returning to the morning, less than a week ago, when her husband and the blackmailer were busted, Mel imagines the piercing yelp of her own misery as she awakens Charlie at 4:35, the words *you bastard* repeated again and again as she rouses him from their bed and pushes him out. She imagines, too, the satisfying thump of his body as it hits the floor, his surprise turning to exasperation and then to anger as she hammers away at him with her fists, each blow fueled by fresh rage mixed with grief, a potent combination, which, before that late night/early morning, she'd never felt even once in her life. Then she sees herself dragging him from the narrow strip of floor along his side of the bed, across the width of the bedroom, out the door and along the parquet floor of the apartment's hallway, shrieking at Charlie like some crazed lunatic, until she manages to shove him roughly out the front door.

In his pajamas, barefoot, and without a key to get back inside this home she and Charlie had shared so companionably until D-Day.

She imagines double-locking the front door with the chain she rarely bothers to use—just to make sure he understands the full meaning of the words "ACCESS DENIED."

She can hear the two-tone sound of the doorbell as Charlie presses it once twice three times and then over again; when that does no good, he will punch the door, using his fists and then the heels of his hands, which have begun to hurt him, turning red and burning painfully. But what does Mel care, let him bang away on the door for the rest of his sorry life, she's not opening it for him tonight, tomorrow, next week, next month, next year.

How does the twelfth of never sound?

Wanna get back into our nice cozy bed? Sorry, never gonna happen, babe.

She's a mosquito, not the dangerous kind that causes malaria or yellow fever, just the annoying kind, the proverbial fly on the wall who sees and hears every fucking thing, and so she can envision Charlie downstairs in the lobby of their building, asking the doorman on the graveyard shift for the master key that will let him back into the apartment.

Sorry, no can do, Dr. Fleischer, Ernesto-the-doorman will report after he speaks to Mel—the broken, enraged partner—on the intercom. *No can do, Dr. F.* He observes Charlie in his plaid pajama top missing a couple of buttons and thinks this tenant is looking pretty pathetic here in the lobby at a quarter to five in the morning in his pj's, the angry wife upstairs unwilling to let him back into their home.

He's witnessed worse, this guy who works the graveyard shift. Tenants, both elderly and young, taken away on stretchers by paramedics in the middle of the night, never to be seen again. Heart attack and stroke victims, and once, an infuriated tenant who tried to run over her live-in boyfriend in the building's underground garage and then was escorted none too gently by the police through the lobby and into a waiting squad car with flashing lights that reflected dizzyingly off the glass doors at the front of the building.

Want a jacket or something? Ernesto will ask Dr. Fleischer standing there so forlornly in his pajamas. But Dr. Fleischer in apartment 17G is so out of it, he can't even answer the simplest yes or no question.

Oh yes, Mel can imagine it all so vividly. Not that it gives her much satisfaction.

Well, maybe a little, enough to keep her going for a half hour or so.

Honestly, who knew disappointment could be so oppressive, so weighty, so hard to lug around with you all day and all night?

Heaven has no rage like love to hatred turned, and doesn't she know it, she who loves and hates and hates and loves and wonders if she will ever settle on one and disavow the other or whether this will be the continuing story of her life.

56
Mel

It's clear Charlie doesn't want to answer Mel when she asks if he and the blackmailer ever had a sleepover together, but she forces it out of him nonetheless.

"Look, you lied to me for so long, the least you can do is tell me the truth when I ask you such an easy, straightforward question," Mel says reasonably, and it's hard to argue with that, isn't it? Even when she can see by the anxious look on his face that he wants to spare her the pain which she can already predict his truthful response is going to bring her.

He tells her it was only one time, the night of the "overnight retreat" with the supposed group of shrinks at Woodstock.

Mel is bent over the dining table, Windexing its glass top with paper towels, and she continues wiping away the smudges left behind by a couple of errant French fries from dinner as Charlie confesses that there was, in fact, no overnight retreat, at least not for him and his pals from the Manhattan Psychoanalytic Society.

"I'm sorry, but it was just one night, that's all. In the grand scheme of things, that's not so terrible, right?" he says, sounding hopeful.

She's still cleaning the table, refusing to look at him, refusing to answer, but her shoulders are shaking.

"I'm sorry," he repeats. "Really and truly."

"Which pajamas did you wear the night of the sleepover?" she's asking him now. But why does she care? Why does she need to know every last detail of every hour he spent with the blackmailer? What good will it do her?

The next morning, as soon as she wakes up, she tells Charlie he has to trade in their Rabbit for another car. "I mean one with a passenger seat uncontaminated by the blackmailer's DNA," she says, unable to conceal her contempt for the very idea of her seat up front next to Charlie defiled by so much as a fingerprint belonging to the blackmailer.

"You're kidding, right?" Charlie says.

"We're not having a fight over this, and I'm dead serious. You're just going to have to suck it up and find us a new car."

"Seriously," she hears him saying now, "I'm crazy about that Rabbit and its quick reflexes, and the thought of having to part with it kinda kills me."

He's looking at her sadly, but she is adamant. "Get rid of the damn Rabbit, Charlie. Case closed."

Before they trade in the Rabbit, Mel takes it by herself on a Sunday for a final spin out to Farmingdale, on Long Island, thirty-five miles from the city, to the cemetery where her mother is buried. Charlie offers to come with her, since she hasn't driven in ages, but she prefers to be alone, she tells him, and then makes him swear he won't take advantage of her absence by going out to bang the blackmailer.

Solemnly raising his right hand in a gesture of self-mockery that makes her laugh, he swears, one more time, that he and the blackmailer will never happen again.

Ever.

And because she has no choice—not if she wants to stay in this marriage—Mel decides to take him at his word.

The modest, granite footstone marking her mother's grave is etched with the words ADORED AND ADORING WIFE, MOTHER, AND DAUGHTER and the dates "Nov. 19, 1924–July 6, 1976"; as Mel stands before it, as she has twice a year these past few years—on her mother's birthday and on the anniversary of the day of her death—she hears herself asking her, in an imperceptible whisper, why this utterly cruel but mundane betrayal of Charlie's makes her feel as if she's dying, as if she no longer wants to live. Though her mother has no answers for her, Mel keeps talking, plaintively, and if she's being completely honest with herself, somewhat pitifully. But she doesn't care; unexpectedly warmed, at every visit, in the presence of her mother's grave, she could stand here forever, she thinks, so effortlessly conjuring the familiar sound and feel of her mother's compassion.

The gates to the cemetery close at four every afternoon; it's time for Mel to get back into the car defiled by the blackmailer's DNA. Walking toward the Rabbit, she sees a new footstone marking the grave of a man whose life ended at thirty-nine, she notices sadly. She stops in front of it to read: "Darling husband and father, how tenderly he loved us" and these are the words that kill her.

57
Mel

In the ladies' room at work, empty when she arrives, Mel hides in a stall, pulling the cover down over the toilet seat and perching herself on top of it, arms folded across her raised knees, a Yiddish-inflected story by Nina Levinthal—which Austin has asked Mel to Xerox for him—safe on the black-and-white ceramic-tiled floor beneath her. Soon she hears the chatty voice of Rebecca, the proofreader, telling someone that her boyfriend will be doing a three-year internship in internal medicine, followed, he hopes, by a couple of years of a gastroenterology fellowship . . . eventually he plans to specialize in patients with inflammatory bowel diseases, though, frankly, Rebecca is saying, *she* doesn't really want to know too much *a-boat* it. Neither does Mel, camped out in a darkened toilet stall with her eyes shut, trying to keep her mind blank, unhampered by even a single thought.

"Hey there," another voice says, and Mel knows it's Sally Steinhart, who, after barely a year and a half of marriage, is presently in the midst of a very public divorce from that adulterous celebrity husband of hers still in Washington but now working at CBS News. Sally and Rebecca are gossiping away *a-boat* the copyeditor and her boyfriend in the Art Department and their continued fondness for S&M; Mel lowers her head to her knees and wonders how long she can stay here in the toilet stall before Austin begins to wonder where she and that requested Xerox of Nina Levinthal's story have disappeared to.

There's the small sound of a lighter being flicked and now

the smell of cigarette smoke floating up and over the toilet stall. "Thanks for the Marlboro," she hears Sally Steinhart say, and as usual, "You know, don't you, that you ought to quit. Me, too, of course."

The door to the ladies' room slams shut; Mel emerges from the toilet stall and goes straight to the sink to wash her perfectly clean hands.

"Hey you, you look like hell," Sally Steinhart offers casually.

"I'm sorry about your divorce," Mel says. "Really sorry." Who knows: maybe if, on the morning of her wedding, Sally had been on that flight back to DC with her husband instead of here in the ladies' room with *her*, things might have gone differently. Or not . . .

"Actually," Sally is saying, "you don't have to be *that* sorry, because thanks to the misery my soon-to-be-ex-husband's caused me, and the whole disgraceful mess he's personally responsible for, my agent was able to negotiate a big fat book contract for me for a novel, where I can put it all to damn good use. Really, it's the most spectacular birthday gift I can think of. And I can promise you that my soon-to-be-ex will be getting everything he deserves in those pages—and I do mean *everything*. In fact, *more* than everything."

Mel loves hearing this; she smiles, for only an instant, for the first time in days.

"Is that a real smile?" Sally asks her. "Or a fake one?"

"Totally real, believe me."

Shaking her head, Sally says, "All my instincts tell me otherwise, and lucky for you, my wise counsel is absolutely free. So let's hear it, Melissa." She puts her cigarette out in the water dripping from the faucet Mel failed to turn off properly after needlessly washing those immaculate hands.

"Do you take insurance?" Mel says. "Can you prescribe psych meds?"

"Yes. And yes. By the power vested in me by me," Sally says, and how can Mel not allow herself to smile for the second time today?

The two of them lean against adjoining, slightly chipped sinks, facing each other, while Mel finds herself so easily confiding in her, as readily as if they were friends—which, Mel understands, surely they are not; she's still an underling, after all, albeit one who's been published by *The New Yorker.*

"All right, that's it, nothing more to report," she says after a three-minute synopsis of what suddenly sounds like a mostly fortunate life that has only recently turned shitty, but she's surprised to realize that not a tear has been shed in the telling; apparently she's made some progress here in the ladies' room today, resting awkwardly against an unwashed sink and looking into the dark eyes of someone who's been there before her.

The expression on Sally's face is pained and in it Mel sees the clear, gratifying reflection of her sympathy. "Okay, Mel, you want my professional advice? What you're going to do is hold on fiercely to whatever is good in your life in the face of what so clearly sucks. You know I'm talking about your career—not your work here at the magazine, which, sorry, we both know is inconsequential—but those stories you're writing, those stories you're telling; that's where your life is, the beating heart of your life." She's staring at Mel sharply. "Are you listening to me, Melissa?"

Yes, she's listening. Very, very carefully, in fact.

"Oh, and you've got to beware of that self-pity, do you hear me? You need to ditch it—every drop of it. It's a lethal poison, a killer, okay?"

Okay, sir.

58
Mel

The blackmailer's name, she learns, is Julia Myerson, a basic piece of information she extracted from Charlie, only because, unbeknownst to him, she felt a sudden compulsion to look her up in the White Pages and find her address and phone number, just in case she ever needed them.

Mel knows this isn't a smart move; most likely it's a dangerous one, but she isn't sure she can extinguish her curiosity. She's about to open the phone book tonight while Charlie's engaged in *Saturday Night Live* in the living room, but surprising herself, she changes her mind and puts the hefty book back in place on top of the file cabinet in their small, second bedroom-of-a-sort—the one she refers to as her office, but which Charlie often mistakenly calls their den, as if they were back in the colorless suburbs of their respective childhoods. Now, pulling out one of the file drawers in the army-green metal cabinet, looking for a folder with her notes for a story she's never been able to get quite right, she notices, at the bottom of the drawer, tucked between folders labeled "TAX STUFF" and "GRAD SCHOOL LOANS" a greeting card in the shape of a bouquet of flowers. Lifting it from the drawer, she sees that the card—which looks pristine, as if it had never been mailed—depicts a photograph of a wicker basket filled with pink roses, peach-colored calla lilies, and Dutch tulips. Inside, in Charlie's handwriting, are the words:

HI HONEY—HAPPY BELATED BIRTHDAY!
LOVE YOU, YOUR ONE AND ONLY HONEY PIE

What Mel hears so distinctly is her husband's voice saying *honey,* that easy, everyday endearment she and Charlie had for one another even before their marriage; the simple truth is that the imagined sound of his voice embracing that single word as he wrote out the blackmailer's birthday card just crushes her.

But then she sees that he'd dated the birthday card—it's the date of their fifth wedding anniversary—and she nearly loses her balance standing there in front of the file cabinet, nearly falls to her knees and onto the floor.

How can I hurt thee? Let me count the ways, she imagines him thinking. The fact that he'd evidently forgotten to mail the card does little to cheer her.

"You husband didn't deliberately mean to hurt you, Melissa, it just he compartmentalized in far-reaching way," Krystyna claims at the start of their appointment tonight.

Nodding his head eagerly, Charlie tells Mel and Krystyna that he barely—if ever—permitted himself to contemplate the damage he was doing, that he just didn't allow himself to recognize, during that year and then some, that he had violated their marriage from every possible angle.

"Yes yes yes!" Krystyna says approvingly. "This, as you well know, Charlie, what we call com-part-men-ta-li-zing."

She explains that Charlie was in a dopamine fog for the months of the affair. "It like being on drugs, you understand, Melissa? You husband's pleasure centers were all lit up, and nothing much on his mind except the pleasure of it all."

"Yes yes yes!" Charlie says approvingly.

Mel recognizes the damn psychobabble. (And when they're close to the end of their two-month relationship with Krystyna, Charlie will concede, apologetically, that he and Mel probably should have found someone better.)

But the agonizing truth, she understands, is that, unaccountably, even on their wedding anniversary, she was far from Charlie's thoughts. Even then, when she was standing right in front of him, he somehow failed to see her.

Hours later, at bedtime, when Charlie is in his pajamas at the bathroom sink, about to brush his teeth, he lets her know with a yelp that he's noticed what she's left there for him on the mirror.

"What's with you and taping things on there? Can't we talk to each other anymore?"

He rips the birthday card off the mirror, then shreds it, and flushes it down the toilet. He apologizes to Mel for what feels, even to her, like the hundredth time; she nods her head up and down from across the bedroom, her back toward him now as she unhooks her bra and slips on a camisole. Ever since D-Day, the day Charlie was busted, she has been dressing and undressing either with her back turned, or behind closed doors, silently letting him know he is no longer entitled to see her naked, or even half-naked.

But how long are things going to continue like this? A few more weeks? Months? How can they live like this, with one of them filled with both anguish and rage, and the other, remorse? How many times will Charlie have to apologize before she finally tells him she's heard enough and doesn't need to hear or see yet another *sorry sorry sorry*?

"Apologies are easy," she informs Charlie now, turning to face him. "Anyone can apologize for anything. Big. Deal."

He tells her she looks like she's been through something; *hell* is probably what that something is, he says, *and* he acknowledges, he's the one who's responsible for that.

Mel believes he would like to reassure her, once more tonight, that he loves her, but that the sadness she knows he sees reflected in her weary-looking eyes, in her down-turned mouth, and in the distinct slump of her slender shoulders serves, yet again, only to make him angry, at both himself and her.

So they get into bed together without those love-you's, set the alarm on the clock radio, and mumble *guh' night.* When he turns toward her and kisses her, her cheek is already damp, and it isn't, she wants to tell him, from her moisturizer.

Lately she's been doing a great deal of talking *sotto voce*, as if telling herself private things, but she knows Charlie's hearing is exceptionally good and there's not a word he doesn't hear.

suchabastard

pieceofshit

whyamIstayingwithhim . . . I'msosostupid

And so it goes. Night after night.

She knows he deserves it, but still . . . who wants to think of himself that way? Who wants to be reminded, night after night, that this is who he is and this is what he's done?

This is what Mel has done with the pajama pants Charlie wore the night of the sleepover in Woodstock.

It will take him all of about ten seconds, she predicts as he hauls himself out of bed this morning, to figure out what he's supposed to make of the assortment of oddly shaped scraps of plaid fabric that have been layered in a disorderly pile on top of his pillow. The bright plaid is green, red, yellow, and turquoise, and as he holds in his hands pieces of what were formerly his favorite pajama pants, the ones he chose to wear the night he and the blackmailer spent at the Dreamcatcher Cottage, he admits to Mel he can't believe how violated he feels.

Violated? Really? Hey, sorry you feel that way, babe!

She hopes that Charlie, one of those shrinks whose specialties include (somewhat hilariously, she thinks now) family conflict, can envision the fury with which she used her scissors, that he can imagine the satisfaction she felt snipping away, reducing his pajama pants to mere scraps, suitable for dumping directly into the trash.

He's telling her now that he understands, but that what

she needs—and here he sounds to Mel like the shrink that he is—is to put aside her anger so they can move forward. He's worried, he says, that this anger of hers will prove lethal to their marriage.

How long will it take, Mel wonders, until it occurs to Charlie that it is *deceit* that is most lethal of all.

Oh, and by the way, she'd like to add, how ironic is it that so often shrinks, sitting there on their thrones handing out advice left and right, are just too fucked-up themselves to see the world with the clarity their patients deserve from them.

59
Mel

Perhaps just to torture herself, she will ask her closest married friends, one by one, in half a dozen separate phone conversations, how each would feel if she happened to catch sight of her own husband sauntering by on a path in Central Park, or along Spring Street in SoHo, or in a suburban mall in Connecticut, holding hands with another woman. Unsurprisingly, each friend will say the imagined sight is enough to make her ill—nausea-inducing-migraine ill.

Then Mel will ask each friend to imagine her husband and this woman standing in a doorway engaged in a lengthy, impassioned kiss.

And then her husband in bed together with this woman, their clothing cast in a heap on the floor of a hotel room or the slut's own bedroom.

And then Mel will say, *Imagine the two of them in bed together not once, but over and over and over again, the adulterous husband telling this woman, each time, how very beautiful she is, and how very much he loves her.*

And then she will say, *Imagine that this scenario will go on, from start to finish, for a year and two months. Right under your nose.*

And then she will say, *Imagine that when confronted, the husband in question—a shrink, by the way—will insist, staring directly at you, unblinking, clueless and unashamed, that adultery is a harmless, victimless activity. As long as the participants don't get busted, that is.*

Stop stop STOP, Mel's friends will beg her.

They will choose the word *hellish* to describe what she has asked them to imagine.

Mel will have one final question for each of them: if they had spotted Charlie moseying hand in hand with the blackmailer anywhere at all, would they have called and told her what they'd seen?

Absolutely not, her friends will tell her. *Not a chance.*

60

MEL

"Dear heart," she hears Austin calling to her, followed by, "can you please ring up Richard for me?" Weird, she thinks, that he makes almost all his own calls, but for some reason these days needs to impress his main man Richard, king of the book critics at *The Times*, by having Mel dial the number and announce, "Please hold for Austin."

When she hears Richard's brusque "Yes, what is it?" she wants to finally let him have it, wants to shriek, *You think I'm an idiot, you think I don't know what a lyingcheatingpig you are?*

"Please hold for Austin," she says, a bit less than politely, maybe even with a trace of rancor in her voice.

Later in the day, while Austin is "out to lunch" in Richard's apartment, there's a call from Lincoln Pastorelli, who insists, as always, on identifying himself, first name and last. Just the sound of his whiny drawl summons up for Mel that image of him on her TV screen several years ago, his belly bulging beneath his ill-fitting turtleneck, his eyes hidden behind sunglasses, Lincoln rubbing his knee with the palm of his hand as he explained to Johnny Carson that no, he never once received a single rejection slip. *That's right, not even once.*

"Lincoln Pastorelli," he's saying to Mel now. "Shall I spell it for you?" He's slurring his words a bit; Mel assumes he's a little hammered.

You really don't need to spell it—I actually know how to spell, believe it or not. And I'm very, very familiar with your name, Lincoln. I know who you are, I know what you look like; I even typed one of your manuscripts in the office at six in the morning. I know what a brilliant writer you sometimes are and I know that you sometimes drive drunk and almost caused serious harm to a friend of mine one night when you were behind the wheel in the Hamptons. Please DO NOT spell your name for me.

"L.I.N.C.O.L.N. P.A.S T.O.R.E.L.L.I."

"Got it," Mel says, and promises that Austin will return his call.

"But when will *that* be?" Lincoln says, sounding kvetchy. "I have to go out soon."

Oh no, you're not going to be driving under the influence, are you?

"Austin will call you, I promise," she repeats.

"Let's hope so," Lincoln says just before he hangs up.

Men are really stupid—let's throw rocks at them.

61
Mel

Apparently Mel has a thing about pajamas, or at least her husband's pajamas. First she cut to pieces the pair he wore on his overnight getaway to the Dreamcatcher Cottage; boy, does she love the name of that place where he and the blackmailer fucked. And now she can't stop herself from checking his pajama drawer every morning after Charlie leaves for his office and before she leaves for work. He routinely and carelessly stuffs his pj's into the fourth drawer of his dresser, a habit which, before D-Day, never bothered her in the least. But post D-Day is a different story, and every morning she neatly refolds his pajamas for him. She realizes exactly what she is doing: she's attempting to restore order to her home, her psyche, her life.

She is on Eighty-Sixth Street tonight, at Gimbel's, looking for nothing in particular but intent on coming home with *something* for herself; she doesn't care what. The merchandise in the store just doesn't turn her on, but then, in the lingerie department, she finds a pair of pajamas that look very cozy, soft cotton ones imprinted with dainty little cupcakes. She's standing in line to pay for them, when, looking more closely in a brighter light, she sees her mistake—those aren't cupcakes the pajamas are patterned with, those are teeny-weeny pies; the words *honey pie* are what come to her. She lets the pajamas drop to the floor, as if, in an unlikely moment of spontaneous combustion, they might burst into terrifying flames. The customer in line behind her, a young mother in bell-bottoms and platform shoes who can't stop talking to her friend, in ruthless detail, about the potty-training boot camp she'd put her toddler through ("It's a three-day affair, and I'm telling you, when it's over, you're done!"), bends down to pick up the pajamas for her.

"You dropped these," she says, and smiles at Mel with her pretty face.

I thought you loved me in a way that was worth everything, Honey Pie, she hears this young mother say, and Mel runs out of the store like a madwoman, or maybe just like someone suffering from PTSD.

62
Mel

Though Charlie isn't a big fan of musicals, which he generally finds sentimental and dopey, Mel had ordered tickets, a month or so before D-Day, to see *The King and I* on Broadway. A lifetime ago, when he was eleven or twelve, Charlie had played the role of Lun Tha, the doomed lover, in a sixth-grade production of the musical. Lun Tha's heartthrob, Tuptim, was played by someone named Heidi Rubenstein, who had a long dark ponytail in sixth grade and a very pretty soprano, and who, Charlie recently discovered from one of his high school buddies, became a real estate broker in Florida. In sixth grade, Mel knows, Heidi Rubenstein and Charlie were an item.

These days, even the thought of twelve-year-old Charlie and his sixth-grade girlfriend causes her pain. *Pathetic*, she thinks.

Sitting in the theater now, several weeks post-D-Day, Mel rests her head on his shoulder. She adores the music from *The King and I* and is feeling calmer than she expected, given the recent unraveling of her life. She listens as the orchestra plays the overture; right before the curtain goes up, a guy seated directly in front of her says, "I don't think she's like, a devil, but she has, like, no heart or anything!"

She leans her head across Charlie's uncomfortably hard shoulder all the way through Act I and the start of intermission. Every so often, he rubs her bare arm affectionately.

Now he's taking her hand in his and she has to admit that listening to what she considers the best of Rodgers and Hammerstein feels heavenly. But ten minutes after Act 2, Scene 2, Tuptim and Lun Tha are doing their thing, singing "I Have Dreamed" so beautifully that Mel wants to shoot herself.

Or kill Charlie first, and then herself.

"In these dreams I've loved you sohhh . . ."

Oh, yeah, she can just picture the blackmailer singin' this tune loudly and clearly.

She who is always so polite is repeatedly socking her husband's arm now somewhere between his elbow and his shoulder as he sits here in his seat in this theater on Fifty-First Street. She can't stop smacking him, all because Oscar Hammerstein's lyrics are just too excruciating for her ears. And for her dumb heart, and her stupid stupid *stupid* brain.

"Ow, stop hitting me! What is *wrong* with you?" Charlie whispers, but then apologizes to her.

The guy in front of her, the one who was talking about the devil who had, like, no heart, is now turning around to scold Mel for the minor disturbance she's creating.

"Sorry," Charlie says. It's his favorite word these past few weeks.

As well it should be, Mel thinks.

"Jesus, can't take you anywhere," he jokes, and they both have to laugh.

They go straight home and into bed after the last curtain call for Angela Lansbury and Yul Brynner.

This will be the first time Mel and Charlie have slept together since D-Day. It's Mel's idea, not his: she surprises him by getting into bed with nothing on but her underwear. It's remembering what a good husband he used to be that ignites her desire to touch him.

First she puts his hand on her breast. "I still love you," she hears herself say, but he's not taking the bait.

She notes the tenderness in his voice when he says, "I just

think it's too soon, babe." His hand is still on her breast, but it's lying there motionless, dead weight that disappoints her. "I still love you, too," Charlie reassures her.

She finds his reluctance terribly painful and worries that he's still galvanized by thoughts of the blackmailer. But in a few minutes, without another word from either of them, he's made his loving, gentle way inside her and both of them remain uncharacteristically quiet as he delivers soundless kisses here and there along her jaw, under her neck, and then upward across her eyelids.

For the moment, anyway, here in their bed she feels both relief and contentment.

She sees, as her husband sleeps, his wedding band glinting in the light from the open bathroom door from which she is now emerging. And she wonders how often the blackmailer had observed that shining metal circling Charlie's finger and been reminded of who he really was—a man married to a wife he loved—even if the blackmailer had preferred to pretend otherwise.

Mel is teary-eyed; she's a twenty-seven-year-old crybaby in need of a dose of maternal love.

63
Mel

She's lucky enough to have found a support group for betrayed spouses after talking with a friend of hers who wrote a piece about it for *New York* Magazine.

"Not that I don't believe in the value of support groups," Charlie says when she tells him where she's going tonight. "But frankly, what's the therapeutic value in hanging out with a bunch of angry, disappointed people who may very well make you feel even angrier and more disappointed than you already do, babe?"

"Well, we'll find out," Mel says.

The group meets at the Church of the Blessed Sacrament on Forty-Sixth Street in Hell's Kitchen, and this first night she attends, she arrives with a bag of extra-dark Pennsylvania Dutch pretzels, a stack of napkins, and a small package of thin, budget-brand paper plates. The group of nine women and four men is seated around a seminar table in a comfortable space that could pass for a classroom in a secular college. There's a blackboard with a trinity of affirmations that have been half-heartedly erased; without any effort at all, Mel can make out the words of the first two:

I CHERISH THE TRUE LOVE IN MY LIFE
THE UNIVERSE BLESSES ME IN SURPRISING AND JOYFUL WAYS

She knows from an information-packed, tell-all newsletter that Howard Banks, the group's leader, seated at the head of the table, is a betrayed spouse whose wife, Cynthia, had been having an affair with the high school boyfriend she dated over thirty years ago. Last winter, Cynthia had managed to reconnect with that old boyfriend and soon began joining him on weekend afternoons at a Motel 6 in Queens while Howard was hard at work selling Ferraris at a dealership in Manhattan. In a former life, he'd been a casting director in Hollywood, but here he is now, taking the bag of pretzels from Mel, dumping them into a sky-blue plastic bowl that he positions at the center of the seminar table, and pausing a moment just before introducing her to the rest of the gang.

"Though we're all friends here, please feel free to use a pseudonym," he tells her for the second time tonight. "You know, just in case you feel uncomfortable sharing your real name."

"No problem," Mel says, exactly as she'd said the first time. Why would she care if any of those assembled here knows her real name? Like her, they've all been broken by the very people who were meant to do their best to shield them, whenever possible, from every sort of grief.

Howard is a pale guy sporting a big gold watch around a hairy wrist, and he's wearing a T-shirt that confesses, OF COURSE I TALK TO MYSELF—SOMETIMES I NEED EXPERT ADVICE! He seems happy with the pretzels he requested Mel bring for the group; others have contributed bowls of chips and colorful jellybeans. Most of the members are middle-aged, but there are a couple of women who appear, like Mel, to be in their twenties, and one of whom, Davina, is visibly pregnant. Mel can't bear to contemplate the sort of man who would cheat on a pregnant spouse, preferring, instead, to send Davina a sympathetic look from across the seminar table. Davina returns her smile shyly. There are metal braces gleaming on her upper teeth and it occurs to Mel that this mother-to-be might actually be a teenager.

"Basically, the only rule we have here is that no one interrupt the member who has asked to speak," Howard explains. "Try and keep that in mind, tough though it may be." He clasps his large hands and rests them on the table; there's a column of red, scaly skin running from each of his wrists up to his elbows. Psoriasis, probably. As if losing his wife to her high school honey three decades down the road isn't bad enough.

"So . . . how *is* everyone?" Howard asks. "Anyone?"

Looking stricken, a diminutive, well-dressed woman in her fifties, whose name is Taffy, says, "Okay if I go first? As some of you already know from last time, it's been almost two and a half years since my husband took off with his whore. She's a French teacher in the high school where he's the head of the department." Her eyes are glassy; she bows her head. "Selfish bastard," Taffy murmurs. "Let's hope the two of them rot in hell for the rest of their stupid lives."

On the blackboard Mel can see the faint letters of the mostly erased third affirmation:

INNER PIECE IS MAKING MY LIFE
BEAUTIFUL EVERY MOMENT

The last time *she* felt some inner peace was the instant before she stumbled upon that letter from the blackmailer, the one who wants to touch Charlie's face with the tips of her fingers and talk to him about everything in the world. It's hard to remember that self, the Mel Fleischer who was privileged to walk comfortably on this earth, privileged to float, for the most part serenely, from one hour to another without this toxic mix of grief and bitterness that now trails after her from the moment she awakens and accompanies her through the course of her day.

"Not helpful, Taffy," Howard says, and the gang around the seminar table nods in agreement. "Here's what I'd like you to do for yourself, okay: first, picture a perfectly clean blackboard empty of words. Can you do that?"

"Whatever," Taffy says.

"Now I want you to make a list of everything that's good in your life and write it on that blackboard. Write down the names of your children and your best friends and your beloved dog and —"

"First of all, I don't *have* a dog, and second, both my kids are in college and feeling free to ignore me except when they want permission to use my American Express card."

"Self-care!" someone suggests. "Put yourself first!" the guy says enthusiastically.

"Let's go back to the blackboard," Howard says, but Taffy is shaking her head, stage-whispering the words *May they rot in hell.*

"She needs to self-soothe," someone else says, a woman whose upper arms are as large and wide as thighs. She's wearing silver hoop earrings big enough to put her substantial wrists through. "Self-soothe like a baby sucking its toes," she adds.

Mel looks around, hoping to catch sight of at least a few smiles, but she sees people nodding in approval, one following the other, all of them, evidently, comforted by the thought of sucking on *something*.

"So what's going through your head now, Taffy?" Howard asks.

"What's going through my head? Okay, how's this for self-soothing: you say the word 'sucking' and I see my husband sucking the tits of the damn French teacher, Mademoiselle Desjarlais, who, no surprise, is young enough to be my stepdaughter."

"You're not helping yourself, Taffy," Howard warns her. "I can tell you're not even trying."

Mel imagines him in the Ferrari showroom, killing himself attempting to sell a $40,000 Ferrari to a young real estate tycoon, Howard offering this and that to sweeten the deal as the customer begins to back away, edging ever closer to the front door of the dealership, and out onto Eleventh Avenue as Howard keeps talking talking talking.

So what's he doing here in Hell's Kitchen at the Church of the Blessed Sacrament moonlighting as a therapist of sorts in his spare time?

Leaning forward, Mel grabs a pretzel from the bowl at the center of the table. "You don't know me, guys, but trust me when I tell you the universe isn't blessing me in ways either surprising *or* joyful," she says, snapping the thick pretzel into small chunks that she lets fall onto the table as she talks. "Speaking of surprises," she continues, and uses the words "big-time adulterer" to describe Charlie. She repeats the words "big-time," just so they get the picture, and they do.

Taffy, sitting beside her, turns to face Mel. "I can't stop thinking about my husband's whore, not even for a minute. I saw the two of them coming out of ShopRite together the other day and I followed them to their car, and then I gave them both the finger. I'm fifty-four years old, giving my husband and his whore the finger in a supermarket parking lot. I mean, what's *wrong* with me?"

"It's not about *you*, Taffy, it's about your not-very-smart husband," Howard says firmly as Taffy bows her head again and begins to cry, but without making a sound.

Mel would have to say she's truly surprised by the dopiness of the support group's "sharing"; they seem to inspire self-pity in each other, she observes, and wonders who could possibly find anything that was said here tonight even remotely helpful.

But she watches herself clasp the small, moist hand of this stranger sitting next to her in a church in Hell's Kitchen, the two of them surrounded by a tableful of people who know what it's like, baby, who know what it's like to be that person just dumb enough to have found yourself married to a big-time con artist. Mel didn't ever want to be that credulous fool; in fact, she was always sure she *wasn't* that person, and possibly even congratulated herself, from time to time, for *not* being her.

She needs to get the hell out of this Church of the Blessed Sacrament and get some rest.

Extracting her hand from Taffy's, she whispers "good luck" into her ear. And takes one more look at the blackboard on her way out.

INNER PIECE IS MAKING MY LIFE
BEAUTIFUL EVERY MOMENT

64
Mel

"I have a gift for you," Mel announces on a Saturday morning. From the kitchen she brings out a paper hat that looks like something from a children's birthday party except that it's covered over in plain white typing paper, and on it, written with a thick black Sharpie, are the words:

EMOTIONAL DUNCE CAP

"Oh, you shouldn't have," Charlie teases, and allows her to set it in place on top of his head and tuck the elastic strap under his chin.

"It's a dunce cap made especially for emotional dunces!" she says gleefully. "Especially for those with their PhD's in psychology!"

"Very fitting!" Charlie says, as if he knows it's what Mel wants to hear, and also, she guesses, because he welcomes the jauntiness in her voice.

"You like?" she says.

"It's a lovely gift," he says, after they exchange a momentary kiss.

Later in the day, after she returns home from doing some errands, she finds a note that Charlie, who is out playing squash with a college friend, has attached with a magnet to the refrigerator door:

Hey, I'm sorry for all the pain I've caused you
Hugs and kisses from your very own Emotional Dunce

What she needs now, she understands, is to graduate from "*He* is the great disappointment of my life" to "*What he did* is the great disappointment of my life."

The million-dollar question is, how does she get from here to there?

65
Mel

Mel will spend over two hours at the magazine this afternoon retyping a thirteen-page poetic but bizarrely incomprehensible piece of fiction, on her wonderful IBM Selectric. The story is his own, Austin confides to her in a whisper. "But shouldn't take you too long," he says as he hands her his manuscript, which is full of angry-looking cross-outs, and carets with long-winded inserts. When she is finished typing and after he has proofed it, Austin has her walk it over to the editor-in-chief's office with a note clipped to its pages.

The next morning, before Austin shows up at the office, that editor-in-chief with the spacious suite at the end of the hallway and those degrees in literature from Cambridge and Yale returns the manuscript to Mel, a look of faint disgust on his heavily bearded face. He has, Mel can see, given an official rejection slip to Austin's very own short story; the note attached to the manuscript is brutally clear. *Austin: Feel free to publish this—ELSEWHERE.*

Surprising herself, she feels a small jolt of sympathy for Austin as she hands the manuscript to him in his small dark office.

Without asking, she closes the door gently behind her as she leaves.

One Sunday, a handful of years from now, Mel will have her first story collection reviewed in *The Washington Post*, along with Austin's own collection and those by a trio of writers whose work she admires. The reviewer will conclude—to Mel's utter astonishment—that *the most accomplished of these, the very best of these, is by newcomer Melissa Fleischer.* What she will once again imagine hearing, upon reading those words in *The Washington Post*, is the sound of Austin whispering, *Seriously, are you KIDDING me?*

66
Mel

She told Charlie, in the vaguest of terms, that she needed to go out tonight and would be home in "a while." He was seated on the living-room couch reading his revered *Journal of Generalized Anxiety Disorder* as she headed for the front door. When he asked where she was going, she shrugged one shoulder and left, the blackmailer's home address on a piece of note paper jammed into the pocket of her blazer. So easy to hunt her down in the White Pages; all Mel had to do to find the blackmailer's address was go to the "B's" and look for the words *Blackmailing Bitch.*

Kidding!

Those words would merely be *Julia Myerson,* but even getting two of her fingers and her thumb to grasp a pen and write out the blackmailer's address was keenly distasteful.

One subway ride later, and Mel has arrived.

Outside the blackmailer's drab, early-twentieth-century apartment building, directly across the street from the Whit's End Bar & Grill, Mel waits between two glass doors—the inner one locked and preventing her entrance into the lobby—hoping an arriving or departing tenant will come along and inadvertently usher her in. She has no intention of confronting the blackmailer; all she wants is to stand at the door to her apartment and . . . what? Well, Mel can't say precisely what it is she's looking for. But as she stands waiting in the small vestibule that smells, oddly, of both sweat and garlic, she sees the blackmailer's name and apartment listed in the tenant directory; just the sight of that particular arrangement of letters and numbers stirs a sickening brew of melancholy that seems to spread, all at once, throughout her.

The lock poppers, when they finally arrive, turn out to be a little boy with a worried expression on his face and the elderly man holding his hand, to whom the boy confides, "I've been afraid of squirrels my whole life, Grandpaw." Mel smiles at the sweet voice of the sciuriphobic as his grandfather holds the door for her.

"Thank you," she says. "Cute kid," she adds.

"He's not mine, not exactly, but thank you," Grandpaw says, and the two of them disappear up a flight of stairs off the lobby. Beyond the stairway, there's a seating area decorated with a mural of determined-looking soldiers on horseback, dressed in Revolutionary War uniforms and chasing after a troop of fierce-looking American Indians, tomahawks raised threateningly overhead. Mel studies them, trying to figure out what war this could be depicting, and decides the artist must have slept through American history in high school, but then she remembers—the French and Indian War, 1754–1763! Bingo! British colonists fighting French colonists and American Indians! There's something disturbingly racist about the mural; probably it's the fury on the faces of those tomahawk-wielding figures, but Mel has already wasted enough time staring at it when, instead, she should be summoning the courage to get herself upstairs to the thirteenth floor, where, the directory shows, the blackmailer lives in apartment F.

Moving toward a bank of dark-pink elevators framed by pink-and-gray-marble walls, she's joined by two women about her age, their breath giving off a strong scent of alcohol. "Both grandmas walked me down the aisle, including the 114-year-old!" one of them says joyously.

"No way, no how!" the other woman says.

Mel holds the elevator door open for them as they stumble aboard, and she's relieved when the two pals exit together on the fifth floor, leaving her all alone, though with the alcoholic stink of their bar-hopping spree lingering in the elevator. On the eighth floor she's joined by a teenager with long, sculpted and polished nails that go on and on for well over an inch. She's carrying a filthy blue backpack with a pin that warns: "Yes, I'm a bitch . . . SO WHAT!" She's there with her friend, who has similarly sculpted nails and a pair of bloodshot eyes. "Yeah, yeah, I totally get it, Jamie, but sometimes you just gotta accept a person for who they is," the girl tells her friend.

The elevator reaches the thirteenth floor all too soon, and Mel goes ashore cautiously, as if someone might appear without warning in the empty hallway and demand an official ID card and the name of the person she's here to see. It's not exactly as if she's breaking and entering, but she wonders if she could be arrested for trespassing, for unlawful entry onto the premises.

Fine! Let them take her into custody, what does she *care? And while she's at the police station, Mel can file charges against the blackmailer for trying to extort a thousand bucks from her husband.*

She finds apartment F without encountering a single person in the ill-lit, uncarpeted hallway, and positions herself directly in front of the blackmailer's door. It's made of oxblood-colored metal, an unappealing brown tinged with purple and red, and as she stands there in front of it, she's aware of the scent of something cooking, and the very particular scent of curry. The tip of her finger is grazing the doorbell, stroking it again and again, and she imagines Charlie's feet, like her own, planted here on the rubber welcome mat, his finger stabbing the bell impatiently as he waits for the blackmailer to come to the door, she who's been readying herself—meticulously shaving her legs and under her arms, smoothing moisturizer everywhere—to be made love to by him. And there she is; Mel envisions her effortlessly, can see that the blackmailer is barefoot and dressed in an ankle-length bathrobe, the hair at her temples damp from the shower, her face rosy with anticipation.

Hey, Honey Pie, she says, and Charlie is all over her in an instant, poking his tongue inside her warm, welcoming mouth and his hand inside the V of her bathrobe and now he's backing her into the apartment, where her queen-size mattress with the freshly changed linens is all set to accommodate them, the comforter already drawn to the foot of the bed they're falling into now, their sighs and murmurs growing louder and softer and louder again as they nibble at each other with some crazy hunger, two people who, at this moment, are absolutely convinced they belong together, now and forever.

Never mind that, according to Charlie anyway, he told the blackmailer—repeatedly—that they had no future together. That he had a wife he loved and would never abandon, not even for his Honey Pie, whose need for him sometimes seemed even more profound than his own need for his wife and those bonds he'd always thought were the very center of everything for him.

You're just so beautiful, Honey Pie, Mel can hear her husband saying.

Imagining all of this now, she feels nothing, just a puzzling numbness that surprises her, and not in a bad way, either. Sometimes, she marvels, it seems like a victory simply to feel nothing at all.

Time to go, she tells herself, and just as she is turning away from the blackmailer's door, she hears movement inside the apartment, footsteps approaching, and then something heavy, possibly a vacuum cleaner, being shoved inside a closet. She can feel her heart knocking around, as if warning her of serious danger.

She turns back toward the door, but only for a moment. She gives it the finger, and mouths the satisfying words *Stay the fuck away from my husband.*

67
Mel

Just after Charlie has left early for work one morning, and while Mel is lingering at the kitchen counter with her mug full of Instant Breakfast, there's a call from her smart, practical friend Lisa, whom she's known since the two of them, together with their own young mothers, walked hand-in-hand to kindergarten more than twenty years ago.

"It's just that if I were the one who had the cheating husband . . ." Lisa is saying, but Mel's trying not to listen. She's heard it all before, from every one of her friends: *Make him sleep on the living-room couch for six weeks or six months, and let him see how he likes it. You need to do something punitive so he'll finally get it through his head that what he's done for the past fourteen months is wrong wrong wrong.*

"So if you want my professional advice, if I were you, I'd make him wear a condom," Lisa suggests. She happens to be an epidemiologist, but that doesn't mean Mel has to fall in line here. "Condoms, every single time, till death do you part. How's that for appropriate punishment?"

"We . . . I . . ." Mel mumbles, and then she's silent. She opens the refrigerator, wanting to top off her Instant Breakfast with a squirt of whipped cream, but then she changes her mind and whams the door shut so hard, all the unpaid monthly bills and their accompanying envelopes stored in a disorderly pile on top of the fridge slide to the floor in a small avalanche. "Goddamn it," she says, bending down to pick up all the paper; some of the bills have slid under the refrigerator and she can't retrieve them.

"Oh shit, you and Charlie are already sleeping together again, aren't you? You never even made him sleep on the couch for a single night, did you?" Lisa says.

"Okay, look, forgive me, but I just can't listen to you anymore," Mel says, and hangs up on her old friend.

She's trying to steer Charlie's attention away from the ever-fascinating weather forecast on the 11:00 news tonight. A meteorologist in a white button-down shirt and crimson tie announces that the moon will rise at 5:42 tomorrow morning and will set at 5:53 tomorrow evening. Moonrise, moonset; they're pretty words, and Mel likes the sound of them.

"Question for you," she addresses Charlie, and says she wants to know whether he at least showered between "dates" with the two women in his life.

Do you hereby swear that you took a shower after you were with her *and before you got into bed with* me*?* She's shouting these words, as if Charlie's hearing isn't up to par, and then when he doesn't answer her, she offers them in a whisper.

"I did, I think, definitely. I mean, most of the time. To be honest, though, probably not always," she hears him say. "But I never took one in her apartment."

"Wait, you couldn't take a shower in her apartment before coming home to me?" *How could you come back to me, walk through the door of our home, with the intimate scent of her body, however faint, still on yours?* she wants to ask him, but the thought of saying the words aloud is repellent to her.

"Actually . . . I was afraid you would notice that my hair was wet."

Seated next to her on their banged-up, rust-colored leather couch, he's looking down at his bare feet now. His long legs are surprisingly furry, she always thinks, his toes ornamented with tiny swatches of dirty-blond hair.

She finds it difficult to keep from laughing as she says,

"Hey, did you ever hear of a shower cap? You know, it's made of plastic and you put it on over your head before you get into the shower? And then, when you're finished, your hair is still dry?"

"A shower cap," Mel repeats. "Have you heard of it?"

"I just never thought—"

"Never thought *what*?"

She thinks of their wedding day, when she went off to the local Long Island beach at noon with a couple of friends to get some color in her face before the ceremony and instead, came home with a painful sunburn. Her face, in their wedding album, was flushed with happiness but also with too much sun, and when she and Charlie made love that night, he was so very careful not to touch her cheeks, her brow, her eyelids, her chin, so careful not to cause her even a moment's worth of pain.

"Never thought . . . at all . . . about . . . what you just said," Charlie confesses. "Thinking didn't enter into it, into what I was doing when I was with her. It was all about the moment. The intoxication of the moment."

Ah, Mel finally gets it: *As her husband the brilliant psychologist sees it, the unexamined life is the only life worth living.*

68
Mel

Only a few years from now, in the not-too-distant future after her first book appears in print, she will be invited by NYU to take part in a panel discussion with a fivesome of young writers, one of whom, Doug Hayward, is already a minor celebrity. The very thought of speaking in public has always left Mel feeling miserably uncomfortable—come on, she's a writer, not a performer!—and she will consider turning down the invitation, the first of many over the years, before forcing herself to say yes.

A half hour before the panel is to begin, she and her fellow writers will learn that a much larger audience will be attending than had originally been expected; the venue has been moved from a common room in a dormitory to a large auditorium on campus. A horrifying thought, at least to Mel. But she happens to have, in the back pocket of her pants, a single miraculous pill falling into the category of a benzodiazepine, a word she will never have heard until a few weeks earlier, when her newest shrink will be persuaded to write a prescription for her after Mel works hard to convince him she's always been terrified of public speaking and needs some help. She's never taken this minuscule pill before, but recognizes there's no way she'll be able to get up on stage in that auditorium without a little help from this benzo.

Her equally shocked and petrified colleagues will, along with Doug Hayward—the only one among them who looks entirely at peace with the world—clamber up onto the stage at the appointed time and take their seats in a row of folding chairs, as directed. The moderator will begin to speak, but no one will be able to respond to her questions except Doug Hayward—and Mel, who will be soaring joyfully and confidently above it all, thanks to that tiny benzo she will so brilliantly think to drop into her back pocket just before leaving home. The others on stage with her will eventually warm up the slightest bit and manage to murmur a few words uncertainly here and there, their voices faint and hesitant, but it's Mel and that minor celebrity of the literary world who will steal the show and all that applause from the audience.

Pretty much every glorious minute of it!

69
Mel

Krystyna had told Mel and Charlie that there'd been a crack in his foundation, one that allowed him to continue to believe, to insist during the length of his affair, that adultery was a harmless, victimless activity. As long as the betrayed partner didn't find out, of course.

But isn't cheating still cheating, dishonesty still dishonesty, no matter how you slice it? Mel keeps asking him.

Well . . . not exactly, according to Charlie. Who argues that his love for the blackmailer had rendered that dishonesty permissible. The love he once felt for her took that dishonesty and kicked its ass, get it?

Nope, she just doesn't get it and she never will.

Listening to Charlie defend this wrong-headed bullshit so disturbs her, that one night in their bedroom with the TV news on in the background, Mel grabs him by the arm and digs her short nails into his wrist, leaving marks that resemble small insect bites and that will remain on his skin over the next few days.

"A great tragedy situation," she hears on the news, as a police officer in Hattiesburg, Mississippi addresses an assemblage of sweaty-looking reporters.

"You hurt me," Charlie says with a touch of whininess.

"*Ohhh,* Charlie, please, I hurt *you*? You know what? You're astoundingly dumb, and as shrinks go, monumentally stupid!" she says to her husband. But soon she's in the bathroom, getting a tube of Neosporin and tenderly rubbing a small swirl of it into all three of the tiny red marks on Charlie's wrist. Then she apologizes, though only for insulting him, not for tearing his skin.

He says—to his credit, she thinks—"You don't ever have to apologize, babe, not anymore. Not for anything, really."

She offers him a fake, theatrical smile, the kind they sometimes like to tease each other with; lying down on her side, she arranges herself next to him on their bed. When he loops his arms around her, balancing his elbows on her hips, she doesn't push him away. Now, in the aftermath of his betrayal—and though not one of her friends believes it when she says so—the familiar feel of those long bony arms encircling her waist still does it for her, still warms her like nothing else.

Later, after they've dumped Krystyna, a psychiatrist named Dr. Wachtel, whom Mel is seeing on her own, will advise her, *Look on the bright side: One day, when he dies and you're sitting there in the front row at his funeral, you won't be anywhere near as grief-stricken as you'd be if he'd been a faithful husband.*

And this is supposed to make her feel better? Really?

Dr. Wachtel is another middle-aged woman who specializes in the aftermath of adultery, and has more than three decades of clinical practice under her shiny black patent leather belt.

But she's unable to understand how much Mel loves Charlie; unable to understand that Mel cannot imagine ever loving anyone but that lyingcheatingadulterous husband of hers.

70
Mel

It's payday, the end of the workweek; the checks are delivered, on alternate Friday afternoons, by Albert-the-mail-guy, a tiny, elderly man in a black suit and white shirt, no tie, and rubbery black shoes. As usual, he says not a word as he hands over Mel's check today. It's just before the end of the lunch hour and there's no one around in the office except the two of them.

Opening the envelope and staring at her check, she's disappointed to see that, as usual, after taxes and Social Security are deducted, she's left with the whopping sum of $272 for two weeks of work.

What was she expecting, a raise? Why the same disappointment every other Friday?

"I have degrees from two Ivy League schools," she whispers to Albert, who looks at her and says, "What's your point?"

"My point," she tells him, "is that I make a little less than three dollars and ninety cents an hour."

Albert is smiling now; this is a first for him, the first time he's ever shown Mel those two front teeth on top that are crossed over each other in a way that she guesses even her father the orthodontist would find a challenge to fix.

"*I* make five dollars an hour," Albert announces. "My job is more important than yours, you do understand that, right?" Mel nods, and Albert says, "'Neither snow nor rain nor heat nor gloom of night stays these couriers from the swift completion of their appointed rounds.' And do you know who said that?"

Coming around from behind the mail cart that he pushes

along the hallway several times a day, Albert leans his elbow against the top of Mel's desk. "It was Herodotus, who wrote *The Persian Wars*, in 425 B.C. Did you know that?"

"I did not," Mel says, impressed.

"And that's why they pay *me* the big bucks," Albert explains.

If you were to tell her now, she wouldn't believe it because, well, these things would never happen, would they, to anyone who sits at a desk with her IBM Selectric at her side, earning take-home pay of $136 a week, but . . . a dozen years from now, she will get a call from Hollywood, someone representing a superstar—an actor and director who, astonishingly, is willing to pay Mel big bucks for the rights to her novel.

Put your feet back on the ground, her agent will say to her sternly. *Put your feet back on the ground and keep them there*," she will instruct Mel, instantly and forever spoiling the moment for her.

But how satisfying it will be to deposit those checks that feel like they've come from nowhere less than heaven—and so many years from now, to use that Hollywood money to pay for her son's wedding.

So why put your feet back on the ground, why not savor the moment when it arrives, you lucky duck, you!

71
Mel

She's observing Charlie as he prepares dinner on this Friday night, watching him carve up—as he habitually does—artichoke hearts to ornament her slice of pizza; to his own he'll add arugula and extra mozzarella. Mel is studying his hands, unmarred by wrinkles or lumpy, bluish veins, the nails broad and pink. On the fourth finger of his left, the plainest of gold wedding bands. And what she is thinking as she observes him is that these are the hands, the fingers, that touched the blackmailer when she was naked. First her left breast and then her right, then both at the same time; these are the very same hands that so urgently, so lovingly, parted the lips of the blackmailer's ladyparts in the moment before he went down on her.

How can Mel entertain these thoughts and still enjoy her favorite meal, that slice of pizza bedecked with those artichoke hearts scented with olive oil?

How can she entertain these thoughts and still approach her husband tonight and thank him for making her pizza just the way she likes it?

How can she entertain these thoughts and not want to shoot herself in the head with a Smith & Wesson nine-millimeter semi-automatic?

Then it comes to her—after she's thanked Charlie, and sunk her teeth into those vinegary artichokes—that, as the teenager in the blackmailer's elevator advised her friend, *sometimes you just gotta accept a person for who they is.*

Sooner or later, Mel may actually be able to embrace this bit of wisdom; maybe in a few days or weeks or a couple of months.

But not right now.

72
JULIA

Using the key left for her with the doorman of the high-rise several blocks from the Mishkins, Julia lets herself into the apartment. She's here to feed and water a long-haired cat named Marshall whose owner is away for three days in Boston at a retreat for drug and alcohol rehab counselors. She quietly drops the keys into a small ceramic bowl on a shelf in the foyer, and tiptoes toward the bedroom, because she knows from previous visits a few months ago that Marshall still hasn't quite warmed to her and doesn't like to be startled. "Hey there, beautiful boy," she says as she enters the room, and is shocked to see Marshall lying listlessly on the floor and Valerie, his owner, stretched out beside him, her head already bowed in grief.

"Oh God, I forgot to call you," Valerie says.

"You never went to Boston?" Julia gets down on the floor for a closer look. She sees at once that Marshall's breathing is labored, and there is something gravely wrong.

"He's the one true love of my life," Valerie says, "and he's got catastrophic heart problems." Her voice shaking, she reports that the veterinarian has already made a house call and will be back shortly with an intravenous catheter and some medication to euthanize Marshall. "He's only twelve, but today is the last day of his life," she says. "His pupils are fully dilated and the vet told me that's a terrible sign."

"I'm so very sorry," Julia offers. She doesn't know what else to add, and asks Valerie if it's all right to pet Marshall, whose chest is rising and falling in a way so alarmingly pronounced, it's painful to look at him.

Without answering Julia's question, Valerie begins ranting about her ex-husband, whom she describes as a faithless piece of garbage, and confesses that it was Marshall who was her only source of comfort, there for her every night, sleeping next to her on her pillow after she ditched her husband. "I kid you not, Julia, when I say that in a heartbeat, I'd take Marshall, my sweet sweet boy, over that loser husband any day, believe me."

Guess what: I personally am in love with someone else's faithless husband, Julia could say, and then what? What would Valerie think of her? That she's made of frayed moral fiber—would that be an accurate assessment? Preferring not to meditate on any of this, she stares at a new poster on the bedroom wall, a large photographic image of a lightly toasted grilled cheese sandwich; the sandwich is split down the middle to reveal oozing, garishly orange cheese inside.

"I see you're a big grilled cheese fan," Julia says, and almost laughs at the sound of her own voice. Hey, she's only trying to render a difficult situation a little easier for Valerie, a woman her own age and in need of comfort.

Marshall is struggling to get to his feet; incredibly, he manages to lift himself from the floor and walk down the hallway to the living room, Julia and Valerie following behind.

"I love you, darling boy," Valerie calls to him. He settles under the piano for a moment, then under the coffee table, and then collapses on the floor next to a wall-to-wall bookcase. He lets out what sounds like a feline cry of grief and despair, and Julia and Valerie are down on the floor alongside him, watching the very last rise and fall of his chest. Julia is not a believer and is convinced she never will be, but she would swear, looking at the utter, deathly stillness of Marshall's body, his wide-open eyes with their fixed and dilated pupils, that she has somehow just witnessed the flight of his spirit from his beautifully fluffy remains. She doesn't know Valerie very well, but feels the urge to embrace her now as Marshall lies so profoundly inert before them.

"I don't expect you to believe me, but I swear his emotional IQ was almost human," Valerie whimpers against Julia's neck. "He gave me unconditional love, twenty-four/seven, when I so needed it. What more could you ask for from a cat?"

Or a boyfriend. Or a husband. Or a father or mother, Julia thinks.

Maybe she should get herself a cat.

When the veterinarian, a youngish, dark-haired guy wearing a wistful smile, arrives ten minutes later, he's bearing now-useless gifts of a catheter and an intravenous overdose of pentobarbital.

It's Julia who greets him at the door.

Too little, too late, she whispers.

"Marshall's spirit has been released back into the universe," the vet explains quietly as he kneels over the body, stethoscope already in place. And Valerie's wail is a sound Julia will never forget.

No more cat-sitting and dog-walking; there's got to be an easier way to supplement that not-very-impressive income of hers.

73
Mel

When her son, Jack, is born a few years from now and Mel becomes a mother for the first time, she will emerge from what she will always regard as the horrific experience of giving birth (*pain, followed by worse pain, followed by agonizing pain* are the words that will come to mind) in a fog of bewilderment and exhaustion. The next day, when a nurse arrives at Mel's bed in the maternity word at Lenox Hill with a clipboard and paperwork to keep her busy, Mel will pick up her still-lucky twenty-nine-cent extra-fine-point Bic pen (its price having doubled to fifty-nine cents, still acceptable) and try her best to scrupulously enter all the information required for the baby's birth certificate. Jack will weigh in at a measly five pounds, thirteen ounces, but will, one month later, plump up to a mind-blowing nine pounds, two ounces.

Working on the birth certificate after the nurse escorts Jack back to the nursery just down the hall, Mel will come to the box that says "mother's occupation" and fill it in as effortlessly, as unthinkingly, as she filled in her address and phone number.

Mother's occupation: short-story writer.

The nurse, an older woman with feathery graying hair and white oxfords that squeak quietly across the Lysol-scented tile floor, will, on her return an hour later, take the completed birth certificate, give it an especially swift once-over, and hand it back to Mel. "What's this?" she will say, and point to "mother's occupation."

"I'm a writer?" Mel will answer, her voice rising at the end of the sentence, as if she were asking for confirmation.

"But I don't understand—what's a short-story writer? I mean, what's a short story? Is it a fictional story? Or a real story?"

"Yes, it's fiction, but often there's—"

"I mean, I've worked in this hospital for decades, since the early sixties, as a matter of fact, and please don't take offense, but seriously, I've never seen even a single patient put "short-story writer" as their occupation, and it just strikes me as odd, you know? Peculiar," the nurse will say, and smile. "Kind of weird."

"I'm sorry, but it's the truth—it's what I am," Mel will hear herself say. "*Who* I am."

"Not a problem, you don't have to apologize." The nurse will glance down at her wristwatch, a rectangular gold face on a band made of brown leather, a more elegant version of the watch Austin wore every day during the few short years Mel was his assistant, and Mel will think—as the nurse says it's time for her to leave now to check on another patient—that it's Austin who would find all this amusing, Austin who would probably note, *Well, she* says *she's a writer, but who knows how long it will take before she sells another story?*

74
Mel

It occurs to her one night while she's cleaning the toilet with a bristly plastic brush and Lysol—the kind that promises to kill 99.9 percent of all bacteria and viruses—that despite Charlie's appalling inadequacies as a husband, no one could dispute the fact that he'd been a compassionate, generous son-in-law to her parents in the years before his steep fall from grace. Her mother, and father, too, had been his biggest fans, especially in her mother's final weeks when Charlie sat with Mel so faithfully at her mother's bedside, as she and Charlie witnessed her losing battle against the ferocious cancer that would kill her within a year and a half of her diagnosis. Although Charlie had a juvenile, life-long fear of needles piercing his skin, he'd donated blood several times for Mel's mother, whose struggle with the most virulent sort of leukemia broke Mel's heart. She can envision her mother, her completely, shockingly, bald head concealed by a black-and-orange San Francisco Giants baseball cap, her mouth hidden behind a pleated, powder blue surgical mask, as Mel and Charlie guided her into a taxi at the main entrance to Sloan-Kettering and accompanied her on one of her last trips home to the apartment on Riverside Drive, where her parents had moved after Mel went off to college. The three of them were seated in the back of that unair-conditioned cab on a humid September morning, her mother's left hand slipped into Mel's right, her right hand into Charlie's left. *What would Daddy and I do without you two angels?* Mel can still hear her saying, sounding nothing like the self-assured, long-practicing Legal Aid attorney she'd been, and everything like a mortally exhausted but grateful mother surrounded by her always-to-be-counted-upon, infinitely responsible daughter and son-in-law.

When she died, and Mel was asked to officially identify her body in its coffin minutes before the burial, it was Charlie who raised the upper section of the burnished mahogany lid and bravely peeked inside. Charlie who kissed her mother's waxy, unearthly pale, stone-cold forehead, sparing Mel and her father from what, she is sure, would have been one of the most harrowing moments of their lives.

The fact that he fucked the blackmailer for fourteen endlessly long months doesn't strip that moment of Charlie's generosity. Or diminish the love reflected in that kiss to his mother-in-law's forehead. Mel knows this to be true, and oh how gratifying, how comforting it feels, to at last be able to acknowledge her husband's goodness.

75
Mel

Though Charlie has been kept in the dark about her plans, she and the blackmailer are meeting for coffee at Caffé Cognoscenti, a cozy place with couches in the back and shelves full of hardcover books. It is near the end of June, ten weeks post-D-Day, and the air-conditioning isn't doing its job, or maybe it's only that Mel is anxious and mildly sick to her stomach. She's in the jeans and espadrilles she wore to the office today, but the blackmailer arrives wearing a loose-fitting, sleeveless black dress and heels. She's already let Mel know, during a quick phone call this afternoon, that she has a job interview later and can't stay long.

It's Mel who engineered this meeting, in a call she made from her desk at work this morning, still unable to pronounce the blackmailer's name out loud, saying only, "Hi, it's Charlie's wife, how are you?" The familiar signs of dread—the thumping heart and perspiry palms—had swiftly kicked in, and she wondered if dialing the blackmailer's number a minute ago was proof that she herself was a psycho for wanting this conversation.

"How *am* I?" the blackmailer said, her voice chilly. And then, a little warmer, "How are *you*, Mel?"

Using her thumb and her pinky, Mel twisted her engagement ring around and around her finger. "I was hoping," she said, "that we could meet, you know, for just a couple of minutes?" She watched Austin drifting down the hallway, the steam from his coffee mug rising toward his face, a manuscript pressed against his safari jacket.

"I gotta go," she told the blackmailer. "But can we meet after work sometime, just for a few minutes?"

"Today is good," she's surprised to hear the blackmailer say. "For a couple of minutes, anyway. Let's just get this over with."

"Thank you," Mel says. *As if she should be thanking the blackmailer for anything.*

So this is what a blackmailer looks like, she sees now; it's a little disappointing, really, to observe, the instant they make eye contact, that she's just an ordinary person in her thirties, though Mel immediately takes note of her allure—the darkness of her hair and eyes, the stylish arc of her eyebrows, the slender bones of her wrists, rather like Mel's own. Okay, she sees what drew Charlie to her. She's pretty enough, but so what?

Soon Mel will find the blackmailer somewhat pathetic, as soon as she opens her mouth and begins to talk, bitterly, of her grievances against Charlie, her disappointment in him and in his failure to keep her happy.

She's recognized Mel from a photograph she'd seen in Charlie's office, the blackmailer says, extending her hand; it's warm and slightly damp, and Mel holds on to it for a split second too long, wanting to know her, wanting to know who she is.

The blackmailer, it's clear, isn't thrilled to see her, Mel with her diamond wedding band still glittery on her ring finger years after it landed there.

It's Mel who needs this face-to-face meeting, Mel who's hoping that the sight of the blackmailer actually, physically, here in front of her might, by some miracle, enable her to "process" (this is psychobabble from Dr. Wachtel, Mel knows) the reality of Charlie's betrayal and then, if she's lucky, help her let go of it.

Dr. Wachtel's most recent recommendation, offered from

her home office in her fancy high-rise on Central Park West, is that Mel concentrate on the long view and on her goal, which is to look forward rather than backward—but how the hell *can* she? She continues to look backward, at everything she'd missed; she keeps looking at her life in the rearview mirror, when what she needs to do is travel farther and farther away from the past until it is no longer visible, no longer relevant.

As if the past could ever be irrelevant. Just pay attention to Faulkner: *The past is never dead. It's not even past.* Who's going to disagree with the great William Faulkner?

How deeply painful it is in this moment to imagine the blackmailer running her manicured fingertips through Charlie's hair and calling him *Honey Pie*.

"Okay, so let's talk," the blackmailer suggests as she and Mel carry their large, identical paper cups of iced coffee toward the back of Caffé Cognoscenti and settle themselves uncomfortably on the ironically named love seat. In an eyeblink, it's obvious the blackmailer is just too close for comfort; she gets up and moves herself into a scuffed leather armchair opposite Mel. Around her wrist is a thin turquoise rubber band; around her neck, a chain with a pair of good-size interlocking silver hearts suspended from it. Mel happens to know Charlie gave the blackmailer this necklace on Valentine's Day, the very same Valentine's Day he'd given *her* heart-shaped gold earrings. Shortly after D-Day, he freely admitted buying both gifts on the same trip to Bloomingdale's, and could not seem to understand why Mel was outraged that they had been purchased together and on the same VISA card.

"But you're my *husband!*" she'd reminded him; sadly, he still needed a reminder. "You're buying Valentine's gifts for your wife and your blackmailer at the same time and that minuscule thing called your moral compass can't be bothered whispering even the shortest, briefest message to you?"

"Nope. No message at all," he said quietly.

Well, at least she appreciates his honesty here.

Yet another thing Charlie couldn't understand was why she was so affronted by the image of the two of them—her husband and the blackmailer—swanning through the Botanic Garden in Brooklyn one spring Saturday, hand in hand, like boyfriend and girlfriend, while she was home in her mini-office, working on a new draft of a story for Elizabeth Greenwell, her dictionary and thesaurus loyally at her side.

"But in that world of ours, mine and hers, I guess that's what we were . . . boyfriend and girlfriend . . . of a sort," he informed Mel the other night in their kitchen, unloading the dishwasher, and then turning to look straight at her, apparently unashamed.

And what world was that, dearest?

The Magic Kingdom? Neverland? Disney World?

Youfuckingpieceofdisappointingshit.

Dr. Wachtel has explained—as Charlie had once explained to Mel about Austin—that anyone is capable of anything in this life. Even a formerly honorable guy who keeps insisting it's possible to "have feelings" for more than one person at the same time.

Feelings?

Why not just say love?

"Hey, in case you're interested, I've decided that his love for me wasn't exactly authentic," the blackmailer is telling Mel now. "And that's why I want him dead."

Mel stares at the thin silvery hearts on the blackmailer's necklace. "Excuse me?" she says. *"What?"*

"Yup, you heard me, I want him dead," the blackmailer repeats. "Or let's just say sometimes that's how it feels, okay?" She raises her hands to the sides of her face, and sweeps her hair back and into a micro ponytail, which she fastens together with the rubber band ornamenting her wrist. "The last time we had an actual conversation, the day he broke up with me,

I couldn't believe what I was hearing, and I just thought—"

"Don't tell me," Mel interrupts. "Do not." Why should she care what the blackmailer thinks about *anything*?

Well, she shouldn't, but she does.

She cares very much. Way too much, in fact.

Everything the blackmailer says is of the greatest interest to Mel. She wants, desperately, to catch up on everything she'd missed during those fourteen months. And too, the writer in her is listening very, very carefully.

"Are you listening to me? I SAID don't tell me!" Mel repeats, but the blackmailer is ignoring her wishes.

"I used to type up just two words on my typewriter to help me get through the day," the blackmailer confides. "Every morning, I'd sit down at my typewriter and type those two little words. Do you know what they were?"

Mel shakes her head "No."

"Can't you guess?" The blackmailer's dark hair gleams beautifully in the overhead lighting in Caffé Cognoscenti. "Come on, take a guess. I'll give you a hint, okay?"

But Mel's in no mood for guessing games. "Fine, just go ahead and tell me!" she says, sounding cranky and impatient, not very likable, she understands, but who cares what the blackmailer thinks of her?

"Those two words were . . . *human . . . garbage!"* the blackmailer says triumphantly. She looks up at Mel, in search of approval, perhaps. "Human. Garbage. Because that's how Charlie deserved to be regarded. *Deserves*." The blackmailer's eyes are glazed with tears now, and much to Mel's surprise, she finds herself reaching into her bag and handing her husband's "affair partner" a couple of tissues. She gets it—she recognizes the fierce anger and the profound disappointment she and the blackmailer share, the darkness that links her and this woman seated across from her who, sickeningly, knows her husband's body as intimately as Mel does.

This woman she'd sort of like to kill but with whom she also feels an undeniable kinship.

Mel's iced coffee is lukewarm and not as sweet as she'd like it to be. She wants to go home, even though she's the one who arranged this meeting between the two of them and she had, in a way, been dying to meet the blackmailer. But she hasn't really eaten since last night, and is still slightly nauseated.

And surprised at how maternal she's feeling toward the blackmailer now.

"Why why why," Mel asks her, "were you willing to waste over a year of your life with this person who was never going to give you what you wanted? Come on, you're nice-looking," she says benevolently. "How hard would it have been to find an appropriate guy for yourself? Why would you ever do this to yourself?"

Evidently the blackmailer needs no more than a second to gather her thoughts, saying, "You know, Charlie may have been an asshole, but to be entirely honest, so was I. And . . . and I was lonely."

Mel nods her head, agreeing with the blackmailer's assessment, and *to be entirely honest*, relishing it.

Now the blackmailer is talking about her crappy ex-husband, and her piece-of-shit father, who slammed her against the walls of her childhood bedroom, and Mel's empathy kicks in forcefully. But then she listens to her say, "I'm sitting there in Charlie's office every Thursday night and I'm thinking, well, here's this lovely guy, this good, decent man who's going to help me—and you know what, this, *this* is what I want for myself—this good, decent guy who's so very different from those—"

"The guy you chose for yourself was my *husband!*" Mel says. "*My* husband!" she repeats as a couple walks past, carrying croissants on paper plates and bottles of fancy beer. They're Mel's age, and the guy, who has hair that droops down his back in a long neat braid, is saying to his companion, "Sure I care about you, Leah, but lovin', I don't know—that's a whole other story." Leah, tall and shapely, suddenly appears devastated, and walks off, with her croissant and fancy beer, back toward the front of Caffé Cognoscenti; her guy drags behind her, looking appropriately self-conscious.

"Sometimes I find myself hoping he'll die of cancer," the blackmailer is confessing now, and Mel stares at her in disbelief. "Or that maybe you'll kill him yourself. Or hire a hit man to have him killed," she says, tears in her eyes. Mel continues to stare at her; instead of outrage, what she's feeling is . . . well, she doesn't quite know *what* she's feeling. Revulsion, but also something verging on sympathy?

"Part of me thinks you're insane," she tells the blackmailer, "but there's a part of me that has to admit I understand where all of this is coming from." It's satisfying, she thinks, to take note of those tears clouding the blackmailer's dark eyes, satisfying to know she's flesh-and-blood and has a beating heart.

To Mel's astonishment, she hears the blackmailer saying she'd like to ask for her forgiveness. "May I do that?" the blackmailer says politely. "And listen, would it be all right if I told you that I've admired your stories in *The New Yorker?* Especially the first one, 'Untroubled Lives,' right?" There's a small, nervous smile arranged on her face. "And now may I ask for your forgiveness? Please?"

Mel wants to answer her, to tell her *no way in hell*, but all at once her mouth is so dry, it seems she's incapable of saying anything at all. The blackmailer apparently has taken her silence for assent, and now she's rising from her seat and soon Mel can feel herself leaning forward, can feel the blackmailer's arms cast tight around her back, her warm face brushing briefly against Mel's own, the delicate touch of a shy kiss against her cheek.

What is the blackmailer *doing*? And why is Mel weeping?

Don't cry, the blackmailer tells her in a wobbly voice. She says there's something else she would like to share with Mel, but then she stops and says *forget it*.

"Are you sure?" Mel asks, because everything the blackmailer says is of the greatest interest to her.

This is when, for the very first time, she is stunned to hear herself say aloud, "Are you sure, *Julia*?"

She's riding home without a seat on a densely crowded subway with grimy floors and graffitied windows, when it hits her that even though she's never written a novel—never even considered writing a novel—she will, the instant she's good and ready, write the only one she's certain she is capable of writing. She hasn't yet written a word, and may very well hold off for years, but she's already confident of the title: *The Blackmailer's Guide to Love*.

Hanging on to the pole next to Mel, a guy in shorts and a Minnie Mouse ski hat addresses his pal beside him, saying, "Just keep on believin' on yourself, dude! And if you wan me to say it again, I goddamn will."

Yes, please say it again, dude. Please do.

76
Julia

Good things are happening, one piece of news coming swiftly on the heels of another. At the conclusion of her job interview, immediately after leaving Charlie's wife at Caffé Cognoscenti, Julia is offered a full-year adjunct gig at Hunter College: two sections of Intro to Writing About Literature, and two sections of Expository Writing. She's fully capable of teaching both, and is relieved that the female professor who interviews her can't possibly discern that she's just about eleven weeks into her pregnancy. When asked about her dissertation, Julia is able to say, truthfully, that she's hoping to move forward with it before the start of the fall semester.

In the fall, she will no longer number dogs and cats among her clients; her job caring for the Mishkins will be coming to an end, as well. Though she hasn't planned on telling Molly and Walter about her pregnancy for a few more months, a wave of morning sickness overtakes her one day in July while she's scrambling eggs for their breakfast; moaning quietly, she stretches herself out on their living-room couch and shuts her eyes.

"What's wrong, Miss?" Molly calls from the dining-room table, where she's seated next to Walter, awaiting those scrambled eggs and some lightly toasted English muffins. "I can hear that you're not feeling so well."

"Does she know we haven't had our breakfast yet?" Walter says. "And does she know how sick I am of reading all about this Richard Pryor guy who set himself on fire?"

"Then stop reading *The New York Times*, my handsome

hero. No one says you have to read every word of it."

"Oh, but I do have to . . ."

The smell of those half-scrambled eggs is going to be the end of her, Julia thinks.

"You look terrible, Miss," Walter tells her. "I hope this doesn't mean we're not going to get our breakfast. Or that whatever you have is contagious."

Julia has to laugh, despite the nausea. "Not contagious, I promise. In fact . . ." Her eyes are still closed as she explains that she's pregnant, but not to worry, she can continue to work for them until the last week of August. When she opens her eyes, she sees Walter's head resting, so childlike, on Molly's shoulder, his face looking sweetly bewildered.

"Thirty-three percent of all people who go to funerals don't realize it's their own," he reports.

"Oh, congratulations, Miss! Mazel tov!" Molly says. Then, "You have a husband we don't know about?"

"*Whose* husband don't we know about?" Walter says.

"The young lady who works for us!" Molly says. "You need to listen more carefully, Handsome Hero."

Nope, no husband, Julia tells them.

"Well, then, here's what we're going to do," Molly says. "We're going to go into the bedroom where Walter keeps the checkbook and we're going to write a nice check for you and the baby. For all the things you're going to need: carriage, stroller, playpen, crib, baby clothes, baby nurse for the first couple of weeks. Whatever you want. And this will be fine with Walter, too, even if he says it isn't."

No response from Walter, who has the TV remote in hand and is enthusiastically engaged in channel-hopping.

"That's so lovely of you, but I couldn't," Julia says, though she's not sure why. Her nausea is fading, and she sits up cautiously. "That's lovely and generous," she says, "but—"

"But nothing!" Molly says. "Did you hear me, Walter?"

"I don't hear well at all," he says. "But I do know that Helen Keller said that if she had a choice between blindness and deafness, she would choose blindness. And I know why."

"I'm going to punch you," Molly says. "Really hard." Then to Julia, "Can you believe this guy? You don't think I would trade my blindness for deafness in the blink of an eye?"

She rouses herself up from the table, and walks along the hallway to the bedroom, holding on to the crook of Julia's arm. "The checkbook's right in *there*," she says, pointing to the banged-up nightstand at the far side of the bed. "Go get yourself a pen."

Julia finds one in the medicine cabinet in the bathroom, lying on a shelf next to a thermometer, a manicure scissors, and the pair of old toothbrushes she uses to clean the grout in the shower. The pen, which is black-and-gold plastic and imprinted with the words *World Jewish Congress*, sits lightly in her palm.

"You know Walter's handwriting is terrible," Molly says, "and I can't really see well enough except to sign my name. So I'm going to ask you to write yourself a check for three thousand dollars and then I'll sign it."

"What?" Julia's eyes are suddenly blurry with tears. "No, that's crazy. Wonderful and incredibly, incredibly generous, but crazy." She and Molly are seated at the edge of the Mishkins' bed now, and Molly takes Julia's hand.

"Listen to me, Miss. Walter and I never had the opportunity to give gifts to our own poor little grandchild, who didn't last even a minute in this world, so please let us do this for *you*, and for your child when he arrives. So write yourself that check and don't tell me I'm crazy. Do as I say or else!" Molly says, and laughs. "We may not be millionaires, but we have enough, and that money is ours to give away. Who better to pass some of it along to than you, who've taken us all over the place to all those doctors of ours and who've worried so much over the flame coming from the burners on the stove and the faucets we always forget to turn off in the bathroom. Don't you think it's our privilege to be able to help you, Miss?"

Woozy with an unnerving mix of gratitude and morning sickness, Julia flops flat on her back onto the Mishkins' bed; and Molly's hand feels featherlight as it rests so daintily now across Julia's forehead.

77
Mel

Sometimes when she's outraged at even the mere thought of Charlie and Austin's faithlessness, she finds herself desperate to spill those toxic beans to his wife. The phone receiver almost slides out of her increasingly sweaty palm now as she and Hillarie shoot the breeze about this-and-that, about things of such little consequence, while Austin treats himself—as usual, in the available apartment downtown owned by his adulterous amigo at the paper of record—to one more wannabe writer who apparently thinks that banging an editor is the surest way to get her work published in one of those highly regarded glossy magazines. According to office gossip, Austin's "lunch date" is not only married, but also the mother of two little children, someone who's done popular TV commercials for Dipsy Doodles and Kraft Macaroni & Cheese, transforming herself into something of a celebrity. But why, Mel will always wonder, would someone like this young married wannabe writer wanna sleep with some middle-aged magazine editor and put everything in her life at risk?

Here's another thing Mel can't avoid thinking about: Does *she* really want to be responsible for swinging a wrecking ball squarely at the heart of Hillarie's marriage? She knows she doesn't, and that her trustworthy moral compass will never grant her permission to take down both Austin *and* his sadly laughable marriage. (Sadly laughable marriages? Chronically unfaithful husbands? Ah yes, once ignorant of both, she's now, at twenty-seven, an undeniable expert in the field and could someday write, she thinks, in addition to a novel, an authoritative doctoral thesis on the subject.) Too bad; since she has to keep all that damning evidence about Austin to herself, she can't confide in Hillarie about her *own* marriage, can't seek even a quarter teaspoon of Hillarie's empathy, can't ever allude to the whole misery-so-passionately-loves-company thing.

But at the very next opportunity—less than two weeks from now—she will, for the first time, deliberately fail to pass along a telephone message to Austin; a message that one of his "ladies who lunch" won't be showing up as scheduled. Mel will watch him heading out at noon, his briefcase loaded up, she bets, with the usual towel, bar of soap, and stick of deodorant, Austin striding so determinedly in his Top-Siders through the hallway and out to the elevator with no idea that his "date" has been canceled, that his trip downtown will all be for nothing.

When he questions Mel about it later, a pissed-off expression on his face, she will simply say nope, no one called to cancel.

A look will be exchanged between them; it will be clear to Mel that surely he has figured it all out. He will never raise the subject again, apparently having decided not to make an issue of it, knowing it will only reflect badly on *him,* an adulterous boss aggrieved because his assistant refused to deliver a message from a woman he was planning to screw.

And Mel will have the pleasure of knowing that she has, at last, subverted him, undermined him, though not in a vindictive way, really—just in a way that will give her a small taste of satisfaction, as if she were somehow finally protecting Hillarie, somehow looking after Hillarie's best interests just this one time.

It will never be enough, but at least it will be *something.*

78
Mel

She went to bed sometime after 3 a.m. this Saturday morning after watching, back-to-back, a couple of B-movies from the fifties. This is what she does when she can't sleep—she switches on the TV in the living room and finds herself unable to turn away from melodramas about blue-collar wives who murder their wealthy husbands and stepchildren, or frustrated daughters who kill the successful businesswomen who gave them up for adoption years earlier.

Staggering from the living room to the bedroom, eyes burning with an unhealthy mix of fatigue and faintly lingering sorrow, Mel eases herself into the double bed she and Charlie have continued to share, and commands all that noise in her head to shut the hell up so that she might actually fall asleep for a while.

At 7:03, hours earlier than usual on a weekend morning, Charlie awakens, shoots bolt upright in bed beside her, yelling, loud enough to spook her, "I'M SORRY I'M SORRY I'M SORRY I LOVE YOU."

He's sorry he loves her?

"I'm drenched in sweat," he confides, and raises Mel's hand to his dampened forehead, then lowers it to his chest, where his heart is pumping at some crazy warp speed. The T-shirt he's wearing is soaked.

He's having a panic attack, Mel realizes, and she leaves him so she can retrieve her single, amber plastic bottle of Valium from a kitchen cabinet jammed with a messy assortment of vitamins, Rolaids, Alka-Seltzer, and two extra-large bags of

M&M's and another of snack-size Kit Kats. *You need to clean up your life, girl.* She brings the Valium and a shot glass full of water to her husband's bedside and lovingly blots the sweat from his forehead with a tissue.

Well, maybe not 100 percent lovingly; possibly 99.5 percent or so.

"So what was *that* all about?" she asks, after he's gulped down the treat she's brought him.

Charlie motions for her to lie down beside him, and she does, resting her chin against his bumpy shoulder.

"Sorry for the melodrama," he says, "but I think it was literally an awakening, big time, you know, in every sense of the word . . . Something in my gut, something so visceral . . ." It was, he tells her, a recognition of that tremendous, painful weight of guilt he's been subconsciously lugging around for so long.

He feels it in *the very depths of his soul*, he's confessing to her somewhat grandly now, and though Mel believes him, that uncharacteristically solemn, highfalutin language of his makes her pause, for only a moment or two, as she contemplates what he's just told her.

But it's what she has wanted from him all along—isn't it?—an acknowledgment of the utter wrongness, the blatant greediness, of the choices he'd made, the cruelty inherent in all of it, and those words "tremendous" "painful" and "guilt" linked together appropriately, even tinged with a trace of melodrama. What she has wanted all along is to have him share in her suffering. And looking at his sweat-shiny forehead, the spots of moisture staining his T-shirt, the trembly hand he's holding up for her to take note of, she hears herself uttering the word *I* followed by *forgive* and then *you*.

How exhilarating, how utterly liberating it feels, stringing that trio of modest words together so neatly all in a row, the words themselves forming a quartet of easy-to-pronounce syllables.

I. For. Give. You.

The toughest words she's struggled with these past couple of months, and yet here she is, saying them aloud, and he, the former lyingcheatingadulterer, is no more. In his place is someone else, yet someone instantly familiar, someone filled with the deepest regret, contrition, and sorrow, and she thinks she hears herself silently welcoming him home.

79
Mel

Charlie arrives home from work sporting a handmade paper badge Scotch-taped to the lapel of his sport coat. It's a perfect oval—about the size of his palm—of plain white paper imprinted with large black letters forming a message that's as blunt and accurate as can be.

I WAS A
DEEPLY
FLAWED
FUCKING
MORON

"You'll get no argument from *me*, Charles," Mel tells him. "Every word is perfection itself, especially 'deeply' and 'flawed,'" she says, and her arms are already around him.

"Oh, and here's one for *you*, babe," Charlie says, easing himself out from under her embrace and bending down to take badge #2 from his backpack.

CAUTION:
MY WIFE
IS OCCASIONALLY SOMETHING OF A
FRAGILE
CREATURE

He tapes it onto the front of her blouse as sweetly as if it were the corsage that Dave Alexander, her first boyfriend, had pinned to the shoulder of the kelly-green-and-white dress she wore to the graduation dance he escorted her to in ninth grade. It was her first official date, and included in the festivities was a pre-dance dinner that was held in the school cafeteria, each plate sitting on a brown plastic tray neatly arranged on those long rows of Formica-topped tables. It is a dinner she remembers so vividly, because of that newly fractured middle finger on her left hand, broken the day before in gym class; that foam-lined metal splint her finger rested in; and the undeniably chivalrous manner in which Dave Alexander had offered to cut up the chunks of white meat on the plate of Chicken Tetrazzini set before her in the cafeteria. *What a gentleman!* her mother had said admiringly when Mel reported back to her later that night.

As for her husband: *A gentleman and a scholar and a deeply flawed fucking moron—an irresistible combo*, Mel whispers seductively into Charlie's ear now.

PART THREE
MARCH 1981
ELEVEN MONTHS POST D-DAY

80
Mel

It's Wayne Morrissey's largesse, flowing through the telephone lines stretching all the way from Seattle (*Damn, baby, why don't we get this ball rolling and you let me talk to my agent about you?*), that leads Mel to a literary agent named Charlotte Widenfeld. When Charlotte hears from Wayne, her star client, that Mel has sold a fifth story to *The New Yorker*, she sends her a letter on official agency stationery, asking if Mel has enough stories for a collection, and inviting her to give her a call.

What? Is this what Charlotte's expecting from her? Enough stories to fill a book?

"I only wish I had enough, believe me, but I have nowhere near that many, not exactly," Mel says apologetically when she phones Wayne's agent.

"This may not be a problem," Charlotte Widenfeld says. "Send me those five stories and give me a couple of weeks and I'll see what I can do for you."

Eighteen days later Charlotte has an offer "firmly in place" from a publishing house for what she refers to as a "partial manuscript," meaning Mel has to get her ass in gear and fill those empty pages over the next year or so.

Austin raises one eyebrow and mumbles, vaguely, *Good for* you, *dear heart*.

Why does she even bother to tell him anything? Why does she want his acknowledgment, his respect—Austin, she reminds herself again, is not her father, so why does she feel the need to earn his blessing?

She calls Charlie with her good news, and then her father, both of whom are more than happy for her, and then Elizabeth at *The New Yorker*, whose excitement is clearly heartfelt. But it's Wayne who offers the most exuberant, congratulatory whoop over the phone.

"Couldn't have done it without you," Mel says from her desk at the end of that never-quite-clean linoleum hallway.

"Oh yes you could've, baby!" Wayne says, probably drunk, Mel guesses, but, what the hell, earning praise from this recognized master of the short story is what life is all about, isn't it?

When Sally Steinhart offers to take her to lunch to celebrate—*your choice, anywhere at all,* she says—Mel knows at once what she wants: Lunch at Tre Scalini on Madison and Sixty-Third, where Austin and Wayne had lunch without her. This time, though, there will be no leftovers in cardboard containers from Wayne; this time around, she'll have that linguini alla puttanesca served to her by a waiter in a black vest, bow tie, and long white apron, a tall, gentlemanly guy who will say, "*Per lei, signorina—buon appetito!*" as he serves her the lunch she has worked so hard for. And she will listen, happily, as Sally says, in the middle of that lunch, cadging yet another cigarette, *So here's the thing, Mel, let me tell you about the only other person from my class at Beverly Hills High School besides me who's even a little bit famous.*

81
Julia and Mel

The baby's name is Sophia, meaning "wisdom" in Greek, and when she turns four months old, on this raw day, a Saturday in March, Julia dresses her in her first pair of jeans and a black sweatshirt embellished with a purple, giraffe-like space alien on the front; underneath the smiling alien are the encouraging words WELCOME, TINY HUMAN! A gift from Rachel, her very best friend from college who was by her side, nearly from start to finish, through Julia's nine-hour labor. Rachel, who had come around to embrace the very fact of this baby, once Julia made it clear—and not half-heartedly, either, but with a decisiveness she needs to show more often, she thinks—that she was going forward with her pregnancy.

Why should there be two happy as weeee? she sings as she eases, one at a time, first the baby's legs and then her arms, into a quilted snowsuit and then positions her gingerly in her stroller, topping things off with a pink blanket trimmed in sateen.

During Julia's elevator ride down to the lobby, a little girl wearing a reindeer headband with red velvet antlers enters with her mother and says, "But Mom, wait, if San Francisco's not in New Hampshire, then where is it?"

"Oh, for Christ's sake, can you please just stop talking about San Francisco!" her mother says. "Just stop!"

A whole new generation of disappointing mothers, Julia thinks, then yells, "In California!" as the elevator arrives at the lobby and she's wheeling the stroller out. But the little girl in those velvet antlers is already gone.

Outside, on Twelfth Street, she looks around for a cab, walking east toward Union Square until one stops for her. It's going to be a pricey ride to the Upper East Side, she predicts, wincing as the driver roughly folds up the baby's brand-new stroller and slams it into the trunk of the cab. But she's no fan of public transportation for her baby, and this is the expensive choice she's made.

Funny thing: When awakened by her hungry, soaking wet four-month-old at 5:30 on this chilly morning, she had no plans whatsoever to bring Sophia, for the very first time, all the way uptown to the Upper East Side today, had no particular plans for the day at all. But looking, before sunrise, into her daughter's lovely blue eyes, into that blue that was a gift from Charlie, it was clear to her what direction the day would take. She and the baby would be traveling today, sixty blocks north and half a dozen blocks east. Because the truth, as always, is that Julia longs to be recognized, right now as the mother of this perfectly beautiful child of theirs.

His beautiful child. *His* and hers.

It's all she wants, really, and she's never felt feistier, more confident, more resolute about anything as she considers the pleasures of being able to give herself what she hungers for. Just as, years ago, she gave herself that small magenta-color burn on the underside of her wrist, the slightly larger one behind her knee, the tiny one on the tender skin between her thumb and index finger.

When she and the baby arrive at their destination—that undistinguished, postwar, white brick building tucked into a side street somewhere between Lex and Third—and she politely asks the doorman to please buzz them up, she knows exactly what she will say to Charlie.

Yours. Mine. Yours and mine.

And you do *understand, don't you, that we'll never not be thinking of you.*

* * *

This is the happiest she's ever been, Mel would swear, showing off to Charlie, yet again, the newly signed and notarized copy of her book contract here in their living room; printed on impressively long, legal-size paper, there's a fifteen-page rider attached, along with a fourteen-part table of contents. She loves the words *Publishing Agreement between "the Publisher" and Melissa Fleischer, hereinafter referred to as "Author"*; loves the words *shall deliver to the Publisher two copies of the literary work now entitled UNTITLED COLLECTION OF STORIES, hereinafter referred to as "the Literary Work."*

And as the doorman buzzes again from downstairs, announcing that she and Charlie have a visitor, Mel knows for certain, on this most intoxicating of days, that she wouldn't dream of trading places with anyone else on earth.

Epilogue

Though it will take almost twenty years for their paths to cross again—here on Madison Avenue, farther uptown this time—Mel will immediately recognize Austin. Nearing seventy, handsome still, his eyes the same blue-green, his hair gray-threaded-with-white, he is sluggishly pushing an elderly woman in a wheelchair, the woman's hair so colorless and thin her scalp is visible everywhere. Astounded to realize this is Hillarie, Mel will guess by the pronounced droop of her head and the saliva glistening on her lower lip, that, like Mel's own grandmother long gone, Hillarie has Parkinson's.

"Austin?" Mel says, her voice tentative, as if there were even the slimmest chance she's mistaken, and then she will proceed to identify herself.

It is a warm, bright day in mid-June, the twenty-first century looming, and Mel has just come from the supermarket; there's nothing more than a pint of hand-packed cinnamon ice cream in the single plastic bag dangling from her wrist.

"Melissa, dear heart," Austin says gravely.

Looking at Hillarie, at the blankness of her gaze as she raises her head slightly and stares in Mel's direction now, and observing the tremor that afflicts both Hillarie's left arm and her right as they rest on her thighs, Mel will suddenly find herself on her knees on this Madison Avenue sidewalk, her hands balanced on the front tires of the wheelchair.

She has the overwhelming impulse, once again, to apologize to Hillarie, but as Mel begins to speak, her voice will turn quivery and give way to an unseemly weepiness she just can't control.

Austin is asking what Mel's doing there on the ground as she rises from the pavement and sees that he's pointing downward, with the index finger of his left hand, to the melting ice cream that has somehow drizzled onto the white leather toe of her Nikes.

Staring at him, at that delicate hand of his, now embroidered with the bulging veins of old age, what she will recall in this moment is how she once found herself mesmerized by the graceful flight of his hand back and forth across the typed pages of Wayne Morrissey's stories, and by the smoke from those endless True Blues drifting silently into the single column of lamplight illuminating his darkened office.

Acknowledgments

With gratitude to Andrea Barrett, Suzanne Berne, Caroline Leavitt, Elinor Lipman, Joan Matthews, D. Randall Radin, Stacy Schiff, and, as always, Robin Rue and Beth Miller. Special thanks to Tom Jenks, who published a story of mine that ultimately led to this novel.

About the Author

Marian Thurm is the author of seven other novels and four short story collections, including the most recent, *Today Is Not Your Day*, a *New York Times* Editors' Choice. She had her first short story published in *The New Yorker* when she was 25 years old. In addition to *The New Yorker*, her stories have appeared in *The Atlantic*, *Michigan Quarterly Review*, *Narrative Magazine*, *The Southampton Review*, and many other magazines, and have been included in *The Best American Short Stories*, and numerous other anthologies. Her novel, *The Clairvoyant,* was a *New York Times* Notable Book. Her books have been translated into Japanese, Swedish, Dutch, German, and Italian. She has taught creative writing at Yale University and Barnard College, in the MFA programs at Columbia University and Brooklyn College, the Writing Institute at Sarah Lawrence, and at the Yale Writers' Workshop.